ALSO, BY R.W. MARCUS

R.W. Marcus

THE PATH OF VENGEANCE

*A Tale of the Annigan Cycle
in Three Acts*

BOOK TEN

R.W. MARCUS

LAUGHING BIRD PUBLISHING
GALAX, VA USA

Published by Laughing Bird Publishing
Galax, Virginia USA

Visit us on the web https://AnniganCycle.com

Cover art by Kilson Spany
Cover layout and design by Laughing Bird Publishing

Laughing Bird Publishing® is a registered trademark of Mark W Phillips

Manufactured in the United States of America
10 9 8 7 6 5 4 3 2 1

First Printing, 2025
ISBN 979-8-9877180-6-3

R.W. Marcus

Dedicated to the memory of
Edgar Rice Burroughs...
with a wink and a nod to
Philip José Farmer &
Quentin Tarantino

CONTENTS

ACKNOWLEDGEMENTS

My Partner in crime, Cheryl Pepper, is always the first to be thanked. She is the one who endures my many outbursts, suddenly verbalizing ideas at odd times and is my trusted and proven proofreader.

Mark Phillips has long been my reliable sounding board and someone who has contributed to this entire project from the beginning.

Team Marcus also deserves a big thank you. My Beta readers: Max Yrik Valentonis, Lynn Marie Firehammer, Dave (Lather Rince Repeat) Holman and Ivy Maxine Alyssa who get to read the first draft and experience the story, warts and all.

My work would be much more difficult without the technical division of Team Marcus. Jessica Pepper R.N. for all her medical advice, Tina Ciatto Garrett for all her equestrian assistance, Kilson Spany for his outstanding artwork, physicist Keenan Pepper and Dave Holman once more doing double duty as resident chemist.

A special thanks go out for this tome to Ernie Womack for his expertise on outlaw ink.

Not to be ignored are those at Laughing Bird Publishing, for agreeing to shepherd this twisted little project.

Without these brilliant and dedicated people this project would have been substantially lacking. My eternal gratitude goes out to these folks standing behind the curtain watching my back.

WELCOME TO THE ANNIGAN

This mostly aquatic planet travels in a geosynchronous orbit around a small yellow sun. It's set far enough back in the solar system's Goldilocks Zone so that it maintains an atmosphere conducive to a wide variety of life.

Sentient creatures, terrestrial, marine or amphibious, share a hyper-fertility devoid of genetic boundaries. Any sentient creature may mate with any other and produce offspring.

Lumina basks in perpetual sunlight on one side of the Annigan. Humans dwell alongside many other sentient races thriving across its various continents and island chains. The fertility enriching rays of the sun, and the warmth of the Shallow Sea, support a vibrant and rich ecosystem.

Although life is abundant there, Lumina is hardly a serene place as you will see. Millennia of feuds, ruthless ambition and individual hatreds forged a fragile peace, barely sustained under the rule of the Great Houses.

Because of the incredible diversity of sentient creatures, all races, genders and hybrids in Lumina enjoy social equality, judging each as an individual based upon their own merits. Beneath the veneer of peace, however, dwells a hotbed of totalitarian torture, raider uprisings and a constant escalating cold war between the Great Houses.

Nocturn languishes in constant darkness on the other side of the Annigan. Only moonlight, starlight and bioluminescence illuminate the land of endless night. Without the warming rays of the sun, Nocturn's oceans are frozen over, but constant geothermal activity heats the land masses, creating a temperate and misty terrain teeming with exotic and predatory sentient races.

Imperialistic cat people rule aboveground and hive nations of humanoid mantises swarm beneath the surface. In the Ocean Deep, a race of sentient octopods dwell in vast underwater cities worshiping the ancient ones of the abyss. You are predator or prey in Nocturn's despotic societies.

The Twilight Lands reside at the fringes of the Annigan and remain in constant gloaming. Here, warm and cold air currents clash, generating a perpetually stormy climate.

Ruled by the amphibian Bailian race, the Twilight Lands serve as a neutral zone for cultures from every corner of the Annigan. Many encounter other races for the first time, and like the weather, their clashes can prove tempestuous.

Only the sun of Lumina keeps back the nocturnal predators of the dark side. Legends tell of a prophesied great eclipse stripping away all boundaries and igniting an apocalyptic war. Until then…

…these are the tales from the Annigan Cycle.

The Path of Vengeance

A trick of the tail
A roll of the dice
A hero lies bleeding
Who pays the price?
For the guilty are pleading
O'er the mourner's cries

ACT ONE

Malice and Forethought

The Grand Turine in the Zorian harbor rang out fifteen bells, indicating the Kan would soon be over. By this time, Karker de Goya found himself longing for the damp mist to recede. The early spring chill on the Southern Docks always seemed worse just before the sun broke through, making the early morning hours miserable.

Thankfully, the plentiful work helped warm him and keep his mind off the current conditions. This morning, he and his crew had just unloaded a shipment of grain from Amarenia. He gave a satisfied nod at the several hundred sacks stacked neatly in a square pile.

"That didn't take nearly as long as I thought it would," said a burly youth with red hair standing next to him.

A smile came to Karker's face and the corners of his normally sleepy eyes crinkled with pleasure. "Yep, you all did a good job, but we're just gonna have to load them up again when the hackney gets here."

"Isn't that the way it always is boss?"

"Yep," he replied with a chuckle.

"When's it due? I might have time to grab a bit of breakfast. The food stalls will be opening soon."

"You got plenty of time," Karker replied. "This isn't due to be picked up until mid-morning."

The young man's face scrunched in irritated bewilderment. "Then why did they get us out here so early to unload it?"

1

"Any one of a number of reasons. Maybe the ship is needed back in Amarenia. Kid, I think you're gonna find that the less you try and guess at…"

"Well, hello there!" came an exuberantly friendly male voice from the street behind them.

Karker and his five-man team turned to see a slender man of average height wearing an expensive-looking ankle-long coat briskly approaching. His angular light-brown features and high cheekbones spoke of refinement, as did his overall deportment. Behind him, a large truck hackney waited with its rear doors open.

"I must say you all have been very industrious this morning," he complimented, walking directly up to Karker and extending his hand.

The team leader guardedly shook his hand but quickly became entranced by the glimmer in his eyes and the radiant smile. Karker found himself smiling back at the stranger, overwhelmed by a sudden feeling of really liking the guy.

"You must be the boss," he said, finally letting go of Karker's hand. "I just want you to know, I think you and your team did an excellent job." He then exuberantly shook each member's hand, looking them in the eye.

"Uh, thanks, I didn't get your name," Karker said when the man faced him again. "Is there something we can do for you?"

The broad grin seemed to grow even larger and he put a hand on Karker's shoulder.

"You know, there is, now that you mention it," he said, gazing around at the dockworkers. "I'm here to pick up this shipment and as you can see, I'm a bit overdressed. Would you all please load these sacks into my hackney?"

Karker knew deep down the shipment wasn't supposed to be picked up until much later, but it didn't matter. He found himself really wanting to please this human and by the willing nods of his team members, they felt the same way.

"Sure thing," Karker heard himself saying before looking over at his men. "Come on, let's get this done."

"Thank you," the man said appreciatively. "I am a bit pressed for time."

The team, including Karker, worked feverishly, loading the back of the truck hackney under the watchful eye and constant praise of the likable stranger.

When they finished, Karker closed the back of the hackney and beamed under the man's grateful nod.

"I can't thank you enough," he said, extending his hand once more. "You all did a great job!"

"Thanks," Karker said, blushing slightly.

"It's nothing," the man said, looking deeply into Karker's eyes. "Forget about it."

He got into the hackney's driver's side and drove off. Karker and his team watched the vehicle join in traffic before disappearing around the corner.

The moment the truck pulled out of sight the entire group of laborers peered around in confusion, all wondering the same thing. What happened to the grain shipment?

"Hey, where's the grain?!" the red-headed youth bellowed. "We just unloaded it and now it's gone!"

Karker looked around in a panic. The neatly stacked sacks they unloaded mere moments ago seemingly disappeared before their very eyes. He didn't know what just happened, but he knew he needed to call someone to report this.

The High Council of the High Holy City of Zor normally met every other Quinte in the Grand Hall of the Forum, unless specially convened for some special or emergency event. The Eldorian sovereign Shom Elder himself, called for a special unscheduled assemblage so he could make a grand announcement, causing widespread speculation through the Goyan halls of power. The mere fact that a ruler of one of the great houses would address the council directly, instead of their appointed house ambassador, piqued everyone's interest.

Hearing that Maluria Konrad would sit beside her longtime friend, King Shom, confounded the full-to-capacity gathering and drew Mazie de Goya's attention from all the way in The Sisters.

She decided to skip the crowds, as usual, and elected instead to watch a broadcast of the High Council meeting on a wall-mounted Larimer screen in her office. She watched as everyone found a spot to sit or in some cases stand, before Balik, the current chairman and the Picean Ambassador, gaveled the meeting to order.

"This special meeting of the Zorian High Council is officially called to order," the humanoid fish announced in a high squeaky voice while gill flaps fluttered over its ear holes. "This session has been called by the Eldorian sovereign and I now turn the floor over to him. Your Majesty?"

She stepped away from the podium and Shom Eldor stepped up to the lectern, smiling out at the crowd.

"Madame chairperson, thank you for the introduction. To my friends and colleagues in attendance, I thank you for meeting me on such short notice. Unfortunately, this announcement simply couldn't wait for our regular gathering.

"House Eldor held secret negotiations with the Amarenian crown, led personally by me and Maluria Konrad. Negotiations destined to have long-ranging implications for anyone calling this part of Lumina home.

"Thanks to the policies and directives Mz. Konrad implemented nearly two grands ago, she brought one of the largest Amarenian rogue provinces to heel. I'm proud to say the resulting peace and productivity produced an increase of a full ten percent for the entire continent! So much so, that the Amarenian government now finds itself in the position of exporting their excess abundance.

"Because of this, House Eldor and the Amarenian crown have agreed to an Eldorian/Amarenian Agriculture Compact, being crafted by Mz. Konrad and me. This future agreement ensures a wonderfully diverse bounty in trade between these lands. It also provides a level of protection against possible food shortages and famine.

"In the coming cycles, this framework of a plan will take shape and provide this governing body a viable working agreement to debate and vote on.

"Until that time I want to thank you for your attention and I look forward to your input."

The council broke into applause and cheers. Shom gestured for Mal to stand, and when she rose, she received a standing ovation. Mazie turned off her Larimar screen and peered over at Miran who sat opposite her desk.

"Well, this certainly isn't good," the mob boss said, her mind racing with the possible repercussions of such a treaty.

Miran's plain tan features drew tight in uncertainty. "How so, ma'am?"

"Too much control of the world's food by one united group. It's worse news for our friends, the Jomake. House Eldor and the Amarenians uniting reduces them to a second-rate food power. Which in turn, will make the financiers over at House Aramos nervous due to their drop in productivity."

"Ma'am, if you don't mind me asking, I mean, first you have Zoteri heist the Amarenian grain shipment and now you're fixated on an agricultural agreement. Why the sudden interest in grain?"

A confident smile crept across the mob boss's face. "Simple, The Sisters' renovation is all but completed and everybody has to eat. I want a piece of that action."

Miran gave a devious smile in return and nodded she understood.

"I need you to get over to Quantara Keep and see how Serkel feels about all of this. You can also arrange for him to take possession of that Amarenian grain."

"How much are you charging him?"

"Oh, there will be no charge. I like to think of it as a gift to show my good faith."

"Yes ma'am. I imagine I'm going to have to use the Howlite again?"

Mazie rolled her eyes. "Yeah, Serkel's an idiot, so you still have to appear as a man. I'm sure as soon as Serkel is informed, he'll want to take House Aramos' temperature on this latest piece of intrigue. I'm going to sit back and let them do the work. For now, I'm going to give my Zorian Guard shadows something to do. The workers are putting the finishing touches on the last of the total renovations over in the Orta Plat and I'm supposed to hammer in the last nail."

The City of Volk rests on the western coast of the continent of Wou. It serves as a major shipping seaport for the entire agricultural body of land and especially the Teeka Rice Collective, dominating the entire northern tip. Its docks count themselves as one of the busiest in the Goyan Islands with a massive warehouse district to accommodate.

Seated in the back of her hackney, Taleeka Konrad watched the Larimar screen displaying the front of a nondescript large storage facility just around the corner. Zerga placed the Magitech viewing chip in a discreet location across the street moments ago on her way to her flanking position.

"Are you sure this is the place?" Taleeka asked, staring at the seemingly vacant structure. "I mean all I see is normal street traffic."

"The Intelligencers said this was where his tracking chip went dead," Zerga confirmed.

"Okay we're going in. Zerga, hold your position and act as lookout. Giddy, have Brzo ready to run in case we have to get out of here fast."

"He'll be ready Tally," Gidaria assured from the driver's seat before scratching the lizard next to her under its chin.

Taleeka then turned to Larzz's massive form seated next to her. "Stick close to me at least until we see what's going on in there. We're going in shrouded."

"Then I get to bust some heads, right?" the half EEtah asked excitedly.

"To your heart's content," Taleeka replied, reaching for the door handle.

The front of the warehouse resembled virtually every other in the Goyan Islands, with large roll-up bay doors and an office door off to the side. Taleeka paused by the single door, retrieved her pistol and cocked it.

"Ready?" she asked, peering over at Larzz standing beside her.

Larzz nodded and she engaged the Etheria shrouding stone in her pocket. "And, *now!*"

Larzz immediately lashed out with a powerful front kick, smashing the unsophisticated lock and sending the door flying open. Inside the simple office, several filing cabinets lined one wall along with a door leading out into the main storage area of the warehouse. An apparently empty desk rested against the other wall. Four men stood around the room's solitary chair, now repositioned in the center of the room and containing a bound, bleeding man, while another man sat leisurely on the corner of the desk.

All their attention immediately snapped to the broken, wildly swinging door but saw nothing beyond it. The leader stood up and his torso exploded, spraying the back of the room with gore.

Larzz charged inside and moved out of Taleeka's range of invisibility to within mere feet of the startled thugs. A single punch to the face of the nearest one produced a sickening crack of breaking bones just before he dropped. A sweep of his other arm toppled the other three while reaching for their weapons. By the time Taleeka materialized with pistol pointed their way, three very stunned thieves peered up at her from the floor.

"Why don't you boys take out your weapons with two fingers and slide them my way," Taleeka said calmly.

All three complied and Taleeka stepped over to the bound man. She studied his thick bald features and golden-brown skin streaked with blood. He peered up at his rescuer with a relieved look on his naturally intense gaze.

"How're ya doing Marinel? You don't look so good," she said, retrieving the knife from the side holster on her backpack.

"I've been better," he said as Taleeka cut his restraints then returned the blade to its sheath. "Tally, what are you doing here? Don't get me wrong, I'm glad to see you."

"Believe it or not I was in the area. When I heard it was you that was in trouble, I figured Larzz here could use some excitement."

"Well, I owe you one," he said rubbing his wrists where the ropes made an indentation. "I caught these pirates trying to snatch a ship's hold full of rice."

"That was probably the rice I came here to broker for," Taleeka said, eyeing the three thugs glowering up at her.

Suddenly a panicked Zerga's voice resonated in Tally and Larzz's head. "Tally, look out!"

Taleeka looked up in time to see a dozen men armed with older Mark Four pistols attempting to rush into the room. The space allowed only enough room for six of them while the other six stood outside barring escape.

Taleeka and Larzz froze in position. The half EEtah slowly raised his hands while the three pirates on the floor regained their feet.

"The bitch here killed the boss," one said, indicating the badly stained back wall.

He then snatched the pistol from her hand while sneering contemptuously.

"Hey, this is one of those fancy new pistols," he said nodding appreciatively. "I say we just kill them and get outta here. If she found us, others can too."

"I say we kill the big one and bring her along for some fun later," another offered. "I call first dibs on fucking her scrawny ass."

Suddenly, everyone heard screams of pain just beyond the door. The group standing in the threshold lurched forward and bodies toppled to the warehouse floor, moving like a wave through the door.

The remaining pirates reeled when they saw massive holes riddling the bleeding bodies of their comrades and a wild-eyed Zerga, with both pistols drawn, bounding into the room. She fired into the closest gunman at point blank, blowing a massive hole out of his chest and spraying his friends with crimson.

Larzz took advantage of the distraction and hammered his fist down on the nearest pirate's skull, crushing it with a loud crunch. Taleeka quickly drew her blade and slashed the one holding her pistol, severing his forearm. He stared down at his appendage pumping blood like a hose and screamed. Before the detached limb hit the floor, Taleeka quickly snatched her weapon from its lifeless fist.

Within the briefest of moments, Zerga performed her waltz of death and gracefully shot the remaining four with astounding accuracy in the crowded space.

"Wow, Tally!" she exclaimed with an excited grin. "These here babies work great!"

One of the pirates moaning on the floor caught her attention and she stepped over to him. She glared down coldly at the man whose shoulder and arm she blew away.

"You were the one who said you were going to fuck my girlfriend," she said coldly.

Zerga then pointed the pistol at the man's crotch without aiming and fired.

"Not so much," she said, watching the life drain from his face. "I'm the only one who gets to fuck my girlfriend."

The rescued trio stared around at the carnage and then back over to the former Quartermaster.

"Well," Taleeka said, obviously impressed. "I can see the enrollment fee for the Valdurian Combat School was money well spent."

◯ ◯ ◯

"You're trying to tell me that a couple of hundred sacks of grain just disappeared?" Tantei asked incredulously. "Like, here one minute and then, poof, gone the next?"

"Yes ma'am," Karker said meekly. "I swear!"

The rest of his crew standing around him nodded enthusiastically, collaborating his story.

Tantei considered saying things just don't disappear into thin air, but reconsidered, given the amount of magic flying around the city at any given moment.

"Alright, stay put," she ordered when she saw Talib crossing the side street dividing the two wharfs.

"What have you got?" she asked, meeting him just out of earshot from the dockworkers.

"Workers on the other dock saw the whole thing. They watched them unload the sacks from that ship and stack them neatly right where they're standing. Then they said a truck

10

hackney pulled up and this solitary, well-dressed guy gets out. They see him shaking hands with the workers all buddy buddy like, and then, all of them loaded the sacks in the back of his truck and he took off."

"Well, either they're all lying or something very strange is going on," Tantei said, before pausing as another option swept across her mind. "Or... tell you what, let's split them up and get a sensitive down here and see if their stories match up."

Talib nodded and stepped away, calling for a psychic while Tantei returned to the group of dockworkers.

"Okay," she said addressing the assembly. "I need you all to separate and make yourselves comfortable. We're going to be here for a bit while one of my associates joins us to take your statements."

The workers shared uncertain glances while nervously shifting about.

"People!" Tantei called out. "The sooner we get this done, the sooner you can get on with your lives. Now, spread out!"

Everyone complied reluctantly and sat around the plaza anxiously glancing at their companions. A half a deci later a marked police hackney pulled up. A female Bailian/Yagur and two men carrying box cases exited the vehicle.

When they moved past the red cordoning rope, they separated. The men moved into various positions in the plaza—where they opened their cases and began collecting evidence using a variety of magnifying glasses and fine tools—while the mostly Bailian-looking female sensitive waked over to the investigators and the seated workers.

Talib gave an amused grin at the differences between the psychic and Tantei. While his partner stood a full head taller with pleasant features and a shiny bald head, the Bailian/Yagur appeared squat with shoulder-length, flaming red hair and small jaguar markings on her light blue face and arms. She dressed in an official-looking suit and smiled warmly when she came up on the detectives.

"We keeping you busy, Rachnia?" Tantei asked, noting the tired expression on the sensitive's face.

Rachnia exhaled loudly and smiled. "This place makes Immor-Onn look like a lazy farming hamlet. You people are wearing me out."

"Think of it as a character-building experience," Tantei quipped.

"I've got plenty of character, thank you very much. So, what's going on?"

"Five dockworkers, all with the same story," Tantei replied, indicating the seated men. "We're going to question them individually and all you have to do is just hang out and let us know if any are being less than truthful."

"One of my easier tasks of late," Rachnia admitted.

"Let's start with that one," Tantei suggested, indicating a dockworker at the far end of the square. "Talib, keep the rest separated and make sure there's no chit chat between them."

Talib nodded and Tantei, along with the psychic, walked over to the seated man.

"Looks like you're up first," Rachnia said, her sharp gaze piercing the interviewee as she stood over him.

The interrogations took a little less than a deci and Talib shot the pair an inquisitive look when they approached.

"Well?"

"Apparently, they were telling the truth," Tantei said with an exasperated shake of her head.

Talib exhaled softly, running a hand through his thick black curls. "So where does that leave us?"

Tantei raised her hand for a moment then looked over at the psychic. "That should do it, Rachnia, thanks as always."

The clairvoyant smiled. "You're welcome. They all should be so easy."

"My question stands, partner," Talib said, watching Rachnia head back to the hackney and waiting evidence team.

"Well, it could be a number of things but I'm leaning towards Zoteri."

"Alright, I'll bite, who or what's a Zoteri?"

"Zoteri, the gentleman bandit," Tantei replied grandiosely. "A high-end thief who uses hypnotism and illusion to ply his trade. Those simpletons didn't stand a chance."

"So, how is it I've never heard of this Zoteri?"

"It's been a while since he's darkened our door. Last time I had to deal with him was right before you started in Investigation."

"But stealing grain?"

"That wasn't just any grain," Tantei explained. "It was a new hybrid out of Amarenia called Gozoa, expensive shit."

"So, where does that leave us?"

"Let's wait until we find out what the evidence team discovered," Tantei replied. "We may just have to wait until the Gozoa hits the streets. Let's make sure our contacts have their eyes, ears and, in this case, mouths on the lookout."

○ ○ ○

The ancestral capital of House Aramos is the city of Aris on Vakai Island in the Goyodian Chain. While the Aramos family calls this home, they conduct most official business of the great human house in the High Holy City of Zor. Some business, however, they keep private and for those situations, the Aramos estate in Aris is perfect.

Under the cover of Kan fog, the swiftly moving vedette boat slowed, then pulled up to the far north end of the Aris wharf. Two hooded figures disembarked, leaving one aboard as a guard. Avoiding the heavily populated main landing and the watchful eye of several armed Forsvara Guards, they

13

approached a short line of public hackneys and got in the back of the first one.

"The Aramos palace," one of the figures curtly ordered, handing the driver a struck gold coin.

"Yes, sir!" the driver, a young man with short red hair said, accepting a large sum of money for such a short trip.

"So, Royal Palace huh?" the driver innocently queried, pulling away from the curb.

The uneasy silence greeting him made the young man swallow nervously, quickly surmising discretion would be the best course of action. After a short ride through sparse traffic, they pulled up in front of the tall wrought iron gate with a guard station, and the two passengers wordlessly got out. Taking his cue, the hackney sped off with the driver relieved to be rid of the unnerving pair.

A tall muscular Forsvara Guard, armed with a pistol at his side, stepped from the small enclosure and stared expectantly at the two.

"Si. Smythe to see Dolan Aramos," the one who interacted with the cabbie announced.

"Is he expecting you?" the guard asked suspiciously.

"Yes," came the singular icy response.

The guard continued his cautious stare while touching his Larimar talking stone in the epaulet on his uniform's shoulder. "A Si. Smythe to see his majesty. He says he's expected."

He paused, cocking his head while listening to the response then looked back at the mysterious pair.

"Someone will be along shortly to escort you," the guard said flatly before stepping back into the booth, all the while keeping an eye on them.

Shortly thereafter, a young, clean-cut, unarmed man in a crisply starched uniform drove up to the gate in a small open-sided hackney and got out. With military bearing, he stepped over to the gate, unlocked it, swung it open and stepped off to the side.

"Si. Smythe, welcome," he said formally, beckoning them into the vehicle.

The one who had not spoken yet nodded and the trio climbed into the hackney. It sped down the long driveway.

They parked in front of the palace entrance. Two Outer Clan EEtah guards flanking double wooden doors snapped to attention when the visitors stepped onto the wide portico and opened the doors.

Once inside, the visiting pair stared around at the military-style opulence. Polished suits of armor stood strategically in the corners, reminding visitors of their illustrious past. Mounted crossed weapons of all sorts, as well as paintings of battles and military figures, lined the dark wood walls.

"Right this way," the aide beckoned them to another set of double doors. Knocking three times in a precise manner, he opened them without invitation, revealing a large office decorated similarly to the rest of the house.

Dolan Aramos, a thin wiry man with a stubbly close-cropped grey beard sat behind a large ornate desk on the back wall. He looked up from his paperwork. His intense ice-blue eyes swept over them and his crisply pressed general's uniform of the Forsvara Guards betrayed the type of man they dealt with.

The Aramos spymaster, Naza Kirkmon, stood next to the Dolan. A thin, clean shaven man with sleepy eyes, he dressed in black robes and a red fez, assessing the strangers suspiciously.

The military sovereign of the great human house of the same name, watched the two men step into his office and pull back their hoods. He recognized King Serkel immediately by his effeminate facial features and long tightly curled blonde hair. Dolan surmised the other, a tall muscular man in his thirties with long brown hair and beard, served as his bodyguard.

"Sovereign Aramos," Serkel said respectfully. "Serkel thanks you for seeing him with no official appointment."

Dolan nodded his acceptance of the greeting. He always considered the Jomake king a little too prissy for his personal taste but respected the fact he managed to forge an empire in the middle of the Goyan continent, counting itself as one of the largest food producers in Lumina. In addition, they rose to become the Imperial Bank's biggest client, so he tolerated him.

"Yes," Dolan said, eyeing the bodyguard, "and the fact we're not meeting in my main receiving hall means this matter is sensitive in nature."

It took a moment for Serkel to get the reference before he discreetly dismissed his guard. Once certain the trio were alone, Dolan got down to business.

"So, what can House Aramos do for the Jomake?"

"Serkel has learned through one of his associates that a treaty is being forged which will greatly impact our futures."

"You mean Mazie de Goya and her knowledge of the Eldorian/Amarenian Compact?" Kirkmon asked.

Serkel, initially taken aback, finally nodded, knowing better than asking how he knew.

"Yes," he answered cautiously.

"I am aware of the treaty," Dolan acknowledged dispassionately. "How does this affect House Aramos?"

"Sovereign Aramos," Serkel answered, genuinely puzzled by the Aramos response, "this agreement will be catastrophic for our two empires!"

Dolan's brow furrowed. "How so?"

Serkel sighed, resigning himself to an explanation. "Sovereign Aramos, this pact between the Eldorians and Amarenians means they will have a lock on the food production. With this concentration of power and output, they will be able to dictate the market to everyone else."

"Especially yourself," Dolan clarified.

"Yes, Sovereign Aramos. This concentration of power means production will go up, prices will go down, greatly diminishing our profits and your loan value to me, as well as a greatly reduced tax base. Serkel is vehemently against such a pact."

Dolan nodded his understanding. "What can be done? These are two self-determining nations. Short of declaring war that is."

"This is why Serkel has come seeking your aid. Your hand reaches far. You can do things the Jomake cannot."

"I see," Dolan said, rubbing the stubble on his jaw. "This is a delicate matter which will require all things to be considered."

"Sovereign Aramos!" Serkel said urgently. "This matter must be addressed quickly. Serkel is convinced if they form this compact, we will begin to feel the effects immediately."

"I agree," Aramos said neutrally, "but these things must be handled carefully. I thank you for bringing this matter so clearly to my attention."

Serkel paused in frustration, his eyes shifting nervously. A long tense moment passed before the Jomake accepted the obvious dismissal. With a slight bow he quickly departed.

Once gone, Naza leaned into his king. "He is, of course, right, Your Majesty."

"I know," Dolan said, staring ahead deep in thought, "but I want to keep the Jomake at arm's length on this one. They are fierce but undisciplined. Handle this as you see fit but keep the Aramos name out of it."

A slight smile crept across the spymaster's face. "Yes, Your Majesty."

"Hey, I remember this guy!" Talib said when Tantei pulled the unmarked police hackney to the curb in front of Majestic Pawn. "He was one of Banavor's minions. We staked this place out for four cycles."

"Yeah, Katan Kotuttavar, they took his arm and kicked him off the monetary council for fraud, but he's still at it. If anyone has a line on Zoteri it's this guy."

"What makes you think he's going to want to talk to us?"

Tantei gave an evil chuckle. "Oh, I know he won't, but I'm pretty sure he's going to want to keep that other arm. It's hard to beat your meat with your feet."

Exiting the hackney, Talib snickered at the vision. "Is that from personal experience?"

Tantei waggled her eyebrows while reaching for the shop's door handle and opening the barred glass door. A small bell rang announcing their entrance and Talib basked in the warmth of the interior.

Glass cases lined the walls of the spacious open room, with shelves above them holding everyday items for sale. On the rear wall, there was a single closed door that served as the only other access point. A dozen human patrons milled about examining the items displayed, attended to by several employees.

"Looks like business is good," Tantei noted, leading the way to the nearest display case with an attendee.

"Hey," Tantei greeted a bright young woman with short blonde hair and a friendly grin. "Is Katan kicking around?"

The woman's smile remained but took on a more serious appearance. "I'm sorry, Si. Kotuttavar is busy at the moment. Can I perhaps take a message and you could leave some contact information?"

Tantei let out a loud exasperated sigh. "I was really hoping to avoid this."

She retrieved her badge placard, prompting Talib to do the same. "Inspectors Talib and Tantei, Zorian Guards, we need to see your boss."

The smile evaporated from the young woman's face, and she nodded nervously before rushing off.

She returned a brief moment later and led them back through the single rear door. The investigators noticed the large safe at the end of the short hallway and twin doors opposite each other. The door to the left appeared fortified and Tantei surmised this held the pawned items awaiting their owners' claim. After a quick knock on the opposite door, she opened it without invitation.

A heavyset man with a round jovial face framed by a thick unkempt greying head of hair and beard sat at a lone desk in the center of a moderately sized office, examining a vase with a magnifying glass in his single hand. He looked up and scowled at the investigators.

"I don't want no trouble!" he blurted, setting the magnifier down.

"What a coincidence," Tantei replied, sounding relieved, "me neither."

"Same here," Talib chimed in innocently.

"So what do you want?! I run a clean operation now."

"And we're about to offer you the golden opportunity to show us what a model citizen you've become," Talib said, causing Katan's eyes to narrow suspiciously.

"What?"

Tantei cast an amused grin at his apprehension. "Word on the street is Zoteri's back in town. Know anything about that?"

The pawnbroker's anxious gaze shifted rapidly from one investigator to the other but he remained silent.

"Katan" Tantei cajoled, "if you're involved, I'm not sure you can afford to lose any more body parts."

"I'm not involved in anything!" Katan said defensively. "I paid my price. I run a clean operation!"

"I'm happy for you," Talib replied, "but you still didn't answer the lady's question."

Katan sighed, his face and demeanor falling in defeat.

"He contacted me last cycle. Said he had something big to move."

"Did he say what it was?" she asked.

"No and I didn't ask. I turned him down right away. I run a clean operation now!"

"So you've been saying," Tantei said, peering around the office. "You wouldn't happen to know where he might be lurking would you?"

Another tense lengthy pause ended with him sighing. "He said I could contact him by our usual means if I changed my mind. He said I'd better hurry because he wouldn't have it for long."

"Now we're getting somewhere," Tantei beamed. "And exactly what would these 'usual means' be?"

◯ ◯ ◯

Taleeka stood at the kitchen doorway, teacup in hand, watching Zerga at the dining room table reassembling her pistol after field stripping it for a thorough cleaning. She marveled at her girlfriend's quick deft movements, rapidly piecing together one of Annigan's deadliest weapons. Once assembled, Zerga slipped the magazine into the port at the base of the handle and ceremoniously placed it on the table before her.

"Wow, are you good at that or what?" Taleeka said admiringly with an impressed nod.

Zerga looked up with a satisfied grin. "Thanks, combat school was intense. We were handed these things on day one and they never left our sides, even when sleeping. They drilled us with timed field strip sessions every cycle, some of them made us wear blindfolds. They called them Break and Build and they could be called at any time."

"That does sound intense," Taleeka concurred, taking a sip of tea.

The conversation paused when Taleeka felt the gentle vibration of her Larimar pendant. She touched it through her blouse and sensed the presence of her mother.

"Well, hey Mz. Tally!" Mal's voice suddenly filled Taleeka's head.

"Mom! Hey, what's going on?!"

"What, I can't just call my daughter?"

Taleeka rolled her eyes and blushed. "Of course you can, I didn't mean…"

"Ah, I'm just fucking with you. I had a couple of things to talk about. First, I hear congrats are in order. You guys pulled the Calden mechanic out of a real tight spot the other cycle. Your father and I are so proud of you."

"Thanks, but that was mostly Zerga, she's got her pistolcraft down!"

"Well, congrats to your honey. The second thing is an invitation."

"Oh yeah, invitation to what?"

"The queen's throwing an impromptu official celebration of the opening of the Durik wharf and the introductions of the eight new Banjas and their crones that I've selected."

"Wow Mom, you're really getting into all that governor stuff. I'm impressed!"

"Hey, the queen tasked me with getting this fucking place moving again and that's just what I've been doing. Not that I haven't had to kick some ass along the way."

Taleeka chuckled. "I'll bet."

"So, you'll come?"

"I wouldn't miss it!"

"And make sure you bring that adorable girlfriend of yours."

Taleeka smiled and peered over at Zerga. "I will, we're practically attached at the hip."

"Good, your dad and I are really looking forward to seeing you. Maybe you can stay afterwards and visit for a few lunas?"

"My schedule's open as far as I know. That sounds great."

"Out-fucking-standing! Okay, a million things to do on this end, gotta go. I love you Mz. Tally!"

"I love you too, Mom."

When the line went dead, Taleeka continued smiling and shook her head.

"What's going on?" Zerga asked, still seated at the table.

"Looks like we're going to a party where we get to meet the Amarenian queen."

"I like parties," Zerga said, nodding approvingly. "I've never met a queen at one though."

○ ○ ○

"Those melons look fantastic! I'll take a dozen," Criada said, pointing towards the bin full of tan orbs.

The food stall merchant, an older woman with greying hair and the light beige skin of a low Amarenian, cocked her head at the skinny young man with a bald head and broad smile.

"Lideri Konrad is hosting the queen in two lunas and I am absolutely buried in the details."

"Those melons are fresh," the merchant said proudly. "They arrived by airship early this morning."

Criada nodded his approval and peered out past the bustling open-air market onto the newly constructed waterfront and the east end acting as a temporary air station until the permanent one could be built. Behind the market the noise of construction filled the air, announcing the city of Durik's return to life.

After choosing several more vegetables, the Konrads' cook, housekeeper and all-around aide took the filled sacks and placed them in the back of his horse-drawn cart. After visiting several other vendors, he finally decided he had procured all he could today. He missed the markets in Taia on the other side of the continent, but he realized his place rested with the lady of the house, no matter where she resided. His love and loyalty to the Konrads ran deep and they treated him more like family than an employee.

Noting the time, he climbed up into the buckboard to get back to Durik House so he could begin preparing dinner. He drove the wagon slowly through the new construction, impressed with the progress and then through the tent city of Durik, about to be replaced by permanent structures. The predominantly female population appeared moderately appeased as they went about their pre-moonless chores.

When he reached the last row of tents, he spied a young Amarenian girl struggling with a large box of fruit. He remembered seeing her in the market and noting how industrious she seemed at such a young age. When he saw her stumble, spilling most of her container's contents onto the ground, he stopped the wagon and got off.

"Here, let me help you," he said, stepping over to the girl gathering her spilled produce and placing them back into the shallow box.

The girl peered up meekly and then looked quickly back down, averting her eyes.

"Don't be afraid," Criada said in a calming tone, kneeling down beside her. "If you want, I can give you a ride to your home. This box looks really heavy."

The girl said nothing, her head down and her hair obscuring her face.

"It's okay," he enticed, reaching for an apple on the ground a short distance away.

When he grabbed the fruit, their hands touched and the girl looked up, her face contorted into a maniacal smile. The air around her shimmered and she suddenly took on the appearance of a clean-shaven young man with dark shoulder-length hair and an angry sneer. Criada recoiled in surprise and the man lunged. He quickly ducked to the side, avoiding the attack, and turned and ran.

Criada barely felt the prick of the tiny dart piercing the back of his neck. His body did feel the almost immediate paralysis and a hand touching his shoulder. He toppled backwards, desperately attempting to breathe as the poison surged through his system.

The long-haired man stood over him and began shimmering. Criada blinked in astonishment, looking up at his own face peering back down at him unemotionally, just before his eyes closed for the final time.

○ ○ ○

A sweaty, naked and exhausted Shom Eldor plopped back onto the bed, watching the last of the orgy goers parading out of his private bed chamber. His seneschal, Attina, once again organized a good one, with twelve in all and a nice mixture of boys and girls as well as a couple of Bailians. The Amarenian Hill Sister stood dutifully at the head of the large round bed offering him a towel.

"Thanks," he said, accepting the thick rectangular cloth. "I don't know how you do it, always finding me a bevy of nubile bodies."

"It's really not that hard sire," she replied, watching her king towel off his chest. "Turns out almost everyone wants to sleep with the king."

"Delicately balanced against the ones that want me dead no doubt."

Attina grinned. "Those are who Koruma is on the other side of the door to prevent."

"Yes, very intimidating," Shom agreed. "Tell me, do you think EEtahs get aroused when they hear sex going on. I know *you* do. You were practically popping out of your pants back there."

"Can't say for sure, but I doubt it. Human sex probably isn't violent enough to get EEtahs aroused."

"Yes, I imagine not," Shom said, before sitting up and swinging his feet over the side of the bed. "Still, I don't think it would be very polite to ask him."

"Probably not. Uh, you may want to consider getting into the bath. You're scheduled to have dinner with the new Whitmar ambassador in a deci."

"Ah yes," Shom said, coming to his feet. "We must maintain good relations with the slavers of the world."

"I believe he has some sort of proposal," she said, helping him with his robe. "Anyways, your bath has been poured and the bathers are waiting."

"Ah, bathers," Shom said wistfully, closing his robe and heading for the door. "It's almost a shame I just had sex."

They met Koruma in the hall and the ten-foot-tall EEtah led the small procession to Shom's private baths, with Attina briefing him on the new ambassador the entire way.

Koruma opened the double doors of the royal baths and stepped inside first. He winced slightly at the smell of perfumed soaps and rolled his eyes at walls and floors covered in expensive blue and white tiles. Two large sunken tubs took up most of the center of the room with benches lining the walls and clothing hooks on the wall beside the doors. Two strikingly beautiful young ladies with mahogany-colored skin, petite upturned breasts and wide smiles greeted them from inside one of the tubs amidst the rising steam and bubbles.

"Good evening, Your Majesty," they said in unison when Shom entered.

"Good evening, ladies," Shom replied salaciously. "I'm feeling extra dirty this evening. I'm going to need you to be especially thorough."

"Yes, Your Majesty," they said through muted giggles.

Koruma, satisfied with the room being safe, stepped back towards the door to wait in the hall when he saw both of the girls raising their hands through the rising steam.

"Gun!" he bellowed, violently shoving Shom out of the way.

Attina drew her pistol just as the two young women fired at Shom's last position, striking the EEtah instead and catapulting his lifeless body through the open doorway into the hall.

Attina fired a single shot at each, blasting open their chests, turning the bubble bath a gruesome shade of red.

Keeping her weapon trained on the floating bodies, she gasped when she reached the tub. The corpses bobbing about in the bath no longer appeared as pretty young ladies, but rather two clean-shaven young men with long dark hair.

Shom joined her, rubbing a sore arm. They heard the sound of palace guards rapidly approaching.

"Looks like we're going to need to reschedule that dinner," Shom noted, staring at the dead men in his bath. "I guess we can count this as a well-balanced cycle. I've been visited by people who want to both fuck me and kill me."

○ ○ ○

"Feel the Shii flow out from your abdomen," Kennari instructed, watching five large Hill Sisters surround a blindfolded Alto.

Alto nodded silently at her instructions, feeling his internal power flowing to his limbs. He spent the last deci in kneeling meditation, concentrating on centralizing and building his Shii, and now the time to release it finally arrived. He realized he must eventually summon this power immediately without the luxury of meditation. However, he felt fortunate because his instructor entrusted him with this powerful new ability.

"And begin," Kennari commanded.

Alto smiled at the tingling sensation coursing through his body. He couldn't see his opponents, but he didn't need to. He felt their presence moving around him. Subtle changes in the air pressure betrayed their positions, as well as the sound of their bare feet across the wooden floor.

He marveled at the sensation of actually feeling the first attacker lunge at him. Easily sidestepping her, he grabbed her arm and sent her plunging into another assailant, sending both to the floor with a loud thump and several groans.

When one grabbed him in a bear hug from the rear, he crossed his right arm in front of him, bringing it up and out, effectively breaking the hold. He then grabbed her already-extended arms and reversed the motion, breaking her balance. With a flowing tug forward, he sent her flying into the Hill Sister advancing in front of him.

By this time, the two he originally threw regained their footing and joined the unmolested one in charging him.

Dropping and spinning with a leg extended, Alto swept two off their feet. He rolled and stood back up when the third threw a roundhouse punch at him.

He brought his hand up in front of him and closed his fist. The muscular woman's arm froze in mid-punch. With a baffled look, she struggled in vain to free it from the invisible grip.

While he held her arm immobile, another Hill Sister lunged at him from the side. With a rapid, open-handed pushing motion from his other arm, he doubled the attacker over with an unseen strike to the stomach.

Smiling at the Amarenian with the trapped hand, he made a rapid jerking motion to his left, sending the startled Hill Sister flying.

Unabated, he heard the others rising to their feet when Kennari called out for the contest to stop.

All obeyed the Geta, and Alto pulled off the blindfold. Glancing around at his startled, vanquished opponents, he bowed reverently.

"Thank you for training with me," he said humbly.

They bowed in return, then faced Kennari and bowed again.

"You are dismissed," she said with a formal smile. "I thank you for volunteering to let my prize student toss you around this luna."

The Hill Sisters left with baffled expressions, not fully understanding what just happened.

"You did well, Mora," Kennari said, approaching him with a proud smile. "Now, you must practice summoning it at a moment's notice."

"Yes, Geta," he replied. "I wish to thank you for traveling here for my lesson."

Kennari waved her hand dismissively. "It was nothing. Air travel makes it easy. Besides, you were ready. This was your final lesson. You mastered the Shii within and can now channel it. I have nothing more to teach you."

"I am honored Geta," Alto replied. "Now, I must go and prepare for the party this moonless. You *will* be attending, yes?"

Kennari's face lit up, and she nodded. "Yes, Maluria was kind enough to invite me."

"It should be something else. With all of Durik-Dor's new crones in attendance, we're ensured an evening bristling with court intrigue."

The Kovos mistress chuckled. "I can hear the whispers and political maneuvering already."

In her twenty-six grands as Commander of the Rophan City Guards, Goyenda de Reet had never encountered a case of attempted regicide. She found it especially baffling with it being *this* king. Shom Eldor, despite initial trepidations, turned out to be the most beloved sovereign in recent memory. She found the concept of anyone bearing animosity towards their benevolent and beloved leader completely inconceivable.

Truth be told, the fifty-one-year-old thought she had seen it all. After joining the city guards at fifteen, the thin, pretty teen with boundless energy experienced a meteoric rise to commander. She secured more arrests than the entire city guard combined, along with a dozen commendations for heroism. She revered Shom Eldor, if for no other reason than the moment he became king he doubled their budget and sent her to Zekoff's class the moment it became available. Yes, for Commander Goyenda this immediately became personal.

She pulled her unmarked police hackney through the wrought iron gates of the royal palace, nodded at the solitary city guard standing sentry and proceeded down the long driveway lined with marked police hackneys. Up ahead, she could just make out the activity around the palace's entrance through the thick Kan fog.

Finally finding a place to park, she slipped her identification placard around her neck and made her way over to the wide portico and open double front doors abuzz with activity.

"So, what do we have, Lewiee?" she asked the patrol lieutenant standing on the busy porch.

The clean-shaven man with salt and pepper hair exhaled loudly and shook his head. "Well, we've got a dead EEtah bodyguard. He took the slugs for the sovereign. You can bet

House Nur's going to be sending out an investigator. Palace security took care of the would-be assassins."

"How's our royal victim?"

"Resting in his bedchamber and surprisingly glib about the whole thing."

"That figures."

"Huh?"

"You gotta remember, he spent a number of grands hanging out with Mal Konrad and her crew. He's used to people trying to kill him."

"I don't know how you ever get used to that," the lieutenant said, before his face suddenly turned grim. "Commander, there's something you need to see."

The two officers locked eyes, then he motioned for her to follow. Inside the opulent manor, two members of the evidence team busily collected and examined anything looking important. When they entered the hall leading to the baths, they caught the distinct odor of dead fish and saw the EEtah body where it lay after being propelled in the attack. A massive pool of blood surrounded the dead man-shark completely coating the floor of the hallway.

"Okay, we've got a mess," Goyenda said, taking in the gruesome sight.

"They were using Mark Six pistols," Lewiee said, stepping carefully through the field of blood.

"That'll do it," Goyenda replied, following her lieutenant into the baths.

Inside the bathing room, the carnage appeared confined to one of the tubs, the water stained a deep shade of red. The torn-up bodies of the assailants, long since bled out, lay on the floor next to the tub. Several members of the evidence team worked around the area under Attina's watchful eye.

"How in the name of the Goddess did they manage to get so close to the king?" Goyenda asked no one in particular.

"They were glamoured as palace bathers," Attina said, pointing to the two shards of Howlite nearby, catalogued with the pistols and other pieces of evidence.

"Well, that's disturbing," the commander noted. "They had access to Etheria."

"It gets worse," Lewiee said, indicating the dead men's upper right arms.

All three peered down at the round solid-black tattoo covering the cap of the arm.

"Talons," Goyenda said concernedly.

"Ex," Lewiee corrected.

"Just as deadly and a lot more dangerous," Goyenda responded. "No chain of command and obviously rogue mercs."

"I'm familiar with the Black Talons by reputation only," Attina said, furrowing her brow at the odd markings. "I thought their symbol was a tribal-style set of claws."

"Until you want out," the commander said. "The only honorable way to leave the special forces of the Aramos Forsvara Guards is feet first. Leaving for any other reason and they black out the tattoo."

"Well, needless to say, these two didn't think this up by themselves," Lewiee said, finally looking away from the dead mercenaries. "Someone sent them."

"Yeah, but who and why?" Goyenda queried rhetorically.

"I don't know, but if there's a chance House Aramos or any other house is involved, this is much bigger than the city guards. I'm recommending that his majesty assign a mechanic to this. Things are probably going to get messy."

The Konrads' Durik house glittered out into the moonless, lighting up the Amarenian coastline like a festive beacon. Even the grounds around the circular two-story mansion basked in the glow of orange Etheria crystals mounted atop strategically placed poles. The mostly female partygoers milled about the lawn with refreshments in hand while predominantly male servants attended to them.

Inside, excitement crackled through the ground floor as the eight new crones from the Banjas, restored after fifteen grands of war and chaos, met their people. Queen Omaris herself, with her long flowing black hair and large entourage, graced the grand parlor, anxious to meet the leaders Lideri Konrad personally handpicked.

Three crones among the revelers carried dour expressions and avoided interaction with the queen or the newly appointed. Former Sardors Hurtig, Skelos and Zamjena, reduced to mere crones of their Banjas, kept to themselves, appearing extremely uncomfortable in the Amarenian formal court dress.

Mal and Alto stood beside the queen with Taleeka and Zerga, chatting away with various guests. Alto cut a striking figure, bare-chested in his white formal Vardee, and Mal appeared comfortable in the floor-length, cinched-at-the-waist, bare-breasted court dress she insisted her crones wear.

"Have you noticed Criada acting strange?" Mal asked softly, leaning closer to Alto.

Both glanced over at their house servant picking up an empty drink glass and placing it on a tray full of used tall, thin glasses with straws sticking out the top. They lost sight of him when he moved off and a guest stepped up to introduce themselves.

"Of late I have noticed him acting a bit unsure of himself," Alto replied. "I thought it might be nerves at putting the party together."

"Yeah, probably," Mal conceded with a nod. "Putting this together was one major fucking undertaking. I'm going to give him a bonus when it's all said and done."

"Most generous my love."

"Yeah, he's a good kid."

No one noticed Criada slip a straw from his pocket, matching those in the empty glasses. Using the serving tray for cover, he quickly raised the straw to his lips, aimed it at Mal and blew. He then spat the straw into an empty glass before entering the kitchen.

Mal, engaged in conversation with one of the new crones, swatted at what she thought to be an insect bite on the back of her neck. Moments later she began shaking her head, attempting to clear it.

"Mom, are you okay?" Taleeka asked, seeing her mother's complexion go pale.

"I... I'm having trouble catching my breath," Mal gasped.

Alto put his hand on her shoulder. "Perhaps you should sit down my love?"

"No, I'll be okay, I just need to..."

With a shaky hand, Mal reached up to touch the back of her neck, it felt squishy and wet. When she pulled her hand away, a large swath of creamy flesh came with it. Suddenly Mal's knees gave way and she began convulsing. Her eyes rolled up into her head and her lips turned blue.

Alto caught her as she tumbled forward and held her while she shook violently in his arms.

"MOM!" Taleeka screamed, watching Mal start foaming at the mouth.

Assisting her into a chair proved to be a monumental feat for Alto as Mal continued twitching violently. Zerga leapt forward in full protection mode, keeping back any overly inquisitive members of the crowd while Alto finally got her into a seat. He braced her to ensure she didn't lurch out of the chair.

Taleeka snapped out her shock and held Mal's shoulders. She searched the faces of the room full of astonished guests.

"SOMEBODY HELP HER!" Taleeka called out in a panic. "IS THERE A HEALER PRESENT?!"

No one answered. Mal gave a final violent twitch before going still and staring straight ahead, her exploded capillaries staining the whites of her unblinking eyes. The foam still flowing from her mouth and nose turned blood red.

Taleeka, mouth agape in horror, peered over helplessly at a stunned Alto. Seeing her not moving, he reached down and placed two fingers on her neck. Finding no pulse, he looked up at his daughter and dolefully shook his head.

"Mom, no!" she screamed before launching into racking, sorrow-filled hysterics just before passing out.

The crowd panicked, crying out in shock and muttering in confusion. From the walls of the house, Defari's howls of sorrow filled the rooms and echoed out into the moonless.

Over the commotion, Tajna Cabela shouted, "Seal off the area, no one leaves!"

Within moments, Security personnel emerged from their anonymity in the crowd, positioning themselves in front of doors. The queen's protection detail swept her from the room while Noorim and Zerga rushed to Alto's side, keeping the anxious crowd away from the immediate area.

Alto, stony-faced in rage, walked over and gently picked up his daughter. He slowly carried her over to the stairs with guests moving aside for them. A guard barred his way at the landing. With one malevolent glare from the swordmaster, the Amarenian sentry lowered her head and stepped aside.

Noorim watched Alto carry his daughter up the stairs to her room before reaching for her talking stone.

"Captain Vanir," she said in her usual austere manner. "Maluria Konrad has just been murdered. I would like to borrow your best evidence team and I need them quickly."

Nodding in satisfaction at the reply, she broke the connection. She, however, still needed to make one more call for help.

○ ○ ○

Cadi Nogol moved slowly and gracefully around the battered room, taking in everything: the broken chair, debris from the table littering the floor and the body bleeding by the front door. She paused and stared at a family portrait in a broken frame hanging crooked on the wall.

Furrowing her brow and closing her wide blue eyes, she concentrated on the fractured rendering. Immediately, her mind flooded with the vision of two women struggling and one's head smashing into the hanging art. Slowly opening her eyes, she turned and peered at two Mahaila Inspectors standing in the open door.

"Well inspector, what do you make of this?" the older of the two asked.

Cadi's youthful pale high Amarenian features remained serious, and she quickly did a last scan of the area causing her black long bobbed hair to sway.

"There was no sign of forced entry, so the victim let their assailant in," Cadi said, pointing at the front beaded door. "The victim was obviously in the middle of her evening meal." Sniffing the air, she nodded approvingly. "Venison with a spicy cream sauce. Smells pretty good. They then struggled, causing all this mess."

She stepped back over to the lopsided frame. "Death more than likely occurred shortly after her head was smashed into this portrait." Cadi then pointed to a trail of blood drops leading to the body. "She had just enough time to stagger over by the door where she fell and died."

"Did your vision reveal who the killer was?" the younger Mahaila asked.

"Not exactly," Cadi replied, "but I got the strong sensation they knew each other well. Who did you say she was?"

"Mirel Leras. She was the next in line to be crone of the Leras Banja," the older inspector reported.

"Hmm," Cadi said, looking back at the rendering. "I get the feeling the killer is in this portrait. Someone wanted to elevate their status in the Leras Banja." She pointed to a woman pictured standing two people away from the victim. "I would start with her."

Cadi stepped over to a desk on the other side of the room. She examined the large round Larimar screen with black Obsidian memory nodules lining the outer edge.

"It looks like she had a bunch of things stored on this screen. You'll probably find the locations of The Sisters portrayed in that rendering and perhaps some even more revealing information."

The talking stone vibrated in her pocket and broke her train of thought. She touched it through the fabric. The voice of her teacher and original mentor, Noorim Sheed, filled her head.

"Greetings Cadi."

"Geta Sheed!" she said surprisedly. "What can I do for you?"

"There's been a high-profile murder in Durik," Noorim stated in her usual deadpan delivery. "The Queen's Envoy is calling you into service."

Cadi felt a twinge of excitement when she heard the summons. This would only be the third time since becoming an inspector for the Mostas' city guards that the Queen's Envoy Service enlisted her aid as a sensitive. Seeing how the Envoys counted themselves as part of the Society of Whispers, their cases superseded anything local.

"Of course, Geta."

"You are needed immediately. Are you in Mostas?"

"Yes, Geta."

"Get to the air station. There will be a ship waiting for you."

"Yes, Geta, immediately."

"Your destination is the Konrads' Durik mansion. I will be waiting. An evidence team from Zor is also enroute."

"Zor," Cadi stammered, finally realizing the gravity of the situation. "Who was murdered?"

"Lideri Konrad. We believe she was poisoned."

"I'm on my way, Geta."

"Good, I await your arrival."

The line went dead and she faced the two Mahailas with quizzical looks on their faces.

"Sisters, I've given you plenty to get started on. I've just been drafted by the Queen's Envoy Service."

○ ○ ○

Tantei pulled the unmarked police hackney off the main thoroughfare and behind a small warehouse on Zor's Southern Docks. The Kan fog had recently risen, shrouding anything on the narrow side street beyond ten yards.

"We seem to be spending an inordinate amount of time here," Talib said when Tantei cut the engine.

"Hey, in this business you gotta go where the scumbags hang out."

"And we've been dealing with our fair share of them lately," Talib said, reaching for his badge placard.

"No badges," Tantei said. "I don't want to spook anyone in this place."

"Yet another sleazy dive bar?"

"A little more upscale, this is officially called a tea house."

"Tea house, huh?"

It's mildly hallucinogenic."

"Okay…" Talib said hesitantly, getting out of the vehicle.

"Yeah, you get good and high then purchase one of the prostitutes. These tea houses serve up a wide range of whores. The one I'm looking for is a Picean named Parola. She used to be Zoteri's favorite. If anyone knows if he's back, it's her."

Talib blinked in surprise as she came around the front of the hackney. "A Picean, really? I mean, they've got fish parts down below. How in the name of the gods does that work?"

"Word is, she can suck the bumper off a hackney."

"Oh."

"She's not the only one. This tea house specializes in Picean prostitutes. On top of that, it turns out human semen tastes like some Picean delicacy. Most can't tell Picean males from females, so the field is open to both sexes and is kinda sought after."

"Just when you think you've heard it all," Talib said, shaking his head in wonder.

"Okay, I'll go in first. Count to fifty and then come in and hang back just in case there's trouble."

The junior investigator nodded, took out his pistol, chambered a round then holstered it. "Ready."

Tantei entered the simple front door, and the place seemed just as she remembered. The smell of brewing tea hung in the air and the large open room contained a dozen cozy seating areas scattered about. Blue-collar working men occupied most of the overly wide, comfortable-looking chairs with naked Picean prostitutes cozying up to them. To the left, a hallway led off to the privacy rooms.

Tantei scanned the crowd and didn't see her old contact. She considered coming back later when she saw a potbellied, slovenly dressed dock worker coming out of the hall looking quite pleased. Parola followed naked behind him, wiping her mouth and carrying a disgusted look. Tantei came up to her, passing her client on his way out.

"How ya doing Parola?" the investigator greeted cheerfully.

The Picean gave a look of surprise then nervously glanced around. "Not here."

Parola then indicated the hall from where she had just emerged, before turning around and walking back down it. Tantei met eyes with Talib entering the front of the bar, making sure her partner saw her before she followed her old contact into one of the privacy rooms.

"So, this is where the magic happens," Tantei said, stepping into a small, spartan room containing only a single short sofa and end table off to the side.

"If that's what you want to call it," the Picean replied. "Haven't seen you around in a while, Tee."

"Yeah, you know, breaking in a new partner and all."

"I get it, well it's a cinch you didn't drop by to reminisce."

Parola's directness caused Tantei to smile. "I heard Zoteri's back in town?"

The Picean's eyes narrowed. "Where'd you hear that?"

"Oh, around," Tantei said coyly, pulling a five secor gold note from her pocket.

"Yeah, he came by a few cycles ago to get his knob polished," she said, taking the money. "Said he was celebrating, something about a big job he just cashed in on. It must have been true because he tipped really big."

"Well, it's comforting to know he's spreading it around. He didn't happen to mention who his generous benefactor was, did he?"

"No, but I got the impression it was only one person."

Tantei nodded and pulled another five-secor note from her pocket. "You wouldn't happen to know where he is, would you?"

"Not exactly," Parola said, taking the note, "but I know Zoteri. When he's flush with secors, he likes the finer things. I'd check the hotels and upscale eateries in the Bogat Plat. He really loves elk steaks, and supposedly there's one place that really does it up right."

Tantei smiled, nodded and turned to go. "Thanks, Parola, I'll be in touch."

"Yeah, don't be a stranger. Oh, and Tee?"

Tantei paused at the door and peered back at the Picean who now wore a sly grin.

"If ya don't mind me saying so, Tee, you're looking kinda tense. I'm getting tired of sucking dicks this cycle. For an extra five, I'll make that little clitty of yours dance, and you'll leave here a much calmer individual."

"Thanks for the offer," Tantei said, returning the smile, "but I've got to keep my edge."

○ ○ ○

From the activity inside and out at the Konrads' Durik House, along with the unknown airships on the lawn, Cadi surmised the evidence team from Zor had already arrived. She looked down on the yard from the four-seater scout craft circling the estate before nestling gently to the ground near the already parked ships.

"Okay Inspector, here we are," the pilot, a low Amarenian with short reddish-blond hair and piercing blue eyes, said from the seat beside her.

"Thanks for the ride, Ensign," Cadi said, popping the canopy.

"Inspector," the pilot said, hearing the potential farewell in her voice. "I've been assigned to you for as long as you need me."

Cadi paused. First, an evidence team from Zor and now her own private pilot; once again, the gravity of the case weighed heavily upon her.

"Oh, I see," Cadi said, retrieving her shoulder bag. "Well, if we're going to be spending time together, I guess I should know your name."

The question brought a polite smile to the pilot. "They call me Tayaar."

"Well, Ensign Tayaar," Cadi said, climbing out of the airship, "get comfortable. I don't know how long this is going to take."

"Uh, Inspector, I was wondering if I could tag along and observe. I'm scheduled to take the modern policing course next grand and I'd like to get all the experience I can."

Cadi considered the request for a moment before nodding her head. "Why not, you may as well get used to looking at dead bodies. Just stay out of the way and don't touch anything."

"I will and I won't," Tayaar said, her face lighting up.

"So, Inspector, if I may ask," Tayaar said on the walk across the lawn, "we have evidence teams. Why bring in one all the way from Zor?"

"This one's high profile," Cadi replied. "Maluria Konrad held prestigious titles both here and in the Goyan Islands. I imagine you're going to be observing the best of the best. Besides, our lab won't be up and running until next grand. They'll just have to send anything they find over to the evidence lab at the University of Marassa in Zor. So, they may as well collect it too. I've got a few tricks in my bag here from my days as a Derik, but we really need a lab for precise readings."

"You were a Venerable Derik?"

"Yeah, for a little while."

"Why did you leave the sisterhood? A Derik Witch is a very prestigious position."

Cadi sighed. "Let's just say it takes a special person to be a healer and midwife. I'm more analytical and questioning by nature. A Mahaila Inspector turned out to be a much better fit for me. Besides, I got bored. In this job, the Queen's Envoy can call me anytime they need hidden things revealed, like now."

"You're a sensitive?"

"I got skills."

At the open front door, they were stopped by a bare-chested Mahaila in red cropped pants with a Mark Six pistol strapped to her hip.

"Inspector Cadi," she said while fishing around in her messenger bag, retrieving her identification and handing it to the guard. "This is Ensign Tayaar, she's with me."

Nodding, the Mahaila handed Cadi her identification back and stepped aside. The moment the pair stepped into the foyer, they heard activity from within the parlor to their right and Cadi deliberately slowed her pace, carefully surveying their surroundings. She paused several times to carefully study an object or wall hanging before stepping through the parlor doorway.

Four gloved, dark-skinned Goyan females in blue jumpsuits with the word *EVIDENCE* stenciled in white on their upper backs milled about the expensive-looking furniture inside the spacious, well-appointed room. They took samples with precision tools, placing them into blue bags marked similarly.

Mal's body loomed ominously, slumped where she fell on the far side of the room. Noorim Sheed stood beside one of the evidence team, closely watching the woman remove a small object from the crack between two floorboards. The two conferred briefly before Noorim made her way over to Cadi, who busied herself studying the room.

"Glad you could make it so quickly," Noorim said flatly, scrutinizing Cadi's companion. "Ensign Tayaar, what is your purpose here?"

"The ensign here is entering the modern policing program next grand and asked to observe," Cadi interjected. "I saw no harm in it."

Noorim nodded with a blank expression and addressed Tayaar directly. "Very well, stay out of the way and do not touch anything."

"Yes, Geta," Ensign Tayaar answered reverently.

"Looks like she was poisoned," Noorim explained. "The evidence team just found the dart which delivered the drug. Alto and Taleeka are still upstairs. As you can imagine they are quite upset."

"I'll talk with them in a bit," Cadi said. "Right now, I'd like to examine the body and that dart."

Before Cadi could get started, Tajna Cabela joined them from the dining hall, her pleasant low-Amarenian features pulled tight in concern. Immediately Cadi picked up on the bad news coming their way.

"We just finished with the headcount and preliminary interviews," Tajna said, running a hand through her shoulder-length blonde hair. "We've got one missing: the Konrads' house servant, Criada."

"You have people out looking for him?" Noorim asked.

"Yes, Geta," Tajna answered, "but it's the moonless and he's got a good head start on us."

"We must not jump to conclusions," Noorim warned. "Criada has been a loyal servant for many grands. He may be held captive or running from the killer or killers. We don't know yet, but it's imperative we find him."

"Yes, Geta," Tajna agreed. "I'll put a few more Mahaila on it."

Noorim nodded and Tajna moved off quickly. Noorim then led them over to the technician who found the dart. Cadi reached her hand out.

"Let's have a look," Cadi said, taking the half-inch-long, bent, metal dart with stripped fletching.

Holding it aloft, she closed her eyes. They opened a brief moment later and the Amarenian sensitive pointed to a spot near the kitchen door. "It was fired from over there. Search the dirty glasses in the kitchen for one with two straws in it."

Cadi pulled a thin roll of white paper out of her shoulder bag. Tearing off a two-inch strip, she returned the roll and placed the end of the paper against the dart's tip. Cadi and Noorim watched as the paper slowly turned three different shades of blue beside one yellow band.

"There are three different variations of the same poison on this dart and something else," Cadi declared.

She examined the strip and then glanced at Mal's corpse.

"I wonder," she said, pulling off another strip of paper.

Cadi gazed sorrowfully down at the dead Lideri. The grimace of pain marred Mal's once-beautiful face, along with bulging, blood blackened eyes and a bloated tongue protruding past foam-covered lips. The poison melted the back of her neck away, revealing liquified muscle and the bones of her spinal cord.

Cadi knelt over the body and dipped the paper into the gelatinous flesh. It immediately turned yellow.

"Just as I thought. This turned out to be a deadly cocktail of a flesh-eating substance and three variations of, what appears to be, a muscle-freezing toxin. It stopped her heart and lungs as well as other important muscles. Of course it will need to go to the lab for specifics."

Cadi then placed her hand on Mal's head and closed her eyes once again.

"She didn't see her assailant," Cadi said. "She thought the dart was an insect bite and swatted it away."

"This explains how it ended up on the floor," Noorim added.

Cadi nodded mournfully as she stood. "It was a painful death, I'm afraid." She then sighed deeply and looked at the stairs. "She can tell me no more. I need to talk to her family."

"We have them quarantined in a bedroom until Maluria's body can be removed."

"This is the part I hate," Cadi said, climbing the stairs. "Grieving families are always the hardest for me. The waves of sorrow flooding out of them can be debilitating."

"I know them personally and count Taleeka as a close friend," Noorim said when they reached the second-story landing. "For that reason, I will let you take the lead."

Cadi nodded that she understood. She acknowledged the Mahaila standing sentry, then knocked lightly on the door before opening it.

She gasped when the door flew out of her hand and slammed shut all by itself. Growling from the barrier followed the mysterious incident.

"Defari, it's ok, they're friends," they heard Taleeka say, and the door swung open.

Alto and Taleeka sat on the edge of the bed facing each other with the father's hands resting assuredly on his daughter's shoulders. Taleeka's eyes appeared red and swollen from crying, but Alto's face seemed an unreadable stone mask to Cadi. She sensed cold and calculating rage radiating from them both. They stood when she entered, giving quizzical looks.

"It was poison," Cadi confirmed. "We're sending it to the lab in Zor for the specifics. Also, Criada's missing."

Neither seemed surprised and Cadi practically reeled from the waves of pure malevolence jetting from them.

"I'm sorry to have to do this, but I have questions I must ask," Cadi said sympathetically.

Alto stood like a statue while Taleeka's face softened at the inspector's delicate position.

"I understand," Taleeka said hoarsely. "Go ahead."

"Did you notice anything strange before the attack?"

45

"No," Taleeka said shaking her head. "She swatted away a bug right before, but that was it."

Cadi nodded solemnly. "That was the poisoned dart. What about you, Alto?"

The swordmaster remained silent and gave his daughter an intricate nod.

"My father has taken a vow of silence until all responsible for this cowardly act are dead. I will answer *for* him until he can speak for himself. And no, he saw nothing unusual."

Cadi and Noorim traded uneasy glances at the news.

"Rest assured, all those involved are going to die," Taleeka stated in a low growl. "I don't care who they are or how far away they may be. I plan on calling on my entire network to assist us. You know, I have gods that owe me favors. I could easily call down their wrath on the guilty. This... this, however, I want to handle personally."

○ ○ ○

As it turned out, the melodic windchimes over the streets of the Bailian capital of Immor-Onn proved to be a soothing element aiding Zau'Berin in her astrological divinations. Ever since helping Taleeka Konrad defeat the greed god, Pa-Waga, four grands ago, the fawn-colored female Singa with a prominent black eye patch left her self-imposed exile in the Os-Tor Forest and moved to the Shining Jewel of the East.

One of only a handful of Singas calling Immor-Onn home, she enjoyed near-celebrity status among the mostly blue-skinned Bailian citizens. With the money she made from the Pa-Waga job, she rented a small two-story apartment in the heart of the city. She chose to live upstairs and used the ground floor to entertain clients. Business for the astrologer and Flavian mage initially got off to a slow start—until she met Mudir.

Convincing the young angular-faced Bailian to manage her existing clients and bring in new ones turned out to be one of the best decisions she ever made. Mudir proved smart, glib and a real hustler. After only a relatively short time, he increased her list of patrons to almost more than she could handle. However, because of his brash entrepreneurial nature, an annoying trait immediately surfaced to Zau. Sometimes, Mudir could be a real schmuck, like now.

Laying back on her single bed in an exhausted heap, the Singa closed her eyes, welcoming a regenerative nap, when her talking stone vibrated on the table beside her. Initially intending to ignore it, the hum continued unabated until she groaned in frustration and touched it.

"Zau baby!" Mudir's enthusiastic, high-pitched voice filled her head. "I got a live one headed your way."

"Mudir, what are you talking about? My last client just left and I'm absolutely spent. You know I need recovery time after I read for someone."

"This one's a real mark. I'm talking problems out the ass and rich! You should be able to string her along for grands. We do not want to miss out on this gravy train."

"Mudir—" the soft knocking on the front door cut her plea short and she gave an exasperated sigh. "I gotta go, she's here."

Tapping the Etheria shard broke the connection, and she rubbed her weary eyes.

"Asshole," she muttered, climbing out of bed.

Padding down the stairs, she listened to the constant timid rapping on the door and wondered what she might be getting herself into. Opening it, a small frail Bailian woman with nervously shifting eyes jumped in alarm.

"I'm sorry," Zau apologized. "I didn't mean to startle you."

"Oh... Uh... Hello, I'm Urduri," the woman said softly, not meeting the Singa's gaze. "Mudir said you might be able to help me. You are Zau, right?"

"I am," Zau replied, attempting to sound cheerful. "Please, come in."

She opened the door all the way, stepping aside, and Urduri cautiously entered. Zau watched her nearly cowering, peering around the sparsely furnished room and staring up at the painted round starfield dominating the entire ceiling, which depicted the Nocturn sky.

"Please have a seat," Zau offered, indicating the chair facing away from the door.

Once Urduri sat, Zau smiled, putting forth the serenest demeanor she could muster.

"So," she said calmly, "I'm what's known as an Arron-Nin Astrologer. My art comes from Nocturn and consists of reading the star patterns of the Nocturn sky, of which this is a representation," she said, pointing to the painting on the ceiling.

The woman glanced up quickly, then downward at the table, completely avoiding any eye contact.

"These are the Tanem Charts," Zau explained, placing her hand on a small stack of thin, six-inch square Ukko Wood cards. "There are six of them, and each contains a section of the map above us."

Urduri stole a quick glance at the cards and nodded.

"Since this is your first session, I need to do a general reading on you. We can get as specific as you want later."

Once again Urduri bobbed her head, and Zau moved the cards to the center of the table.

"What I would like you to do is place your hands on top of the cards and think about your life in general. Take as much time as you need. When finished, slide the cards over in front of me. Don't tell me anything, and we'll see what the cards say."

Urduri did as asked and, continuing to smile, the Singa astrologer picked up the cards and began arranging them in overlapping patterns. After the third configuration, the smile vanished from Zau's face, replaced by confusion. With the next layout, her eyes went wide in shock.

"What is it, what did you see?!" Urduri blurted anxiously. "Is something terrible about to happen to me?!"

Zau slowly looked up at the fearful woman, her own face a mask of dread. "Something terrible has already happened, but this is not about you. I'm sorry, but the reading is over. You must leave immediately."

With Zau's declaration, the mousy Bailian suddenly found her backbone and became indignant.

"But—but I've already paid!" she sputtered. "Mudir assured me you would be able to help me!"

"Mudir will give you your money back," Zau assured, taking the woman by the arm and leading her to the door.

"I'm truly sorry," Zau said, opening the door and guiding her out, "but a reading is impossible right now."

Once she left, Zau quickly made her way upstairs and packed a few things, then grabbed her talking stone.

"Hey Mudir, that woman you sent, Urduri, she's on her way back to you. You need to give her her money back."

"What?!" came the shrill reply.

"Yeah, I couldn't do the reading. I've got an emergency I've got to attend to."

"Zau, what are you talking about? She was a meal ticket!"

"I'm sorry, Mudir. I started the reading on her, but the charts contained a message for me instead. One of my dearest friends has been killed and her daughter needs me. I'm going to be leaving. I don't know when I'll be back."

"You can't do that! We have a contract!"

"Sorry, Mudir, this is more important than any contract."

"You can't do this to me!"

"I don't really have a choice. I'm leaving now."

"You walk out on me now and you'll never work in this town again!"

"I'm sorry, Mudir, I really am, but I gotta go."

"Fuck you, Zau!" came through just before the line went dead.

She pocketed her Larimar and headed down the stairs. Just before exiting, she lifted her eyepatch, and a blue phantasmal globe projected from her eye out in front of her. Already weary, she didn't possess the PSI needed to open her own Flavian Portal. She would need to locate the nearest permanent one.

○ ○ ○

The news of Maluria's murder the previous cycle swept across Lumina like a tidal wave. In the various halls of power, the news brought varying reactions.

In the Eldorian ancestral capital of Rophan, Shom Eldor sat in stunned silence, completely forgetting about the attempt on his life. He found it difficult to grasp the realization his longtime friend, adventuring partner and one-time lover would never be seen again. Even though he hadn't seen much of her since she moved to Amarenia, he still felt an immense hole in his heart.

Joc' Valdur, Pierce Calden and Tate Whitmar, already sovereigns in their own rite, reacted only slightly less stunned than their Eldorian counterpart. Mal and her companions had proved valuable assets in times of trouble.

They all dreaded the unavoidable symphony of death Alto would play out wherever the guilty parties resided.

In Immor-Onn, Queen Shula broke down in tears seated on her throne holding court. Mal's contributions to saving her land and people would be added to the history books.

In the Aramos capital of Aris, Naza, Dolan Aramos' spymaster, approached the Aramos king during a morning council meeting and whispered the news in his ear, Dolan silently nodded, his face remaining expressionless.

"Be sure to send the finest flowers," Dolan ordered quietly, "with a note conveying our condolences and a decent excuse for why I'm not attending.

"Yes, Your Majesty" Naza answered with a solemn nod.

○ ○ ○

The rising moon brought little solace to Konrad House Durik. An air of gloom hung over the estate like a thick pervasive fog. Mal lay on her back, hands crossed on her chest, on a narrow table in the parlor with a white funeral shroud covering her. She would lie in state until House Nur transported her to Makatooa for immersion. Mal specifically requested this funeral method because Makatooa was where it all started.

Several rows of chairs faced the body for those wishing to pay their respects. Currently, Taleeka, Zerga and Alto sat alone, staring forlornly at their dead loved one. Every so often, Taleeka leaned her head on Alto's shoulder and Zerga reached over to hold her hand.

Noorim watched from the doorway, feeling the waves of anguish flooding the room. She had spent all morning on her Larimar tablet, managing Society of Whispers business. She became alarmed after reading the report of the assassination attempt on the Eldorian king around the same time Mal died.

Initially considering it an odd coincidence, she soon realized such events rarely were coincidental. She anxiously awaited Cadi's report. Her protégé received a call at moonrise that a mounted Mahaila patrol found the body of a young Goyan male, shot in the head, on the beach just north of Durik.

Turning away from the mournful spectacle, Noorim approached the front door and the two Mahaila guards stationed there. Stepping through the beaded doorway, she noticed the swirling blue field appear in the trunk of a large tree a hundred feet away beside the road. Both guards immediately tensed up, hands gripping their pistol handles, and looked to Noorim for guidance. The Amarenian spymaster recognized a Flavian Portal opening, though little else. She signaled the guards to hold but remain ready, staring intently at the swirling vortex.

Both guards' mouths dropped open when the fawn-colored Singa with a black eyepatch stepped from the portal. As the portal closed behind her, Zau held up a furry palm when she saw the startled Mahailas handling their weapons.

"Greetings, I'm Zau'Berin. Where are Alto and Tally?"

Noorim knew Singas only from reading about them, but for the two Mahailas, this exceeded their experience entirely. Both stood dumbfounded, watching the humanoid lioness approach. Noorim sensed no aggression, and hearing the Singa use her friends' names alleviated her concerns. She nodded to the Mahailas for them to relax.

"I am Noorim Sheed," she introduced herself with quiet authority. "I will take you to them."

"Thank you." Zau nodded following Noorim and addressed the Mahailas as she passed them. "Aren't you Amarenian City Guards?"

Both managed weak nods.

"I recognized the uniform," she explained.

Noorim indicated the door. "Right this way."

During the short walk to the parlor, Noorim suppressed numerous questions, sensing all would soon be revealed. Zau paused at the parlor door and stared morosely at the funereal wake. The Singa watched her mourning friends for a brief moment, steeling herself.

"Thank you," Zau said quietly to Noorim before entering.

Noorim lingered in the doorway, watching Zau approach the seated pair. Both immediately rose.

"Zau!" Taleeka cried out, wrapping her arms around the Singa in a sorrowful hug before breaking into wracking sobs.

Zau comforted her friend, patting her sympathetically. Breaking their embrace, Zau clasped forearms with Alto and they patted each other's backs.

"I came as soon as I found out," Zau said.

Alto silently nodded, prompting her to glance at Taleeka.

"He's taken a vow of silence until all involved are dead," Taleeka explained.

Zau nodded that she understood and then stepped over to Mal's shrouded body. She placed both hands on Mal's shoulders, lowering her head sorrowfully. Standing there, Noorim heard sniffles from the Singa and saw her shoulders shake with emotion.

"You will be avenged, my dear friend," Zau said before facing father and daughter. "How did this happen?"

"Poison dart," Taleeka replied.

"Do you know who did this?"

"Our main suspect is the Konrads' housekeeper, Criada," Noorim said, stepping forward. "He was the only one missing after her death. The straw used to deliver the dart was found on a tray he had used, and the kitchen door was left ajar."

"I'm here to help in any way I can," Zau said confidently.

"I am certain your abilities will be welcomed," Noorim said, touching her talking stone. "Yes, Cadi, what have you discovered?" A short, one-sided conversation ensued, with Noorim finally saying, "I understand. I'm on my way."

Turning to the mourners, she said, "Cadi discovered something about that body on the beach. I must go."

Taleeka glanced at Alto, who made several slight gestures.

"My father says he will remain at his wife's side. As shall I."

"Mind if I go with?" Zau asked.

"I do not mind at all," Noorim replied. "If your arrival is any indication, your skills may prove useful."

Taleeka then looked forlornly at Zerga. "Zerga, I need you and Gidaria back in Zor."

"But Tally," Zerga protested.

"I need someone to run my operation while I'm gone. I'll meet you in Makatooa for the immersion ceremony."

"Tally, I don't want to leave you."

Taleeka gently grasped her arm. "I know. I don't want you to leave either, but I need someone I trust running things back home."

Zerga's face fell, and she slumped in defeat. "Alright."

Taleeka touched her talking stone. "Giddy, I know you're going stir-crazy in Durik. Fire up the *Vastus* and pick up Zerga. You're both headed back to Zor."

Taleeka tapped the stone again, nodding at her girlfriend. "She'll be here shortly."

"Our destination is just up the coast," Noorim said to Zau. "I will get horses."

"No need," Zau said, lifting her eyepatch.

All but Taleeka and Alto gasped when the blue translucent globe projected from her eye.

"Looks like the portal that brought me here is still stable," she said, lowering the patch and smiling at Noorim. "What say we take a stroll through the Middle Realms?"

○ ○ ○

Major Kimball Monteur of the Eighth Eldorian Lancers listened to the tent flaps rattling from the constant breeze rushing down Kalani Pass. He felt fortunate the noise drowned out the rather heated exchange between the Eldorian and Jomake representatives in attendance. Above the massive shelter, the two white flags of truce fluttered wildly, indicating peaceful intentions, although current behavior suggested otherwise.

The eastern side of the Goyan Mountains belonged to the sovereign territory of House Eldor. It connected with the Jomake Empire in central Goya through the Kalani Pass, fought over for thousands of grands—first with House Aramos and lately against King Serkel and his Jomake.

Major Monteur could clearly see the reason for the conflicts. The hundred-yard-wide ravine provided the only path through the Goyan Mountains, a vital lifeline for anyone wishing to avoid either a perilous trip over the peaks or a lengthy detour thousands of miles out of the way. Fortifications at each end of the pass ensured no unofficial encroachment from either side. The center of this cleft in the mountains also served a diplomatic purpose as the meeting place for Eldorian and Jomake negotiators settling differences between these two agricultural powerhouses.

Monteur considered himself foremost a gentleman and found negotiators on both sides extremely boorish. They hammered out most mundane squabbles in this tent, which commonly grew quite contentious, but they held upper-level meetings in the Zorian Forum, hopefully with a more civilized decorum.

Monteur, slightly overweight and of average height, cut a striking figure with his naturally squinting eyes, large black handlebar moustache and shoulder-length black hair combed straight back under a decorated tan beret. When in uniform, he adorned it, at his own expense, with flourishes of yellow ribbon and gold piping along the collar, cuffs and buttons. His pants, tucked into expensive knee-high riding boots, also bore gold piping running down the sides.

However, Major Kimball Monteur seldom wore his uniform. The military dandy, nicknamed 'fancy pants' behind his back, counted himself among the most dangerous humans in Lumina. The Eldorian Mechanic carried the codename Reaper due to his high body count within the Society of Whispers.

Monteur sighed wearily, finding these temporary assignments tedious, akin to dealing with bickering children. Yet orders must be followed, and he needed to maintain his cover as a military liaison.

He felt immediate relief when the talking stone in his pocket vibrated. Stepping just outside the tent, he tapped it through the fabric of his trousers, and the voice of Jasusa de Bogor, spymaster for House Eldor, filled his head.

"Reaper, we have a situation. There's been an assassination attempt on our sovereign's life. I need you at the royal palace in Rophan immediately."

The Eldorian mechanic paused, unsure he heard correctly. Shom Eldor held the esteem and love of nearly every citizen.

"Pardon me," he said confused. "You *did* mean… Shom Eldor?"

"Yes," came the terse reply.

"Is the sovereign all right?"

"Yes, but you are needed immediately, Reaper."

"On my way," he said before tapping the stone off and stepping back into the tent.

Two Eldorian aides stood behind the negotiator, who leaned over the table, gesticulating wildly while making a point. Monteur approached one aide, whispered into his ear, and then left.

Hopping onto his motorized Ukko bike, he started the Etheria engine and headed for the fort at the Eldorian end of the pass. He needed to secure an airship quickly.

○ ○ ○

The palace in Rophan still reeled after the assassination attempt. With the lifting of the Kan of the third cycle, evidence teams had long since departed with their collected trinkets, the bodies had been removed and the clean-up proceeded quickly. Attina supervised the refilling of the tubs after their thorough cleaning, inspecting the removal of blood stains from the surrounding floor.

"How is his majesty?" came a raspy voice from behind.

The Hill Sister seneschal spun around to see the smallest EEtah she had ever encountered. He stood only six foot four, dressed in a simple blue shirt with black pants tucked into sturdy-looking work boots. However, the Yudon harpoon strapped across his back marked him as a Sunal EEtah deserving respect.

"He's fine," she said, quizzically tilting her head. "A little out of practice at being shot at... but basically fine."

"Fassee, from Adad Sunal," the EEtah said, noting her questioning look. "I'm here to investigate the death of Koruma, his bodyguard. Standard procedure when one of our kind dies inland, especially in a city."

"Attina," she introduced herself, offering her hand. "I'm the king's keeper."

"Then you are definitely the person I need to talk to," Fassee said, joining forearms with the Amarenian female almost as tall as himself.

"Adad Sunal?" Attina said, sounding confused. "Koruma wasn't from your house?"

"Yeah, but House Nur sets the assignments, and they seem to think I have the most experience dealing with humans. Speaking of unusual, you generally don't see Hill Sisters in your position."

Attina chuckled. "That's a long story. Shom and I go way back."

"And you're on a first-name basis with the king," Fassee noted.

"Like I said, we go way back."

"I believe you," the EEtah investigator said, peering around the room. "So, this is where it happened?"

"Yep, your guy died valiantly, taking two rounds meant for the sovereign. It gave me time to take out the assailants."

"So, you were present when it happened?"

"Standing right about where we are now."

Fassee nodded. "Sounds like he followed his training—"

"Attina! So good to see you," came a boisterous drawl from behind, causing both to turn. "Terrible circumstances mind you, but then, that's why you sent for *me*."

Attina smiled recognizing Major Monteur. Fassee studied the well-dressed human as he approached gracefully. He wore his shoulder-length black hair pulled back, sporting the largest handlebar moustache the EEtah had ever seen. His ornate walking stick caught Fassee's attention.

"Hello Monty," Attina greeted warmly.

"You, my dear, are as lovely as ever," Major Monteur crooned, taking her hand and kissing it. "I understand his majesty is unharmed?"

"Yes, he's in his private chambers. He just found out his good friend Maluria Konrad was killed. Monty, this is Fassee, an inspector from Adad Sunal. Fassee, Major Kimball Monteur, our resident mechanic."

"Ah," Fassee said, shaking hands. "I had a feeling I would run into someone in your profession before too long."

"Yes, well, House Eldor is rather good-sized and I find myself constantly having to fix things," he said before turning to the seneschal. "Attina, how did this happen?"

"My next question," Fassee added.

"Two assassins glamoured as the king's bathers. Between the EEtah taking the hits and me taking them down, they failed."

"Thank the gods!" Monteur said earnestly. "Any idea who they were?"

"No names yet, but they were Zoldak."

Monteur's face scrunched in frustration. "Mercenaries!"

"Zoldak?" Fassee asked.

"Mercenaries, like Monty said," Attina explained. "The Zoldak Group are almost exclusively ex-Black Talons from House Aramos' Forsvara Guards."

"I see," Fassee replied. "So, they weren't just malcontents."

"I'm afraid you are correct sir," Monteur said with a rap of his walking stick on the floor. "Which means, even though the assassins themselves are dead, those that sent them are very much alive, for the time being."

The statement caused Fassee to chuckle. "I like the way you think."

"I imagine you have the bodies stored somewhere?" Monteur asked.

"Yes, they're in cold storage over at Clerria House."

"Very well, that is where I shall begin."

"Alright, it looks like this is an easy assignment for me," Fassee said. "He died in the line of duty. I'll arrange for his body to be returned and put him up for a commendation."

○ ○ ○

"Well, at least the neighborhood has improved," Talib said, watching the upscale buildings of Bogat Plat pass by the hackney's side window. "How do you know he's going to be at this eatery?"

59

"Elk steak."

"Elk steak?"

"Yep, my people say our boy is crazy go-nuts for elk steak. So, I did some asking around, and this place called The Butcher's Table serves up the best. It's also the featured item on the menu this evening."

"Okay, that's where. How do you know when?"

"Supposedly it sells out fast, so you have to get there early."

An impressed Talib nodded his head while Tantei parked the hackney just down the street.

"Hold off on the badges," she advised when Talib pulled his placard from his inside jacket pocket. "Keep it handy but let's not go flashing it around."

The junior detective nodded, and both got out of the vehicle. Moving down the sidewalk toward the eatery, they couldn't miss the long line of well-dressed patrons spilling out the door and snaking down the block.

"Wow, the food must be good," Talib said. "I wonder how come I've never heard of it?"

"Because this place is way out of both our price range."

"Really?"

"From what I understand, one meal will set you back about a cluster's pay."

Talib whistled appreciatively, and they made their way past the crowd into the lobby. A beautiful young hostess, with long black hair, seductive eyes and an evening gown displaying ample cleavage, manned a podium at the dining room entrance, smiling sympathetically as they approached.

"I'm sorry," she said with a pout. "There's a two deci wait for a table."

"Oh, we're not here to eat," Tantei said softly, flashing her badge from inside her jacket. "Might we have a word with the manager?"

A concerned look spread over the hostess' face, and she waved at a balding, clean-shaven man in an expensive suit standing just inside the dining area, monitoring a small army of formally dressed servers. Seeing her signal, he nodded and promptly headed their way.

"Yes, Tira?" he asked, leaning in close.

"Si. Torner," she said meekly, "these two from the Zorian Guards want to speak with you."

The manager nodded and faced the investigators with a polite smile. "Torner de Zor, I'm the manager. What can I do for you?"

"Inspectors Tantei and Talib," Tantei introduced subtly. "We need to check your dining room for a person of interest we need to talk to."

"Oh dear," Torner said. "I hope there's no danger to our diners."

"I seriously doubt it sir," Talib reassured. "He may not even be here. If he is, we'll be considerate."

The manager gave a weak smile of approval, and the duo made their way into the dining room. Standing along the wall out of the servers' way, they scanned the sea of diners.

"Do you know what he looks like?" Talib asked without taking his eyes off the crowd.

"It's been a while," Tantei replied, searching the tables, "but yes, I do. He doesn't know me *though*... and bingo!"

The pair started for a table near the front of the room with a lone occupant sawing away on a large slab of meat. He appeared thin, with a clean-shaven baby face and short dark hair. Impeccably dressed, he handled his personal knife and fork with refined precision.

"You brought your protection, right?" Tantei inquired cautiously.

"In my pocket."

"Good, because without that Etheria bauble he could suggest you dance naked on the table, and you would."

"That's a disturbing thought."

"Tell me about it. I'd have to watch."

Talib rolled his eyes, and they silently sat down on either side of the dining thief.

Zoteri paused from cutting a bite of elk and glanced at the investigators flanking him.

"I beg your pardon?!" he said incredulously, his face contorted in outrage.

"Relax, Zoteri," Tantei said with a broad grin. "We're with the Zorian Guards. We want to talk."

"Talk about what?" he asked indignantly. "And I'd like to see some sort of identification."

Both showed their badge placards, and his demeanor shifted from offended to haughty.

"I'm afraid I have nothing to talk about with you. Kindly move on."

"Nice try," Tantei said, "but it won't work on us. As for nothing to talk about, what say I get the conversation rolling." She paused, savoring the frustration on his face from his powers failing.

"So, you blow back into town and all of a sudden you're shitting gold."

"We know it was from that grain heist from the docks almost a cluster ago," Talib stated definitively, leaning towards him.

"I don't know what you're talking about," Zoteri stated angrily, locking his gaze with Talib.

"Oh, will you give me a fucking break," Tantei protested, drawing attention away from her partner. "That job had your name all over it. Look, we're not interested in you. We're after bigger fish, you know, like the people who hired you."

An angry, resolute look descended on Zoteri's face, and he calmly set the knife and fork down.

"I said, *NO,* you cannot sit down!*"* he loudly announced to the room. "You can't jump the line! All these people waited their turn, get in line!"

"Alright asshole," Tantei growled. "Now, you're just flat-out pissing me off!"

"Please get back in line!" Zoteri yelled, directing his outburst towards the line waiting in the lobby. "Are you just going to let them cut in line?! Somebody, do something!"

The suggestion spell worked, and a dozen angry customers broke off the line and advanced on the table, protesting loudly. They swarmed the investigators, shouting and berating them for the supposed infraction. Both looked around nervously until Tantei stood and pulled out her badge, holding it aloft.

"Zorian Guards!" she yelled authoritatively. "We're questioning a suspect, not jumping in line, so back off!"

Her announcement did little to quell the crowd, and she saw the manager making his way through irritated customers. Her heart sank when she noticed Zoteri's empty chair.

"What! Where did he go?!" she demanded incredulously.

"He must have slipped away in the confusion," Talib offered, coming to his feet.

The crowd still pressed in, and the manager finally arrived just as Tantei lost her temper.

"I said back the fuck off!" she demanded, drawing her pistol.

Sight of the weapon immediately quieted the mob, several gasped out loud.

"We were questioning a suspect that *you* allowed to escape!" Tantei berated. "I've got half a mind to arrest all of you for obstruction!"

"Inspectors, please," the manager begged.

Tantei heaved a frustrated sigh and put the pistol away. Her suspect had escaped, and it really wasn't their fault.

"So much for discretion," Talib said wearily.

The moon had just risen over the Amarenian coastal city of Durik and a wide-eyed Cadi gazed around in awe at the rapid restoration progress. Amarenian workers and slaves of both sexes busied themselves with various tools, and the sound of construction filled the air.

"You know, it's still kind of strange to see the female slaves with the Whitmar brand," she said, staring out the hackney's window.

Noorim looked over from the driver's seat with a quizzical expression. "Why so?"

"I don't really know, I guess growing up, all I ever saw were male slaves."

"Since House Whitmar took over providing slaves and indentures, they've vastly improved the system."

"I guess," Cadi replied wistfully. "This place is changing so fast, for the better, I'm sure. You know, with Lideri Konrad gone... I just hope the next Lideri continues what she started."

"I believe the queen will choose wisely," Noorim said, parking the hackney by the wharf entrance.

"I hope this crone turns out more helpful than the other two," Cadi said, stepping out. "I mean, considering these three had the biggest axe to grind with the Lideri."

Cadi slung her luroh over her shoulders so that the twin holsters rested precisely on her hips, adjusting her badge and rank crest where the straps crossed between her bare breasts. With a quick final check, she nodded her readiness. Noorim, dressed in her black Vardee, led the way.

"You would think being crone of your own Banja, you'd send someone to receive a shipment," Cadi remarked, falling in behind the spymaster.

"It betrays much about her personality," Noorim replied, staring straight ahead.

Walking down the round deck connecting the various docks extending into the ocean like wheel spokes, they eventually reached one bustling with more activity than the others. Indentures disembarked from a recently docked Whitmar slave ship and curiously peered around at their new temporary home. The punishment slaves followed, under considerably heavier security.

Zamjena Barkerr watched a short distance from the gangplank, carefully eyeing each new arrival. The new leader of the Barkerr Banja appeared dressed for business with her gold cropped pants, jeweled sandals and bare chest.

A younger high Amarenian, presumably her assistant, stood beside her holding the leashes of two kneeling nude male slaves.

"Zamjena Barkerr?" Noorim qualified upon approach.

The young crone snapped her head toward the interruption with taut lips and narrow eyes. "I remember you from the other moonless. I answered all your people's questions. What do you want?"

"Thank you for your prior cooperation," Noorim said in her typical monotone. "I have just a few more questions."

"As you can see, I'm busy!"

"I will attempt to be brief."

Zamjena scowled, watching two more slaves pass by, before sighing in resignation.

"Very well, ask your questions."

"You, as well as the other two former Sardors opposed Lideri Konrad, did you not?"

"It was my predecessor who opposed Lideri Konrad. She paid for it with her life. You were there as well as I."

"Yes," Noorim confirmed. "I imagine you harbored resentment seeing your Sardor gunned down before your very eyes?"

"Konrad had been kidnapped. It was within her rights."

"That was not my question. I asked if you resented her for it?"

"At the time, yes."

"Enough to have her killed?"

Zamjena huffed loudly. "So that's what this is about. You think I arranged to have the Lideri killed?!"

"You and the other two Sardors had the strongest motives. We've already eliminated the others. So, I ask again. Did you resent her enough to have her killed?"

The crone's lips pursed with anger. "No, I did not! In fact, my Banja was one of the first to reap benefits from her new policies. I had no reason to want her dead."

Noorim paused briefly, then nodded. "Very well, I thank you for your time."

The pair walked away and Zamjena resumed inspecting a line of punishment slaves being led single file by ropes around their necks.

On the return to the hackney, Noorim glanced at Cadi beside her. "Well?"

"Valorous, I hate to push us into a dead end, but she was telling the truth."

They reached the hackney just as a Mahalia officer approached.

"Uh, Valorous, I was hoping you could help me," she said, embarrassed.

"How can I help?" Noorim asked as the pair stopped.

"I have to show you."

Noorim and Cadi exchanged curious glances.

"Very well, show us."

She led them to a small building at the end of the dock. Opening the thick door, they felt a blast of cold air escape. The room seemed empty, save for a dozen brown-skinned Goyan bodies lined against the back wall.

"These bodies are awaiting transport back to the Goyan Islands for funeral rites. There's been a mix-up, and no one's come for them in quite a while. I was hoping you could expedite things?"

Noorim and Cadi stared in shock, then exchanged startled looks. Criada, the Konrads' housekeeper, lay among the others.

"When was that body brought in?" Noorim asked, pointing at Criada's corpse.

The Mahalia checked the tag on his toe. "Well over a cluster ago."

"Before the party," Cadi noted suspiciously.

"I will make some calls," Noorim said, pointing at Criada. "I want that one on an airship to the University of Marassa this luna!"

○ ○ ○

Major Kimbell Monteur made sure to call ahead and did not wear his Lancer uniform into Aramos territory. The central garrison for the Aramos Forsvara Guards sits on the outskirts of the city of Sury. The encampment came before the city, nestled on the western coast of Vakai Island, where forces could quickly dispatch. Sury rapidly sprouted beside it, ready to service the army's needs. Just north of the main garrison, a smaller, walled-off compound known only as "The Camp," houses and trains the infamous Black Talons, the special forces of House Aramos.

Monteur stepped off the transport airship and watched the ground crews scurrying to the cargo bay hatch. A serious-looking, clean-shaven, young man in a crisp uniform stood at the bottom of the ramp to greet him.

"Major Monteur," he welcomed officially, eyeing his expensive blue suit and ornate walking stick. "I was unaware you would be out of uniform."

"I'm afraid I'm not here in that capacity today," Monteur replied congenially.

He thought the young man's statement was odd but remembered the decidedly martial tone House Aramos adopted with Dolan Aramos's ascension to the throne.

The young officer nodded. "I'm Lieutenant Pekor, Commander Varozy's aide. He's expecting you."

Their brisk walk, conducted mostly in silence, was interrupted by the crack of a whip striking flesh. A male voice cried out in pain just out of view.

Pekor shook his head sadly. "He's going to get another lash for that outburst."

Monteur looked over at the lieutenant in disbelief. "You're not allowed to utter anything, even when being bull whipped?"

"Discipline must be maintained," he said, staring straight ahead. "Weakness must be driven out of the body and mind. Just last cluster, I received ten lashes for the collar of my uniform being soiled. I did not cry out once."

Stepping through a small outer office, they stopped at a plain wooden door with Varozy's name on it. Pekor gave it three quick raps, opened it and stepped inside. Coming quickly to attention, he saluted.

"Sir, Major Monteur," he announced, then stepped to the side.

He exited and closed the door once Monteur entered the room. A clean-shaven, tall, fit man with a bald head and seemingly permanent scowl stood from behind his desk and offered his hand.

"Major Monteur, you said it was urgent."

"Yes, quite urgent as a matter of fact," Monteur said, noting his overly firm handshake.

"Please have a seat."

Both sat down, and Varozy leaned forward, arms resting on the desktop.

"Alright, what exactly is this urgent matter for the Eldorian Lancers?"

"Actually, I'm not representing the lancers on this visit, hence no uniform. I'm on assignment for the E.I.S."

At the mention of the Eldorian Intelligence Service, the commander cocked a wary eyebrow.

"Oh."

"Yes, I'm sure you've heard of the assassination attempt on his majesty, Shom Eldor, two cycles ago?"

"Yes, terrible news."

"Well, the assassins are quite dead. However, I've been tasked with getting to the bottom of things and find out who sent them."

"An important assignment, to be sure. How does this concern the Forsvara Guards?"

"Commander, the assassins were members of the Zoldak Group."

"That's disturbing," he said, his brow furrowing. "Many ex-Talons choose the mercenary way of life. Unfortunately, once they're given the black and leave, we no longer control them nor keep track."

"I surmised as much," Monteur said, sitting forward anxiously. "Actually, I was hoping I might get a look at your roster of the Talons who have been 'given the black,' as you put it."

Varozy shook his head vigorously. "Major, I'm sorry, but that's out of the question and, quite frankly, way over my pay grade. Politicians must handle this request."

"Official channels will take forever. I mean, we're all familiar with what happens when politicians get involved. First, they talk it to death and then do nothing."

"Major, quite frankly, my hands are tied, and even if I did have the authority, I would be reluctant to give them to you. The Black Talons are an extremely elite military unit used for our most sensitive operations. Handing over *any* of their names, current or former, could compromise security. After all, you did identify yourself as an agent of a foreign power."

"I see," Monteur said dejectedly. "Well, you understand I had to give it a try?"

"I understand completely. I wish you good fortune with your assignment," he said, coming to his feet.

Monteur recognized a dismissal when he experienced it.

"Thank you for your time, Commander."

"Wish I could have been more help," he said when they shook hands.

Once alone, Varozy touched the Larimar talking stone he wore in a band around his wrist and envisioned Naza Kirkmon, the Aramos spymaster.

"Yes, Commander?" rang out in his head.

"Riddle Master Naza, I just had a very interesting visit that you are probably going to want to hear about."

○ ○ ○

Zoteri knew he needed to be careful ever since finding out the Zorian Guards considered him a suspect. He knew he shouldn't take another job so close to the last one and should leave town, but he just couldn't help himself. This new client paid big money for relatively low-risk heists. She called herself Miran, and he knew she worked for someone bigger, someone he probably didn't want to know about.

She told him to meet at the same place as last time, a dive bar on the southern docks called Outlanders. The place provided plenty of private, darkened alcoves perfect for plotting away from prying eyes and ears. At this time of the early evening, it would'nt be busy. The after-work patrons already left for home, and the late crowds hadn't arrived yet.

The Grand Turine in the Zorian harbor rang seven bells when he arrived. Ordering an ale at the bar, he found a remote booth and settled in. He didn't wait long before the masculine-looking woman with light brown skin and a bald head entered. She wore a similar outfit as last time, simple pants and just a tunic opened on the sides, revealing her petite breasts. This time, however, the unusual buckle on her wide belt caught his attention.

She nodded when she saw him, ordered her ale, and joined him across the table.

"We gotta be careful," Zoteri said tensely. "The Zorian Guards are on to me."

"I know, my employer wanted me to discuss that with you. But first, I gotta hit the privy."

Zoteri nodded, and she got up. She moved around to his rear and disappeared from view. After waiting for several long moments sipping his ale, he felt a presence behind him.

Before he could turn, he felt the thin wire wrapping around his neck and being snapped tight. He gurgled and thrashed, unable to scream as the garrote cut off his air, slicing into his neck. In a panicked gesture, he grabbed the handle of his mug and slammed it back over his head. He heard the glass shatter, Miran's cry of pain, and felt his head soaked with liquid.

The garrote dropped on the table in front of him, and he saw her unusual belt buckle comprised the handles of the murderous tool. Miran fell sputtering and gagging to her knees, covering her bleeding face. He grabbed at his throat, coughing, before lashing out and kicking her in the chest.

She cried out once more, toppling backward onto the floor. The conflict attracted the attention of the few patrons present, as well as the bartender, who yelled, "No fighting!" at them but did little else.

Zoteri, still sputtering and clutching his throat, ignored the bartender and quickly made his way to the door. Glancing back to make sure no one pursued him, he saw Miran getting to her feet, still covering her wounded face.

Fully realizing he just cheated death, the gentleman bandit knew he didn't need both sides of the law stalking him. He needed to choose a side, and one side had just tried to kill him. This left him no other options and only one place to turn. Slipping out into the Kan fog, he beat a direct path to Judgment Square.

○ ○ ○

"Aw, come on Tay, I'd do it for you," Tantei pleaded, sitting forward in her chair.

"I don't know Tee," Talib replied guardedly, shaking his head. "I think it would be kinda awkward."

"Are you telling me you've never been out on a double date before?"

"That's exactly what I'm telling you."

"Boy, talk about living a sheltered life."

Talib gave a weak smile. "Sorry."

"Look, I really want to go out with this guy, but getting someone to go out with his friend is part of the deal."

"You just want what's swinging between his legs," Talib said, straightening a stack of papers on his desk.

A shocked look crossed the female investigator's face.

"You say that like it's a bad thing."

Talib shot her an unamused glance, prompting Tantei to launch into a fresh round of persuading.

"It's only dinner. It probably won't last more than a couple of deci. Afterwards, you two can part ways and I'll spend the Kan riding the pony. Did I mention I'm paying?"

Talib stopped shuffling papers and peered cautiously at his partner.

"You, in fact, did *not*," he said, seeing the hopeful look on her face. Sighing, his shoulders slumped. "What's her name?"

Sensing a crack in his resolve, Tantei pounced.

"Her name is Husong, and she's cute. She works as a file clerk in the land office."

"You've met her?"

"Once, she seems really nice, very accommodating."

Talib sighed again. "Alright, I'll go."

A broad grin broke out on Tantei's face. "Great! I'll set it up for a couple of cycles from now!"

"Fine, whatever," Talib said, returning to his paperwork. "I just hope Si's massive penis is worth it."

"Rumor has it that it's big enough to take down wild game. I can't wait to take it out for a ride."

The desk sergeant poked his head through the partially open door. "Uh, investigators, I've got a guy out front who says his name is Zoteri. Says he wants to turn himself in."

Talib and Tantei shared surprised glances before addressing the sergeant.

"Put him in Interrogation Room Two," Tantei said, a twinge of hope creeping into her voice.

"Yes, ma'am," the sergeant said before disappearing into the hall.

A mood of cautious optimism permeated the walk to the interrogation room. Once inside, they found Zoteri fidgeting nervously at the table.

"Right off the bat, I want to apologize for the other cycle in the restaurant," Zoteri placated the moment they entered.

Tantei gave a wry chuckle as they sat down. "Actually, it was pretty clever. You couldn't affect us, but the other diners, that's another story."

"As I recall, it wasn't that amusing at the time," Talib added.

"Yeah, well, anyways, sorry."

"Apology accepted," Tantei said, leaning forward. "So, what's with the sudden change of heart?"

"You have to get me protection."

"Protection comes with a price, my friend," Tantei said confidently. "What do you have for us?"

"The person who hired me was a woman named Miran."

"Mazie's right hand," Talib noted. "She replaced Drugo."

"Why steal a shipment of rare grain? It would be noticed the moment it hit the street."

"They didn't say."

"What were they going to do with it?" Talib asked.

"I don't know."

"What did *you* do with it?" Tantei asked, unhappy with the last two answers.

"I drove it to a warehouse in Kimadorn, where I left the hackney and cargo. The second half of my payment was there waiting for me. Nobody was around. From there, I got a ride back to Zor."

Jomake, Talib thought. *What do they want with grain? They literally grow tons of it.*

"That's it?" Tantei confirmed.

"That's it. Now, about that protection."

Tantei nodded in satisfaction, then reached into her pocket. Pulling out a five secor gold note, she placed it on the table in front of him.

"Alright, I'll drive you to the air station myself. That's enough to get you passage anywhere in the Goyan Islands. Why the need for protection?"

Zoteri's eyes narrowed fearfully. "I just came from an encounter with this Miran. She said she had another job for me but it was a trap!" He pointed at the wound the garrote left on his neck. "The bitch tried to kill me!"

$$\bigcirc \; \bigcirc \; \bigcirc$$

Monteur saw Zor's skyline from the back of the air taxi. He felt mildly disappointed at the Aramos commander's unwillingness to help but, in a way, almost expected it. His next course of action would be trickier and much more dangerous.

He knew of an upscale bar in Zor's Shimol Plat called Posh. Wealthy and influential people hired the Zoldak Group there. He needed to call and make a reservation, specifically asking for the manager, Rodrick. Of course, no one by that name worked there, but the code word secured a meeting.

While reaching for his talking stone to make the call, it vibrated in his hand. Pressing it, Spymaster Jasusa's voice filled his head.

"Reaper, there is a new development you need to be made aware of."

"You have my attention," he calmly replied, realizing even if the pilot couldn't hear her, he must keep his side of the conversation guarded.

"We just received word from the Amarenians," Jasusa explained. "Maluria Konrad's assassination happened at the same time as the attempt on his majesty. Both assassins were Zoldak, and both used Etheria to glamour themselves to get close to their victims. Unfortunately, Konrad's assassin succeeded. Even though the methods differed, this appears to be a coordinated attack."

"I see. Yes, this is an important development," Monteur said, attempting neutrality for the pilot's benefit.

"The Konrads, as well as your counterpart in the Queen's Envoy Service—a young high Amarenian named Cadi Nogol—will accompany them to Makatooa. Maloria Konrad specifically asked for immersion there. Meet them there, put your heads together, and see what you can uncover."

"A most sensible plan. I'm en route."

The connection ended, and Monteur put the Etheria shard away.

"We have a change in destination, my good man," Monteur said to the pilot, who turned an attentive ear. "Makatooa, if you please."

Alto had not left Mal's side since her death and refused anything to eat or drink. Taleeka, along with Zerga, Cadi, Noorim, Zau and her father, brought the body to Makatooa two cycles earlier.

Mal specifically requested immersion in Makatooa, where it all began. The temple on the wharf there, EEtah's House Nur, hosted the small private immersion ceremony but proved much too tiny for the expected memorial size. Pierce Calden, current sovereign of the great house, arranged through his brother, the mayor, to use the grand ballroom of the Calden estate.

Mal lay in state, bathed in sunlight from the floor-to-ceiling windows, on a low stage at the back of the immense room. A sheer white burial shawl covered her body, tastefully concealing details of her mutilated remains.

The ever-present Alto levitated a few inches above the stage in a kneeling position next to her, while Taleeka stood beside her swordmaster father. Zerga and Zau stood off to the side of the stage, watching the long line of mourners waiting to pay their respects.

People started arriving a deci prior from all across Lumina. Joc' Valdur embraced Pierce Calden when their small delegations arrived, as did King Shom, who almost shared the same fate as his shrouded friend.

Everyone stared when Kumo the spider-woman arrived carrying a small box. All six of her eyes squinted in sorrow and two horizontal black mourning bands adorned her swaying pendulous breasts. When Taleeka saw her, a sad smile crept across her face.

"All the way from the Os-Oni Mountains," she said aloud to no one in particular.

Kumo got in line, and when she passed in front of the kneeling Alto, she placed a comforting hand on top of his head. She lingered a moment before moving on to Taleeka.

"The queen sends her heartfelt condolences," Kumo said, her meek, squeaky voice laden with sadness. "She wanted to give you this gift from the Cevot people."

"Thank you, Kumo," Taleeka replied. "You have been a great friend to my family. Please thank the queen for me."

"I have been authorized to extend you any aid the Cevot empire can offer. We owe you and your family a great debt."

"An offer I may just take you up on, my friend," she said, hugging her.

Queen Omaris of Amarenia and Queen Shula of the Bailian Empire crossed paths as the next mourners, their entrances causing quite a commotion. The two allied monarchs greeted each other warmly, and the contrast between Omaris' pale white skin and Shula's pale blue appeared striking.

The monarchs of House Aramos and Whitmar did not attend due to their contentious relationship with the Spice Rat. Still, because she held the title of Hero of the Realm, House representatives came in their place.

Taleeka glared suspiciously at the two minor court officials, knowing they attended only in an intelligence-gathering capacity. She caught Noorim's attention in the crowd, glancing at the two spies and directing her attention to them. The Amarenian spymaster gave a knowing nod. They would be closely monitored and fed prepared snippets of false information throughout the memorial.

Monteur arrived in all his finery near the end of the event; his expensive black suit accentuated his dark handlebar moustache. Making sure he placed himself last in line, he offered his hand to Taleeka and gave her a serious look.

"Glad you came, Monty," Taleeka said, shaking his hand.

"My presence here is two-fold," he said, lightly rapping his walking stick on the floor. "First and foremost, to say goodbye to my dear friend, your mother. Also, I, along with my colleagues in the Queen's Envoy Service over there, have information for you."

Taleeka nodded and held a finger up to her lips.

"Give me a moment," she said, peering around the ballroom full of milling guests and settling on the two spies.

She then looked over at Zerga, winked, and nodded at the potential enemies in their midst. Zerga's eyes narrowed knowingly, indicating she understood, and walked over to a group of four extremely beautiful human women chatting nearby. All four tittered when she spoke in hushed tones. Zerga then returned to Zau's side while the four women surrounded the Aramos and Whitmar representatives, openly flirting with their beguiling looks and seemingly enamored conversation.

With the diversion in place, Taleeka motioned at Monteur. "Alright, those two are occupied. Let's find a place to talk."

They commandeered a back office, and after Taleeka introduced Cadi and Noorim to the Eldorian mechanic, they got down to business.

"You said you had information," Taleeka said, searching their faces for any sign of good news.

"Yes," Monteur spoke first. "It appears the attack that killed your mother was coordinated with the attempted assassination on my king. All were glamoured members of the Zoldak Group."

"Mercenaries," Taleeka stammered.

"Not just mercenaries," Monteur added. "Aramos mercenaries."

"They wanted to kill both my mom and Shom! In the name of the Goddess, why?!"

"We feel it was because of the agricultural compact about to be forged between our two nations," Noorim stated flatly.

Taleeka shook her head in disbelief. "Once again, why?"

"We're not entirely sure," Monteur said. "We don't have all the pieces, but I'm certain there are more players in this little drama. I tried the official route, petitioning the commander of the Forsvara Guards for information on their Black Talons. He was less than helpful."

"I'll bet!" Taleeka said, twirling a ringlet of her hair. "Alright, this is disturbing, to think House Aramos might be behind this."

"We need more information," Monteur said with furrowed brow.

"You're right," Taleeka concurred. "I think it's time I paid an after-hours visit to our Aramos friends in Sury."

"I must return home and continue the investigation from there," Noorim said, "but it appears the bulk of the work will be here. Cadi will remain and aid you."

"Okay, let's keep each other in the loop," Taleeka said grimly. "Now, I've got to go put my mom in the water. My dad's still in shock, but with her gone, it's gonna be all but impossible to keep him restrained. People are going to die, that's a given. I just want to make sure they're the right people."

ACT TWO

Unraveling

The mid-autumn chill, intensified by the thick Kan fog, blanketed the City of Sury and the adjacent garrison of the Forsvara Guards. Up above, a shrouded *Vastus* slowly circled the three-story headquarters building in the center of the large military compound. Taleeka sat in the captain's chair, facing the rear of the airship, and stared at Cadi, whose eyes remained closed in deep concentration.

"We're coming up on it now," Cadi said in a distant voice. "It feels like dead center, top floor. A large concentration of Etheria and psionic activity."

Taleeka spun and looked past Gidaria through the thermal image windshield bathed in a dull bluish-orange. She clearly saw the roof of the building, framed by a bright orange glow around the edges.

"Looks like they've got some sort of alarm or trap on that roof," Taleeka noted.

"Or both," Gidaria said, watching the heat signatures moving around on the ground, "and there's quite a bit of activity going on down there for this late in the Kan."

Zerga nodded from the seat across from Cadi and patted the carbine in her lap. "Yeah, and if you get spotted, I don't like our odds."

"Relax, I have no intention of going down on that roof," Taleeka said, with a devious grin.

"We're over it," Cadi said, then came out of her light trance.

"Okay Giddy," Taleeka said. "Hold right here."

Gidaria hovered the craft ten feet above the structure while Taleeka got up and went back into the cargo bay. She returned moments later carrying a large suitcase, set it on the deck by the bottom cargo doors, and opened it.

Cadi and Zerga got up and peered into the open case. A large obsidian storage device dominated the entire top half, while the bottom half contained several recessed areas filled with Etheria apparatuses.

Taleeka removed a Larimar tablet and laid it on the Obsidian. Next came a three-inch-wide mirrored cylinder, telescoped out to three feet in length, followed by a roll of fishing line. She caught the quizzical look on her girlfriend's face and gave a sad smile seemingly on the verge of tears.

A four-inch-long baton with an orange Trinilic tip came out next, and Taleeka examined it with a satisfied smile.

"Okay, I think we can get started," she said, placing the baton with the other items. "Giddy, open one door and hold her steady."

One of the bottom doors slowly dropped open, and a brace of cool, crisp air rushed into the ship. Staring through the opening, Taleeka surveyed the roof below and then grabbed the mirrored cylinder. Unraveling a section of fishing line, she tied it to one end of the tube and carefully lowered it down. Both friends watched Taleeka gingerly set the tube on one end on the roof.

"Hey, what do you know, it worked," Taleeka said, causing further confusion on her friends' faces.

"The mirror reflects back whatever nastiness they have going on down there, so it appears invisible," Taleeka explained.

She then attached another line to the baton and sent it down with the Trinilic head leading the way. Again, the friends followed the object down and watched Taleeka thread the baton into the mirrored sleeve.

"Trinilic punch," Taleeka said. "Okay, Cadi, let me know when I get through. You should feel any psionic leakage through the hole."

The Amarenian nodded, sat back in a seat along the hull, and closed her eyes. Taleeka tugged on the line, and a silent orange flash erupted from the mirrored tube. She then glanced at Cadi, who sat silently. Two more jerks on the line, and Cadi opened her eyes.

"You're in."

"So far, so good," Taleeka said, pulling the punch back into the ship.

Only two items remained in the suitcase, an Amber Etheria cone and a delicate coiled chain of Etheria Diamonds. Attaching the cone to one end of the chain, she plugged the other end into the top of the Larimar tablet.

Lying on the ship's deck, Taleeka carefully lowered the cone toward the mirrored tube. She missed twice due to sudden wind gusts. On the third try, she threaded the Etheria into the top hole in the tube and fished it through the roof. When the device met something solid, Taleeka nodded in satisfaction at her two friends, then got to her feet. Stepping over to the Larimar tablet, she touched the upper right corner, and the screen came to life.

"And here we go," she said, watching fields of data written in Aramos-Ya rapidly scrolling across the tablet's surface.

"Are you sure that Obsidian has enough storage?" Zerga asked, watching the information fly across the screen.

"Yeah," Taleeka said with a head bob. "It's not a psionic charge, it's only data."

"You're stealing it?" Cadi asked skeptically.

Taleeka shook her head slowly without looking up. "Just copying it."

The answer seemed to placate the Amarenian law enforcement officer, and Taleeka chuckled ironically.

"But I'm not above it," Taleeka quickly added. "Remember, you're not representing the Mahailas. Right now, you're with the Queen's Envoy Service. Mahailas don't steal, in fact they *catch* thieves. The Envoy Service is a lot more... *flexible.*"

Cadi squinted skeptically at the justification but didn't press the matter.

The data dump proceeded uneventfully for almost a deci when Gidaria called out from the cockpit. "Tally, we've got some gusts coming in from the north."

"Keep it as steady as you can. We're almost done here," Taleeka said, checking the progress on the screen.

True to the pilot's words, the *Vastus* began pitching slightly and Gidaria attempted to steady the wheel.

When the ship rocked more violently, Taleeka anxiously watched the mirrored tube teeter and then topple over. Immediately the rim of the roof started strobing and a loud persistent clanging filled the air.

"Tally, we gotta get out of here!" Gidaria warned shrilly.

"Almost done," Taleeka calmly reported, keeping her eyes on the screen. "Zerga, open the side hatch. If anyone gets onto the roof, make them wish they hadn't."

Zerga hefted her carbine, rushed to the hatch, opened it, and knelt with weapon ready.

"Done!" Taleeka finally proclaimed after Zerga fired at the advancing guards. "Giddy, straight up!"

The airship rapidly ascended into the thick fog, with Taleeka reeling in her dangling equipment.

"Okay," Taleeka said as the hatches closed. "Let's head for home."

"Okay, you were right, she's cute," Talib said softly. "This is still awkward."

"Will you relax," Tantei replied, staring across the dining room at their dates, already seated. "People do this kind of thing all the time."

"Yeah, well, this is a first for me," Talib said, following his partner to the table.

Once they sat and made introductions, Tantei and her date, Colgado, traded lustful stares, while Talib found himself in the dreaded position of keeping the conversation going. Not that he blamed her; he didn't prefer men, but admittedly, the man was stunningly good looking. His coffee-colored skin almost seemed to glow, and his long black hair tumbled about his face in tight ringlets, accentuating a shadow of facial hair.

The date chosen for him appeared just as attractive with similarly colored skin, alluring eyes, and reddish-brown hair. Talib quickly decided if he bore the burden of leading the dialogue, he would concentrate on *his* date, Husong. Tantei would be on her own.

"So... Hi, Husong... um..." he began with an awkward laugh. "So, how do you know Tantei?"

"I met her at the Land Office," Husong answered, with a shy smile, "over paperwork."

"Paperwork?" he asked, hoping to move the conversation along and get her talking. "What kind of paperwork?"

"Lots of it, lately," she said with a laugh. "It's all I do. Nothing exciting like being an *investigator,* like you."

"Exciting? I guess it is sometimes," Talib conceded modestly, "but most times it's paperwork, just like you. Well, that and following up on a bunch of dead-end leads."

"Have you ever had to shoot anyone?"

"No, but I've come close a few times."

"That's definitely better than my job," Husong said through a sensuous pout. "It's paperwork all the time, and even worse lately."

"Oh, how so?"

"Well, you know they're converting all those soup kitchens in The Sisters? Guess who got stuck with the permitting and paperwork?"

"I didn't know they were doing that," Talib said, his demeanor changing from congenial to intently interested.

"It doesn't surprise me you didn't know. We just finished ironing out the details. They haven't started work yet."

"You're talking about Mazie?" Tantei asked suddenly, her attention diverted from the amorous staring contest across the table.

"That's the one! You've heard of her?"

The investigators traded knowing looks.

"Yeah, we've heard of her," Talib said with a smirk.

"But I hardly ever see her," Husong continued. "I mostly deal with her assistant, Miran—what a bitch!"

"So, I've heard," Tantei said wistfully.

"You said converting," Talib said. "Exactly what are they converting them to?"

"Five grain storage warehouses and two industrial grain mills," she answered. "The warehouses were the things that had to be worked out. You need special silos to store that much grain. They just didn't get it."

"Oh?" Talib asked, raising a single inquisitive eyebrow.

"Oh yeah," Husong confirmed. "Grain dust in that quantity is highly explosive. It's bad enough way out on a farm, but these are in the city—a newly renovated part of the city at that. Then, there's the citizens living nearby. Mazie initially didn't want to spend the extra money, but the rules are pretty clear. They only came around when I explained how much of their hard work would be destroyed if one of those warehouses went up."

"Not to mention the casualties," Talib added.

"That didn't seem to bother her as much," Husong replied, with a sorrowful shake of her head. "Like I said, she's a real bitch!"

"You said they haven't started yet," Tantei said, completely ignoring her date. "Do you know when?"

"Yeah, construction is scheduled to begin next cluster. They're doing all of them at once. I just can't imagine how much that costs."

"She can afford it," Talib said thoughtfully. "Mazie's got deep pockets."

"How did she get so rich?"

"She rebuilt The Sisters with her own money," Talib explained. "So, she collects rents from *everyone* in The Sisters."

Husong appeared genuinely shocked. "Is that even legal?"

Talib shrugged. "Sure, as long as the city gets the taxes, they don't care. They're just happy they didn't have to shell out the gold to do the rebuilding. Some of it was pretty extensive."

"Tell me about it," Husong said with a sigh. "I worked on that too."

"Something similar happened back in Makatooa several grands ago," Tantei offered. "The only problem is we know it's dirty money that got the ball rolling."

Husong continued her confused stare. "Well, if you know it's illegally gained money, can't you do something about it?"

Tantei gave a helpless look and shook her head. "Knowing and proving—two completely different animals."

○ ○ ○

Naza Kirkmon sat in his darkened living room, listening to the Grand Turine in the Zorian harbor ring out a very late ten bells across the fog-shrouded city. The Aramos spymaster, accustomed to obedience, bristled at his daughter Panni flaunting her curfew and worrying him. The fact he always kept a discreet protection detail following her didn't matter. The beautiful sixteen-grand-old young lady always knew her daddy could be wrapped around her finger, but since her mother, and his beloved wife Solira, died last grand, her rebelliousness increased significantly. He gave a wry chuckle to the empty room. He found it darkly ironic he could manage hundreds of dangerous operatives but not his own daughter.

The rattling door handle and fumbling with the lock made him sit up and prepare for the inevitable conflict. As the door swung open, he sighed in relief when he saw her silhouette quietly entering.

When she closed the door, he reached over and tapped the crystal by the end table, lighting up the room. She froze in position at being caught yet again, before locking the door and turning to face her father.

"Are you aware of the time, young lady? You were supposed to be home a deci ago."

"I know," she said, her voice hollow, her gaze distant. "I was out walking and lost track of time."

"How many times have I told you it's not safe for someone your age to be wandering around during the Kan?"

"I'm not worried," she said, starting off for her room.

"Don't walk away from me when I'm talking to you!"

She halted, and a bored look descended on her face. "What?"

"Look," he said, changing his tone to conciliatory. "I know it's been hard on you since your mother died, but you've got to work with me if we're going to get through this. And I know you're 'not worried,' you're young. The young always think they're invincible, but I worry because I know you're not."

"I know, I'm sorry," she said, gazing downward.

"Come on," he said, stepping up to her and opening his arms.

He embraced her, but she kept her arms at her sides, and he gently patted her back.

"Everything is going to work out fine, Pooka," he said softly. "Your dad loves you."

She nodded, and when he let her go, she walked lethargically away, still keeping her head down.

Watching her heading towards her bedroom, he noted if her condition didn't improve soon, he would probably have to seek professional help for her, if she would even accept it. Sighing heavily, he reached over to turn out the light when his Larimar talking stone tingled in his pants pocket.

"Yes?!" he said tersely.

Standing at her bedroom doorway, Panni watched her father's face grow stern. She hated the frequent calls at all hours, but the ones late in the Kan upset him the most.

"I'll be right there," he said after listening for a few moments.

He then turned towards his daughter.

"I have to go," he said, grabbing a jacket and donning his fez.

"You're always gone," Panni said bitterly. "You were never there for me and mom!"

"Panni, we'll discuss this later. I've gotta go," he said, slipping on his jacket before exiting.

Outside, he used his talking stone once more, requesting the first available airship to pick him up. Within five centi, a small scout ship descended on the lawn in front of him, and he got in.

"Sury," he ordered, "quickly."

A speedy skirt of the upwinds put the spymaster on the scene within fifteen centi. Seeing the commotion on the roof of Forsvara headquarters, he ordered the pilot to let him off there.

"What have we got, Varozy?" Naza asked, approaching the circle of Forsvara military police. Commander Varozy stood in the center questioning them, his face betraying the seriousness of the situation.

"Well, sir, like I said in the call, we had intruders. They punched a hole in the roof just above the main Obsidian data storage."

"And the alarm on the roof?"

"Well, sir, they somehow got around it for the most part. When they finally tripped it, we had no idea how long they'd been up here."

"How did they get up here in the first place?"

"By airship. It was shrouded, but with the Kan fog, it would've been difficult to see in the first place."

"Was anything damaged or stolen?"

"Nothing apparent, but the location is troubling. If this was a data breach, the consequences could be catastrophic."

"I agree," Naza said, focusing his sleepy eyes on the small hole punched cleanly through the stone. "This may be a minor incident, but I'm putting all operatives and units on alert. If there was a breach, we'll know it soon enough."

"Sir, there is one thing," Varozy said hesitantly. "Five cycles ago, an Eldorian mechanic requested information on the Talons who've resigned and may have joined the Zoldak. I, of course, refused, but..."

"A most interesting coincidence," Naza said. "Perhaps it's time to bring the Talons in on this one. The Eldorian won't be an easy target. Let's get him and find out if he's the guilty party."

"Yes, sir, he said his name was Monteur."

Naza paused, and a cruel, knowing smile crept across his face. "You're definitely going to need the Talons on this one."

"Sir?"

"Major Kimbell Monteur's code name is Reaper. What does that tell you?"

"I see, sir."

"Put several of your best on it, but have backup and replacements ready, just in case they fail."

"Yes, sir."

"And Varozy, the guards on duty when this happened are to receive twenty lashes at the lifting of the Kan."

○ ○ ○

Taleeka surveyed the three large Larimar screens on stands around the far end of the dining room table at Konrad House West and gave a satisfied nod. In the table's center, between the monitors, sat the large Obsidian storage device attached to each screen by an Etheria Diamond filament.

"Well, it looks like this is going to be our hangout for the foreseeable future," Taleeka said, placing her hands on her hips. "Nibira's skills sure would come in handy right about now."

Zerga gave a weak smile. "Actually, my experience inventorying and auditing with the Quartermasters will probably come in handy."

"That makes me feel better," Taleeka replied, smiling back. "I just wish Cadi hadn't been assigned to the Zorian Guards. We could use her, but at least she'll be close."

"What exactly are we looking for?" Zerga asked, with a touch of intimidation.

"Mom died eight cycles ago on the sixth, so just before and just after, we look for payment information. In the cycles before, we look for orders, internal memos, anything linking the Talons or Zoldak Group. We also need to check the rosters for any Talons leaving the unit."

Alto silently maneuvered his hands in an intricate pattern, and Taleeka nodded, thankful for their mysterious bond and understanding. "Okay, Dad, the rosters are yours."

"I'll take the financials," Zerga offered.

"That leaves correspondence to me," Taleeka proclaimed, just before her Larimar necklace tingled beneath her shirt.

Pressing it through her clothing, she peered upward. "Hey, Tantei. What's going on over in Judgment Square?"

"Tally, I hate to ask, but I need a favor," the investigator's flustered voice sounded in Taleeka's head.

"It's what I do."

"Well, we're pretty sure Mazie is working some new scheme involving agriculture and cornering the grain market. Our sources tell us she's ready to start next cluster, so we don't have a lot of time. We need to know what's going on."

"Really?!"

"Yeah, we want to bring in her number two, Miran, but we need an interrogator. Now that Rafel's dead, we find ourselves at a loss. Can you help us out?"

Taleeka thought for a brief moment before responding. "As a matter of fact, one immediately comes to mind— someone Rafel trained. Let me make a call. Oh, and Tantei, because this involves Mazie, you don't even owe me one."

"Gee, thanks, Tally!"

"In this case, it will be my pleasure. I'll have them report directly to you."

"I'll be expecting them. Who is it, by the way?"

"We'll let that stay a secret for right now. I don't want our hand tipped."

"Got it. Thanks again."

The line went dead, and she tapped her stone once more.

"Intelligencer Kem!" Taleeka greeted.

"Taleeka Konrad," came the familiar voice at the other end. "It's been a while."

"Yes, it has, my friend, and I find myself in need of a favor."

"Well, I owe you a few, so ask away."

"This one involves your very special skills and we don't have the luxury of time."

○ ○ ○

Air Station Three dominates the Shimol Plat in the High Holy City of Zor, ranking as the largest transportation hub in all of Lumina. At all times during any given cycle, airships of various types—commercial, industrial, and military—glide in and out of the wide rectangular opening to the flight deck, regardless of Kan fog. On this particular cycle, as the Grand Turine in the harbor rang seventeen bells indicating the morning well underway, Flight Zero Two Three arrived directly from the port city of Makatooa to the northeast.

A demure female with attractive light brown features and short brown hair, dressed in a blue suit top and red skirt, disembarked first. She walked at a determined pace, her overall demeanor radiating confidence. She preceded a young Bailian female with bright blonde hair contrasting starkly against her pale blue skin, also dressed in business attire and carrying an oversized Larimar tablet. Trailing behind the pair, a muscular giant of a man, with a bald head and overall jolly disposition, muscled a huge travel case through the crowd of passengers. The noise from the crowds made communicating difficult, and she winced slightly from the mix of perfume and body odor.

Kem Aleki, spymaster for the City of Makatooa and master interrogator for the Society of Whispers, led her small entourage to the hectic front entrance of the air station and a line of waiting hackneys. She paused and surveyed her surroundings before reaching into her pocket and retrieving her Larimar talking stone, shaped in an oval and lined with multicolored Etheria nodules.

"Okay, Tally," she said matter-of-factly. "I just landed. Where do I report?"

○ ○ ○

The cool morning breeze felt good ruffling the fur on Zau's face. The warmth of the sun and the smell of a steaming cup of tea on the table in front of her added comfort. The roadside open-air café in Zor's Tuath Plat provided a welcome change from the monotony of the current job Taleeka assigned her. Fortunately, the eatery sat just around the corner from Konrad House West where she stayed. The Singa enjoyed watching the various sentients calling the High Holy City home pass by on the busy street.

She took a sip of tea and nostalgically harkened back to the days of flying into adventure with her friends, sighing with a wistful smile. Recently, she led a solitary existence, preparing for the task Taleeka assigned upon their arrival— monitoring Mazie's Flavian activity. The job proved tedious but necessary.

When she sensed the tingling in the artificial eye under her patch, relief filled her, appreciating the proximity of the café to her current abode. Before leaving the house each cycle, she adjusted the setting to monitor only the single Flavian Portal. Someone had just used the portal in the soup kitchen's office. Dropping two struck copper coins on the table, she downed the rest of her tea and rapidly left.

Miran considered the collection of rent in the newly renovated Seven Sisters the favorite part of her job. However, the process proved tedious. Along with two money bearers and two guards, a representative of House Whitmar accompanied them to take people into servitude if they couldn't pay.

Having finished a large apartment building, with only one apartment left, two small merchants would complete the cycle's work. Checking her Larimar tablet, she noted the occupants of this last apartment paid late the previous quinte, and the Whitmar agent took custody of their son. After five cycles of cleaning public privies, the parents finally bought out his contract. Miran hoped it would differ this time.

"Rent collection," Miran announced after knocking on the simple wooden door.

The door cracked open, and an apprehensive female face peered through the narrow opening.

"Rent collection," Miran repeated.

Slowly, the door opened, and a woman in her mid-thirties wearing a simple green dress stepped aside. Miran entered, immediately noticing the smell of cooked food permeating the air. A boy and girl sat eating their evening meal at a round table. Miran surveyed the apartment's interior, finding it well maintained as per their rental agreement. Only the matter of collecting the single gold piece rent remained.

"I'm sorry," the woman said meekly, bowing her head, "but I don't have all the rent yet."

Miran's icy stare prompted the woman to continue nervously. "It's not that we don't have it. My husband doesn't get paid until next cluster."

"That is between your husband and his employer," Miran replied dispassionately. "Mazie has provided affordable housing, has she not?"

"Yes," the woman admitted. "May the Goddess bless Mz. Mazie."

"You know what is required," she said, turning to the Whitmar agent to her right. "What have you got, Percell?"

The woman sadly nodded and looked over at her children staring expectantly at her.

The slaver, a skinny older man in Whitmar court attire, consulted his own Larimar tablet. "Brothels."

Miran nodded. "Very well, the girl."

"No, please!" the mother cried out. "She's too young!"

The mobster remained unfazed. "Have her ready for pickup at the lifting of the Kan. I suggest you round up the money quickly. She'll be on her back before mid-cycle."

They left the mother sobbing and made their way to a series of storefronts situated around a dead-end alley. At the rear of the narrow side street, they approached a delivery truck hackney parked in front of a pair of double doors at the end of the alley.

"Alright, Amat the tailor is next," she said, indicating the doors. "He's always good for it, so wait here."

"Don't you want one of us to come along?" one of the guards asked.

"No!" Miran snapped. "Stay with the money!"

"Yes, ma'am," the guard said fearfully.

They watched her walk down the alley, stepping behind the delivery truck and out of sight. Moments later, the hackney driver appeared and climbed back in his cab. They stepped aside as he backed out and pulled into traffic.

After he drove away, they continued waiting, staring at the two closed doors at the end of the alley until one guard shook his head.

"This is taking too long," he said, starting down the passage. "I don't like it."

He walked down to the doors, found them locked and pounded loudly. Eventually, a thin older man with long hair and an apron dotted with pins poked his head out.

"Where is the tax collector?!" the guard demanded.

"I have seen no tax collector," he proclaimed in confusion.

"The one who came in with your delivery just now."

The tailor shook his head. "I have received no delivery this cycle."

"Then what was that truck doing back here?!"

"I know of no truck. I have been working up front."

"If you're lying to me!" the guard snarled, brushing past the merchant.

"I am not lying!" the tailor protested, watching the man search his small shop.

The tailor watched panic set in when the guard found no trace of Miran. Saying nothing more, the guard rushed back out the doors.

"That hackney! Miran's gone!" he yelled.

○ ○ ○

The mood around the dining table at Konrad House West felt somber and studious. Taleeka, Alto and Zerga sat staring at their Larimar screens, intently scrolling through vast fields of data related to the Forsvara Guards.

Zerga sensed a building tsunami of grief and sadness emanating from Taleeka. She turned to find her girlfriend staring blankly at her screen with silent tears streaming down her face. She realized the inevitability of this moment ever since her mother's death. Taleeka dealt with her grief by compulsively focusing her attention on finding and punishing the murderers, but Zerga knew the reality of the loss would eventually catch up to her.

Zerga's expression softened empathetically and she reached out, taking her grieving girlfriend into her arms. Taleeka broke down into racking sobs in her embrace. Alto peered across the table at his distraught daughter and grimaced, more determined than ever to destroy those responsible for his family's grief.

After several long moments of anguished tears, Taleeka raised her head from Zerga's shoulder, wiping her eyes and sniffling.

"I'll be alright," she managed to choke out.

Zerga kissed her gently on the forehead and stroked her hair. "Baby, it's okay. You cry as much as you need to. It's not good to keep that kind of emotion bottled up."

Taleeka managed to smile weakly. "Like my dad, I'm saving most of it for the bastards that orchestrated this."

Zerga nodded sympathetically and Taleeka returned to her screen. "One thing's for sure—I won't catch them sitting around blubbering and feeling sorry for myself. I'll do my grieving when they're dead."

The trio continued their search for several more decis until Zerga perked up. "Hey, I may have something here!"

All eyes fell on the former Quartermaster as she pointed at the Etheria tablet before her. "I've got a sizable payment to the Zoldak three cycles before your mom's death. Naza, the Aramos spymaster, authorized it."

"That would be on the third?" Taleeka asked.

"Yep."

"Let's see what the chatter was at that time," Taleeka said, scrolling furiously on her screen.

"Nothing on the third," she reported, swiping the display. "Let's see about the day before."

After finding the proper pages, Taleeka studied them until she froze. Her hands trembled slightly and a thin stream of tears began flowing. Zerga perceived these tears as anger, not grief. When she placed a comforting hand on her shoulder, Taleeka glanced over at her with a scowl.

"It's not every day you see your mother's death warrant," she said hollowly.

All crowded around Taleeka's screen and read the royal order from patriarch Dolan Aramos to Riddle Master Naza, directing him to kill the agriculture compact, using any means he deemed necessary.

"Well, we now know who's responsible," Zerga said with one arm around Taleeka's shoulder, "and, to keep House Aramos at arm's length, they used Zoldak mercenaries."

Taleeka looked over at Alto as he started making patterns with his hands.

"My father says they will all pay, and I agree. For the maximum effect on those at the top, we'll start at the bottom. My mother died horribly. I want those sons of whores at the top to know what's coming. I want them to drown in their own fear."

○ ○ ○

Six cycles passed since Mal's funeral, and the Amarenian City of Durik, as well as the Dor surrounding it, still reeled in shock. Even those who initially opposed her, admitted the quality of life increased tenfold for everyone in the two grands since her appointment as Lideri. Agricultural output reached levels allowing for exporting, and unlike before, the Durik's seaport hummed with activity. Holding the fragile new government together through its first monumental test would not prove easy.

Tajna Cabeli stood in an open bedroom doorway at Konrad House Durik and watched Noorim pack, wondering how Mal's death would affect political stability in the capital of Mostas.

"It was good working with you," Tajna said reflectively. "Terrible circumstances, mind you."

"Yes, I lost a good friend," Noorim answered, "and I fear her mother's death will send Taleeka down a very dark path. Her wrath, however, will not compare to her father's. I have trained with Alto Konrad. I have seen, firsthand, what he is capable of."

Tajna nodded in agreement. "Are you heading straight back to Mostas?"

"Yes, I must report directly to the queen, to assist in appointing a new Lideri."

"The sooner the better. I'd hate to see things descend back into chaos without a strong leader."

"Use your network to keep things together until your new leader arrives. Anyone promoting a return to anarchy must be dealt with immediately."

"I understand," Tajna said, nodding, "but I sure could use Cadi's help."

"Her assistance to the Zorian Guards is necessary. Even though Lideri Konrad was not a native of Amarenia, she held positions of high honor. Her death cannot go unpunished. The investigation has now shifted completely to the Goyan Islands. Once the guilty parties have been identified, no force will be able to stop the coming carnage."

$$\bigcirc \ \bigcirc \ \bigcirc$$

Miran awakened experiencing two very different yet conflicting sensations. She lay naked, flat on her back against a soft padded surface on the hard floor. They had tightly restrained her with legs spread, bent and elevated in a sling.

It felt anything but pleasurable and prompted her to test her bonds. Unable to move, she could only peer around at her surroundings. The stark, windowless room contained only a four-foot-tall oblong mechanical contraption at her feet. Two short rods protruded from the sides and two levers, several feet long, jutted from the top.

She felt her stomach knot when the solitary door opened and three sentients entered. A large partial EEtah hybrid with a pleasant deportment held the door for a Bailian female with bright blonde hair. She carried a long wooden case which she set next to the mechanical device before opening it.

A thin human female with short brown hair came in last, held herself with an air of authority and walked over to Miran, staring down with an eerie smile. Keeping her smirk, she glanced over at the contents of the case, nodded approvingly and sat down cross legged on the floor next to Miran's head.

"Hello," the Human said in a friendly voice. "My name is Kem, I thought we might have a little chat and avoid any unpleasantries. I would very much like to know about your employer's relationship with the Jomake and about her upcoming new endeavors with grain."

"Fuck you," Miran spat angrily.

Kem's smile turned lecherous and she stood. "You know, it's very fortuitus you would say that. That's exactly what I had in mind."

The Bailian extended her hand, reached into the case and retrieved a smooth dark wood phallus approximately five inches long.

"Kopit," she called, summoning the quarter EEtah.

Kopit walked over and stood behind the female mobster's head. Keeping his cheerful appearance, he savagely lashed out, grabbing her head and wrenching her mouth open.

Miran struggled in vain as the sentient's powerful grip held her firmly in place.

"I was fortunate to learn from the best," Kem explained, holding up the rigid wooden penis for her to examine it in the light. "Unfortunately, my two greatest teachers, Rafel and Ve-Qua are now dead. This means it's up to me to pass this art along to the next generation."

"Cha-Tra," she called, holding the stiff member out.

Miran watched helplessly as the Bailian took the phallus and moved over beside Kopit. Under Kem's watchful eye, Cha-Tra placed the tip in Miran's mouth. She winced at the smell and taste of mineral oil.

"Slowly now," Kem instructed, while Cha-Tra pushed the artificial cock further into her mouth, "just until she gags."

When the tip touched the back of Miran's throat, she started to convulse and the Bailian halted, pulling it gently out. Using her thumb and forefinger Cha-Tra marked the gag point on the shaft and Kopit let go of her head.

"Huh," Kem said appraisingly. "Obviously not a lot of experience sucking cocks. No matter, this works on everyone. Alright, hook it up."

Keeping the spot marked, Cha-Tra pulled out what appeared to be a small domed cage, opened at one end with a large rubber phallus attached to the top of its dome. She flipped it over and attached the wooden dildo on the underside of the rubber one, so it came up to the gag mark. Once finished, she handed the bizarre double dildo to Kem.

"What are you going to do?!" Miran heard herself pleading.

"Why, exactly what you suggested," Kem said brightly. "You see, my predecessors I mentioned before, had a thing for blood. Blood can be so messy. I prefer a different kind of mess. Now, last chance to talk without making a mess."

When Miran remained stubbornly silent. Kem looked over at her two companions.

"Let's get her attached."

Kopit immediately swung the machine between the bound woman's legs and Cha-Tra reached into the case once again. Miran's eyes went wide when the Bailian pulled out two more wooden cocks, one slightly smaller than the ten inch long, two inch thick one. Cha-Tra knelt in front of the machine and deftly threaded the larger dildo on the top rod and the smaller one on the bottom. She then produced a sizeable jar of lube and slathered both shafts.

Kopit held the device up to Miran's exposed vagina and anus while Cha-Tra threaded them into her. Miran cried out upon being entered. Kopit slowly worked the levers back and forth on top, causing the wooden intruders to rhythmically slide in and out of her orifices.

"I know what you're probably thinking," Kem said, picking up the dildo cage. "This isn't so bad, even if you haven't taken it in the ass before. Believe me, after the first deci it gets really old. Kopit is very strong too. He can keep this up for a long time. Now for the fun part."

Kopit broke away from the levers and once again gripped Miran's head, forcing her mouth open. Kem placed the tip of the phallus inside her mouth. When the brute pulled away, Kem slipped the cage over her head, so the wooden penis lodged in her mouth and her head stuck out the open end.

Kem stood smiling with satisfaction. Miran fearfully watched her then get undressed while Kopit returned to the levers, mercilessly pumping the hard wooden dicks in and out of her.

"I know I offered you the chance to talk, but after asking the second time, I really didn't want you to. I was just too horny. Soo…"

Kem straddled Miran's head and Miran reeled at her muskiness. The master interrogator slowly impaled herself on the rubber phallus jutting upward with a moan.

"You know it's impolite to talk with your mouth full," Kem said breathlessly when she heard Miran's muffled cries. "Hopefully, we'll chat when I'm finished. Oh, and just so you know, I'm quite the squirter."

The knock on the interrogation room's outer door drew all the investigators' attention toward the disturbance. The door opened, revealing Cadi's attractive pale white face with ice blue eyes framed by a long bob of black hair.

"Excuse me, this is where the desk sergeant said I should come," Cadi said hesitantly.

"Ah yes, the Amarenian investigator," Vanir said, taking his feet off the table and sitting up. "Come in, come in!"

Relief crossed Cadi's face as she stepped into the room, just as a piercing scream followed by racking sobs echoed from the next room. Concern quickly replaced her relief as she looked toward the noise.

Vanir waved her in with a pleasant demeanor and shook his head dismissively. "It's okay. We're conducting a little interview."

"I'm Cadi Nogol from the Queen's Envoy Service," she said, just before a fresh round of tormented cries came from beyond the door.

"Yeah, I got the call from your boss, Noorim," Vanir said over the rapid bumping and gagging noises filling the room. "We've been expecting you."

Vanir made the introductions over the torturous din and Cadi's nervous, shifting gaze.

"It shouldn't be much longer," Vanir said, as the sounds of a female in the throes of pleasure joined the other conflicting noises. Finally, she heard a massive orgasm over what sounded like someone drowning, followed by silence.

"So, Queen's Envoy," Talib said, attempting to distract from the awkward situation.

"Yes, my boss felt you could use a sensitive in your investigation and both our governments have a stake in its outcome."

"Well, that's good," Tantei said, "because things have been moving slow on our end. Maybe you can help spur things along."

Cadi smiled modestly. "I'm here to help."

Suddenly, the door to the interrogation room opened and a naked Kem stepped through carrying her dress. Sweat covered her thin frame and she breathed heavily. Her abdomen, neatly trimmed pubic patch and the inside of her thighs appeared soaked with female ejaculate. She nodded confidently and tossed her clothes over the back of a chair.

"It's almost done," she reported. "One last important detail to attend to."

Cadi eyed the naked spymaster apprehensively. As a new member of the Society of Whispers, alongside the Bailians, she hadn't yet been introduced to enhanced interrogation techniques. The barbarian Sardors of Durik Dor reportedly rarely engaged in torture, but those incidents hadn't amounted to much.

"The sentient in the next room is a broken soul," Cadi said, remorsefully.

"Yes," Kem confirmed without shame. "You've got to tear them down first. Now I've got to put her back together as something useful. In fact, this may just break the case wide open for you."

"Well, damn if that isn't good news!" Tantei said, reaching for her boss's whisky bottle and glass on the table. "Anyone want to join me in a celebratory snort?"

Vanir cocked an eyebrow as he watched his senior investigator pour a glass of amber liquid.

"I wouldn't be so quick to celebrate," Vanir cautioned, holding out his glass. "Mazie's proved slippery before when we thought we had her."

"Aw, come on boss, don't crap on our moment," Tantei whined while filling his glass.

The intelligencer paused at the door and glanced back at Vanir with a confident look. "I should be ready to brief within the deci."

○ ○ ○

Kem gently stroked and patted Miran's back as she sobbed in her arms. The two lay naked on the padded floor covering the interrogation room.

"There now," Kem soothed in her ear. "Doesn't it feel good to get that off your chest? Like a giant weight has been lifted."

Miran nodded and her weeping abated into sniffles. Kem smiled in satisfaction at finally breaking her. She proved to be exceptionally strong, but three hours of nonstop double penetration, accentuated by as many of Kem's head soaking orgasms did the trick. She especially loved the gagging sounds when she bore down on her end of the dildo.

Soothing and comforting her, Kem completed the final phase of utterly breaking her will. The spymaster knew she could easily make the female mobster her own sex slave, but she really preferred men. Besides, she considered people she subjugated of either sex, boring after a very short time.

"Our time together has been special," Kem purred in her ear, "but soon we're going to have to say goodbye."

"No, please don't leave me!"

"Shh, you know I can't keep you. You belong to Mazie."

"No, she'll kill me if she finds out about us!"

Kem gave a mischievous giggle. "Then make sure she doesn't find out."

"But I love you!" Miran proclaimed. "I'd do anything for you. Please, let me prove it. I'm yours!"

"Really?"

"Yes, please, anything!"

"If you want to prove it," Kem asked lovingly, staring into her tear-filled eyes, "will you testify in front of a judge against Mazie for me?"

"Yes," Miran breathlessly responded, then broke down into muffled sobs against Kem's chest.

"Good girl," Kem praised, gently stroking her hair. "You're going to tell everything, just like you did to me, aren't you?"

"Yes, everything."

"Good girl."

○ ○ ○

Monteur knew two men were following him at a discreet distance, just far enough back to see him without being obvious. He figured they had to be Talons, waiting for the right moment to strike. Deciding to give them what they wanted, he abruptly turned into a narrow side street in Zor's newly renovated Karo Plat, stepped into the first recessed doorway he came upon, and waited.

He smiled knowingly when he heard their confused mumblings approaching, before stepping into view. Both large men wore gray cloaks, unruly beards and surprised looks.

"Gentlemen," he greeted with a tap of his cane on the cobblestones. "I must insist on knowing why you are following me."

Their startled expressions quickly turned hostile as both stepped forward scowling. Monteur finally got a clear look at them and noted the mole high on one's cheek and the other's sinister sharp nose. Both reeked of smoke.

"We're here to take you to someone who wants to ask you a few questions," said the one with the mole.

"Oh," Monteur said, raising an amused eyebrow, "and who, exactly, might that be?"

"You'll find that out when we get there," the other replied, pulling a pistol from under his cloak.

Monteur eyed the weapon and looked back up at the man with a bored expression. "Let me guess. That's a Mark Five pistol, standard issue for all Black Talons. That means the person who wishes to chat is Riddle Master Naza. Tell me, does he still wear that ridiculous looking fez?"

Both men grinned briefly at the mention of their superior's headdress, but their serious expressions quickly returned.

"Come on, let's go," the man with the mole demanded, waving the pistol.

"Oh, for the love of the gods," Monteur bemoaned. "Will you please put that thing away. You know as well as I do that you're not going to shoot me."

"Oh yeah? Why not?"

"Because at this range there will be barely enough left of me to identify my body, and I can assure you, the dead are poor conversationists. I also seriously doubt Naza sent you here to shoot me. If so, you would have done it by now."

The gunman paused, considering the logic, then chuckled and put the weapon away. "You're right, so I guess we've got to do this the hard way. Which leaves it up to you, old man. You can either walk or be dragged."

"Really not much of a choice when you put it that way," the Eldorian mechanic said, reaching inside his jacket.

Monteur quickly pulled out a small double-barrel pistol and shot the man with the mole. His face froze in shock when the bolt punched a small hole in his chest, catapulting him against the alley wall. Gripping the bleeding wound, he slid down the barrier, leaving a red trail behind him.

The other fumbled for his weapon in stunned disbelief, but Monteur trained the Magitech derringer on him.

"I would advise you to hold, sir."

The Talon froze and looked up fearfully.

"While you are under orders to bring me in alive for questioning, I labor under no such restrictions," Monteur said, pulling the trigger.

The slug grazed the man's side, sending him spinning to the ground. Landing on his knees and clutching his wound, he screamed in agony.

"My apologies, sir," Monteur said, putting away the empty pistol with a perplexed look. "I must be losing my touch."

He grabbed the bulbous, decorated head of his cane and pulled a thin-bladed sword from its camouflaged sheath. The injured Aramos soldier fearfully watched the light glint off the mirrored steel when Monteur lunged at his chest and plunged the blade through his heart, killing him instantly. A small kick freed the blade and sent the man onto his back, eyes lifeless.

Sighing, Monteur wiped the blood from the sword on his victim's shirt and slid it back into the cane. He reached into his pocket and retrieved two struck silver coins. As he did with all his kills, he placed a coin between each of the dead men's lips.

It seemed to him the only honorable thing to do.

The meeting called for more chairs than Vanir's office contained, so everyone met in Conference Room Two. Vanir sat at the head of the long table, took a long swig from the half-filled glass in front of him and curiously eyed the slender woman with light brown skin and short brown hair he had met only two cycles prior. Intelligencer Kem certainly had managed to impress him. Being able to snatch her target and glean the information in such a short amount of time solidified her reputation as a master interrogator. She sat at the other end of the table with a knowing grin and twinkle in her eyes.

Seated next to each other on one side of the table, Talib and Tantei leaned forward expectantly.

"So, how was your pony ride the other Kan?" Talib whispered to his partner.

Tantei scoffed and shook her head. "Disappointing," she whispered back. "He had more than enough equipment, he just didn't know how to use it."

"And all of us normal guys heave a sigh of relief."

"Okay, so what have we got?" Vanir asked, kicking things off.

"She was tough," Kem said with a nod. "I thought I was going to rub her pussy right off her."

"Now there's a visual," Talib noted sarcastically, with an amused grin.

The statement got a chuckle out of Kem and she continued. "Yep, it's all about the grain. Mazie and the Jomake are working together to be the next big player in the world of agriculture. They want to give House Eldor a run for their money. That stolen grain was a gift to Serkel to seal the deal as it were."

"What do the Jomake need grain for?" Talib asked, his face scrunched in confusion. "They already control virtually all the farmland in central Goya."

"It wasn't for the grain," Kem explained. "It was for the seeds."

"Yes," Cadi agreed. "They were a special hybrid with higher yield, better flavor and more resilient under colder lower light conditions. This is yet another crime perpetrated on my people."

"Well, the grain's gone, that's a given," Tantei said. "You can bet the Jomake have the seeds and the best we can hope for is to somehow try and get them back."

"Yeah, and we've got nobody to go after," Vanir said, taking another sip. "We put their thief in the wind for his cooperation and neither Mazie nor Miran actually stole it. No judge will even hear the case."

Talib shook his head, deep in thought. "And our thief said he drove the grain to an empty warehouse in Kimadorn where he left it and picked up his last half of payment. No witnesses."

"Sounds like the trail and the whole damn case just evaporated before our eyes," Tantei said, sitting back in her chair.

"Perhaps," Kem said slyly. "But there could possibly be something bigger going on."

Everyone's attention turned to the Calden intelligencer.

"Miran said that Shom Eldor's announcement about the Eldorian Amarenian Agriculture Compact upset Mazie greatly. She saw it as a direct challenge to the deal she was working on with the Jomake. She saw an Eldorian Amarenian agreement as critically disruptive to supply and pricing. Mazie actually paid a visit to... wait for it... Dolan Aramos, to discuss it personally."

Talib softly whistled. "House Aramos, what do they have to do with this?"

"Money, what else?" Vanir answered. "The Imperial Bank holds the notes on just about every farm in the Goyan Islands. If Mazie could convince Si. Aramos that this will affect his bottom line, it could prompt him into some kind of desperate action."

Talib suddenly gasped. "You mean maybe desperate enough to kill Maluria Konrad and Shom Eldor?!"

A stunned silence descended on the room, with everyone solemnly considering the junior investigator's deduction.

"Holy shit!" Tantei stammered. "You may just be right!"

Vanir took a long drink, then set the nearly empty glass back on the table. "If that's true, this just got way bigger than the Zorian Guards can handle."

"Word in the society is that House Eldor has already dispatched a mechanic," Kem said, raising her eyebrows.

Tantei exhaled loudly. "I predict this is going to get hot. The Konrads are already out for vengeance."

"You know," Vanir said, stroking his beard, "this may just work out to our benefit."

"How so, Chief?"

"Yeah, how so?" Talib parroted.

"Well, like I said," Vanir explained, "this is too big for us. All we can do is stay out of the heavy hitters' way and let them get the job done."

"Not much else we can do," Tantei said.

"What about House Aramos?" Talib asked.

"What about them?"

"If Aramos bodies start turning up all over the city, they're going to expect us to investigate, won't they?"

Vanir chuckled slyly. "Well, there's investigation and there's *investigation*."

The confused look on Talib's face made Tantei smile knowingly and nod. "It's all about how aggressively we pursue it. Basically, we go through the motions."

"Heck, I can do that, I think."

"Good lad," Vanir praised, draining his glass.

"Any chance of this Miran getting back to Mazie?" Tantei asked. "If she finds out we know..."

"None," Kem replied smugly. "She's agreed to testify against Mazie."

The investigators sat in stunned silence, staring at Kem's satisfied smile.

"I agree," Cadi said. "I can feel her completely under the intelligencer's influence."

"Do you think you could have shared that with us a little sooner?" Vanir asked good-naturedly.

"What, and miss these looks on your faces?"

"Wow, this changes everything!" Talib said, his face lighting up.

"It sure does," Tantei agreed.

"We need to bring the I.P.'s office in on this," Vanir said, lifting his glass and finding it empty. "Karta's going to want to handle this personally, I imagine. Where is she?"

"She's locked in the interrogation room with a guard on the door," Kem replied.

"Well, okay," Vanir said. "You two get our star witness someplace safe and sit on her until we can get her in front of an Imperial Judge."

"Sounds good, Boss," Tantei said, getting to her feet at the same time as her partner and Cadi.

"Intelligencer Kem, thank you for your assistance on this one," Vanir said when she stood.

"You're welcome, but I should probably stick around. She might get spooked if I'm not here. She's doing it for me."

"Whatever it takes," Vanir said. "One thing I would ask of you before you become a babysitter. Please share the contents of this briefing with the Konrads."

"You bet," Kem replied, joining the three investigators at the door. "I'll head there now."

"Captain, if you don't mind, I'd like to tag along with your investigators," Cadi said.

"Welcome aboard," Vanir said, glancing at the empty whisky glass. "We can use all the help we can get, especially from a psychic."

Once gone, Vanir grabbed the bottle, filled the glass again and touched his Larimar talking stone with a smile. "Hey Karta, you ready for some good news?"

○ ○ ○

Despite working with the Konrads on numerous occasions over the grands, Kem found it odd she had never visited Konrad House West. While she could have conveyed the information that she acquired from Miran with a call, the Calden Intelligencer figured that, already being in Zor, she would report the news personally. Besides, curiosity got the better of her. When Mal and Alto moved to Amarenia, Taleeka bought the two townhouses on either side and converted them into one big mansion and base of operations.

After leaving Judgement Square, she sent Cha-Tra and Kopit back home to Makatooa and made a quick call to Taleeka. A ten centi hackney ride later, she stood staring at the Amarenian-style beaded door at twenty-three hundred Kasada Drive in Zor's mostly residential Tuath Plat.

She pressed the doorbell and looked up at the small Larimar panel above the door so her face could be clearly seen. A moment later, the rigid field of large beads loosened with a clack. Having no experience with a beaded door, she stepped through cautiously, slowly making her way through the four-foot-deep entryway.

When she stepped out of the elaborate doorway and into the foyer, Peshk stood smiling. Once Kem completely cleared the door, Peshk pulled a lever beside it and the beads snapped back into their fixed state.

"Greetings, Kem," the Picean said, gill flaps fluttering. "I am Peshk. Taleeka is in the study, if you'll please follow me."

"That's some door," Kem noted, staring at the interlocking spheres.

"Yes," Peshk replied austerely. "We had security issues with the old one. This way."

She led Kem through the spacious living room and down a short hall. When Kem heard panting from inside the walls following them, she gave the Picean a quizzical look.

"That is Defari, the Konrads' dog."

Upon hearing her name, the canine spirit gave out a solitary bark, making Kem flinch in surprise.

"I thought Alto's dog was in his sword."

Peshk smiled and nodded. "It's a long story."

At the end of the hall, an open door led to a room with an immense picture window taking up much of the far wall. Normally, the view would be of Narian Bay were it not for the thick Kan fog. An ornate hearth blazed on the wall to Kem's right, and floor-to-ceiling bookshelves filled with tomes lined the others.

Zerga sat at a large ornate desk facing the wall of windows, with Taleeka standing over her shoulder. Both scanned a list of names displayed on a large Larimar screen attached to an Obsidian storage device.

"This is a list of all the Talons who left the unit in the past three grands," Zerga said.

"It's a good place to start," Taleeka replied, placing a hand gently on her shoulder.

"And I'm here to make things a little easier for you," Kem said, offering a conciliatory smile before stepping into the room. "How you holding up, Tally?"

Taleeka shrugged, her eyes weary. "You know—bouts of hysterics, punctuated by murderous rage. Plotting how I'm going to kill the bastards is the only thing keeping me sane, but that's nothing compared to my dad."

"Speaking of which," Kem added, "I have information you *both* are going to want to hear."

"He's up in his room," Taleeka said. "I'll take you there.

"Thank you, Peshk."

The Picean nodded and left, but not before insisting they clear the dining table when they are done, returning its original purpose.

Taleeka leaned down and kissed Zerga on the top of her head.

"Keep digging," she said softly.

Zerga nodded. Taleeka motioned toward the door. As they went up the stairs, Taleeka leaned in close and spoke softly.

"You know he's taken a vow of silence until those responsible are dead?"

"I did not," Kem replied.

"He spends most of the cycle in solitary meditation. It's the only way to contain his usual inclination for vengeance, which is now off the charts. I've managed to keep him restrained by assuring him we only need to kill the ones responsible. My dad has a rather heavy hand when it comes to doling out revenge. Just ask the Onay."

They stopped outside a closed door. Taleeka knocked twice.

"Dad, Kem Aleki is here with information."

No reply came from within. Taleeka waited a brief moment, nodded at Kem, then opened the door. The room appeared almost bare, with a rolled-up bedroll tucked in a corner and a low table. Alto sat cross-legged in the middle of the room, levitating several feet off the floor. When Taleeka closed the door behind them, Alto opened his eyes.

"Go ahead," Taleeka prompted.

Kem briefly stared at Alto floating before beginning. "I was called in by the Zorian Guards on an assist. A grain shipment from Amarenia had been stolen and Mazie was suspected to be behind it. We couldn't get to Mazie without an elaborate operation, so my team snatched her number two, Miran. I just finished an interrogation session with her, and Captain Vanir mentioned I should share my findings with you."

When Kem revealed the plot and the players, Alto's serene expression turned into a scowl. Uncrossing his legs, he stood and made several hand gestures to his daughter.

"My father thanks you for this information. We are indebted to you."

A quick single knock and Zau rushed into the room, an excited look on her face.

"Alto, Tally," the Singa said breathlessly. "We've got Flavian activity at Mazie's."

"Don't tell me, let me guess—Quantara Keep," Taleeka said.

"If it was just there, I'd say it was Miran."

"That is not possible," Kem interrupted. "She's being held in Judgement Square. She's agreed to testify against Mazie."

"Impressive," Taleeka praised.

"I was taught by the best," Kem said humbly.

"Well then, our traveler is definitely Mazie herself," Zau confirmed, "because her next stop was the Aramos palace in Aris."

"Thanks, Zau. Stay on it."

The humanoid lioness nodded and left. Taleeka stared at her father's face, recognizing the look of retribution there.

The time had finally come to take him off the leash.

A beautiful autumn day with brilliant sunshine and a slight warming trend settled over the Goyan continent. Monteur loitered by a food vendor's stall, sipping on a cup of tea, enjoying the sun on his face. He currently surveilled two men he surreptitiously followed since spotting them last cycle. He recognized them the moment he saw them as Zoldak, which he fought against when he rode with the Eldorian Lancers. Thinking they might lead him to something or someone of substance, he decided to withhold an attack. So far, this plan only led to boredom watching the two go about their day.

Currently, they sat at an open-air eatery, enjoying a mid-cycle meal. Both men looked similar, in their late thirties with long dark hair and beards. They appeared unarmed, but Monteur knew they, more than likely, carried pistols under their light jackets.

When they finished wolfing down their lunches, the two Zoldaks got up to leave. One of them headed to the public privies, located in an alley away from the food vendors, where the smell would not offend diners, while the other waited for him outside, grimacing from the odor. Monteur crept quietly up to the edge of the furthest privy and peeked around the corner.

He saw Alto Konrad, in long black robes, step out of the shadows of a nearby back alley. Taleeka Konrad grimly walked at this side, cudgel in hand.

Hearing movement behind him, the Zoldak waiting outside the privies turned to see them and drew his weapon. Alto raised his hand and extended it, open palm forward. An invisible force knocked the Zoldak to the ground and the gun out of his hand.

Before he could lift his head, Alto stood over him. With a single kick of his foot, Alto sent him flying upright, into the side of a stonewall building. Alto summoned the chi and threw it against the mercenary, pinning him against the wall. The Zoldak struggled vainly to escape, panic mounting to the point where his bladder released and urine stained the front of his pants.

Alto's fingers grazed the mercenary's right forearm, twisting it unnaturally backwards. Breaking it at the elbow with a loud snap. The mercenary went to cry out in pain when Alto's other hand covered his mouth. He shook his head and looked straight into the Zoldak's eyes as his fingers touched his captive's left arm, also breaking it backwards at the elbow. Muffled screams echoed off the walls.

The privy door kicked open and out leapt the other Zoldak, gun drawn on Taleeka's head.

"Let him go or the bitch dies!"

Monteur raised his cane, stepped around the corner of the privy and brought it down hard, crushing the man's skull. The mercenary dropped his weapon and followed it to the ground.

Taleeka looked over to Monteur, and then down at the fallen and bleeding Zoldak with a pleasantly surprised grin. In stark contrast, Alto's intense gaze and hands never left his captive.

"By all means, carry on," Monteur said, stepping over the body.

In smooth stroke, Alto swept his free hand across the Zoldak's knees, shattering them both. He screamed into Alto's hand, tears of pain flowing down his cheek.

"You heard the man," Taleeka said, turning her attention to the frightened prisoner. "Now, if you want this pain to stop, tell me where I have to go to hire someone from the Zoldak Group? What would I have to do to enlist your services?"

The Zoldak visibly trembled from shock setting in. Urine ran down his legs, pooling at his feet, and, from the smell of it, Taleeka figured he had shit himself as well. His eyes desperately shifted between her and her enraged father.

"It... it's a lounge in the Shimol Plat called P... P... Posh," he stammered, sobbing in pain.

"Okay," Taleeka conceded. "Now we're getting somewhere. And?"

"Ask to see a m... m... manager named Rodrick. Ask him if he h...has a private room for a large party. He'll ask how l... large, and you tell him how m... m... many of us you want to hire. He'll mention a price. If he l... likes your answer and th... thinks you're legit, you go back to his office, p... p... pay him, and tell him where t... to show up. It usually takes a f... f... few cycles to round up the men depending on how m... many you need."

Taleeka nodded in satisfaction and stepped back beside Monteur.

"Okay, okay," the pinned man pleaded. "I've t... t... told you what you want to k... know!"

Taleeka sneered. "You know, every time I think of you Zoldak bastards, I see my mother dying. Now, you're all going to die as well—all the way to the top."

She nodded to her father and Alto slapped the mercenary's face with the back of his hand. The Zoldak's head spun completely around backwards, facing the wall behind him with a distinct crack. Alto stepped back and dispassionately watched the crumpled body slide down the wall into a pile on the ground.

"Thanks for the help back there, Monty," Taleeka said. "What are you doing here?"

"Following those two," he answered. "I do believe our goals are aligned."

Alto joined them and made a few quick hand gestures at Taleeka while staring at Monteur.

"My father says that while he appreciates your help, the kills are his. Please do not stand in the way."

"I wouldn't dream of it," Monteur assured in a drawl. "I fight for sovereign and house. You fight for family and honor. The latter always supersedes the former. I will assist any way I can. It's just... the attacks that took your mother's life and nearly took my king's—it all seems so pointless."

"Oh, they had a plan and a point alright," Taleeka said with a sneer. "They just didn't realize it's going to cost them everything."

○ ○ ○

Out of habit, Shom Eldor started off towards Joc' Valdur's old office in the Zorian Forum. Attina walked by his side and two bodyguards from the First Eldorian Lancers trailed them.

"Uh, sir," Attina said when they reached the halfway point. "I think we're going in the wrong direction."

The Eldorian monarch stopped, brushed aside a strand of blonde hair from his forehead and peered around, searching for a landmark.

"By the gods, I do believe you're right," he acknowledged before glancing back over his shoulder. "Sorry about that, Lancers. I keep forgetting he's moved to larger quarters."

"This way, sir," Attina said, taking the lead.

She led the procession down a side corridor and then back the way they originally came. When they arrived at the ornate double doors of the Valdurian sovereign, Shom eyed the intricately carved entrance appreciatively.

"How come my office doors aren't this fancy?"

"Because you don't have an office here, sir," Attina reminded.

"Oh, right," Shom replied, bemused.

Attina opened one of double doors. Inside, the large outer office of the Valdurian monarch hummed with activity. Two Picean assistants tapped away on Larimar screens dominating their desktops and several human runners carried stacks of papers. The Valdurian crest hung for all to see on the back wall beside the door leading to Joc's office, where an outer clan EEtah in a green jumpsuit stood guard.

The two lancer bodyguards flanked the outer doors when Shom and Attina entered. Both assistants looked up from their work.

"Your majesty," the nearest one greeted with a smile. "Sovereign Valdur is expecting you. Go right in."

"Thank you, Yissha," Shom said flirtatiously. "You're looking especially lovely today."

"Thank you, sir," the humanoid fish replied, blushing.

Shom knocked quickly and stepped through with Attina following. The spacious yet simple office contained the usual rich-looking dark wood and leather furnishings Joc' seemed fond of, and he rose to greet them from behind a wide baroque desk littered with papers.

"Shom, good to see you," he greeted his old friend. "And it's good to see you finally taking your security more seriously. What's important enough to warrant this unexpected meeting?"

The two shook hands and they all sat down.

"Well," Shom said, his demeanor grim. "I'm afraid it's started."

"And what might that be?"

"The Konrads, that's what."

Joc' sighed heavily. "Given Alto's propensity for vengeance, it was only a matter of time. What happened exactly?"

"My mechanic, Reaper, had been sniffing around Talon headquarters and getting stonewalled. Shortly after, they had a break in and sensitive information was stolen. Because of Reaper's inquiries, they naturally assumed he did it."

"Was it?"

"No, we believe it was Tally Konrad."

"I see."

"Two Talons attempted to snatch him and died in the attempt. Then a few cycles later, both he and the Konrads had a run-in with two Zoldak. Taleeka was with him and mentioned they were going to kill their way to the top. Right before Alto broke one of the Zoldak's necks."

"Given what happened to Mal, I'd take her at her word."

"We've got to get out in front of this," Joc' said. "Publicly condemn this and put ourselves at arm's length from the Konrads. The last thing we need is a war between the human houses."

"On the other hand," Attina chimed in. "The Talons and Zoldak have been a thorn in our side for a while now. This could be an opportunity to thin out their ranks with no effort on our part."

Joc' nodded thoughtfully. "We should both send our ambassadors to see Dolan Aramos and assure him of our having nothing to do with it."

"Which by the way," Shom said, raising a forefinger for emphasis, "is currently true."

"Currently?" Joc' replied with a raised eyebrow.

"Oh, who are we kidding. Dolan Aramos is a total ass who has militarized House Aramos to the point of it actually becoming a threat to peace in Lumina. They've wedded themselves to the Jomake and their loose wheel leader Serkel. It's just a matter of time before they try something stupid and dangerous."

"With the killing of Maluria Konrad and the attempt on your life, we're way beyond 'stupid and dangerous.'"

"Indeed," Shom said with a nod. "Well, if Tally Konrad *did* steal the information from the Forsvara Guards, they have all they need to roll through House Aramos. This could get heated."

"*Could* get heated?" Joc' scoffed. "I can guarantee that fire's already burning."

○ ○ ○

Khabel de Nier counted herself as one of Goya's foremost grifters. At thirty-two she managed to amass quite the reputation of separating marks from their gold. No scheme seemed too elaborate or daring. Few could resist her beautiful chocolate brown features, captivating eyes and smooth, lyrical voice. She met Taleeka Konrad several grands before and the two immediately got along. She also happened to be in Taleeka's debt.

Two grands ago Taleeka assisted her in an elaborate sting on a high-end rug dealer for which the daring teen accepted no cut of the take. On this Kan however, she would finally call the bill paid. She considered herself lucky too. The task Taleeka wanted her to accomplish seemed simple enough and Taleeka would normally do it herself, but being a Hero of the Realm came at the cost of anonymity. She couldn't take the chance of being recognized.

All things considered, Khabel expected it to go smoothly. Taleeka had prepped her well.

Dressed regally in flowing gray robes with wide gold trim and high arching shoulders, she stepped from the luxury hackney Taleeka rented for her. Then, with an air of wealth and authority, she entered the glass double front doors of Posh Lounge.

The low light, from several chandeliers hanging high above, revealed a large room with a bar in front of a tall glass liquor cabinet in the back. A small stage jutted from the wall to her left, with small round tables spaced discreetly apart filling the rest of the room. Being early in the Kan, only six well-dressed patrons sat at the bar, with as many tables occupied. Spying a waiter in an expensive-looking suit delivering drinks to a table, she waited until he finished before approaching.

"Excuse me young man," she said with a beguiling smile. "Might I have a word with the manager? I believe his name is Rodrick."

The server, a clean-shaven young man of no more than twenty, fell immediately under her spell of riches and power.

"Yes ma'am, I'll get him immediately."

Nodding her thanks pretentiously, she watched him disappear into the back. Moments later, he returned with a tall, bald man with a meticulously manicured stubble of a beard, dressed in a similar suit as his employee.

"I'm the manager," he said, introducing himself while the waiter returned to his duties. "May I help you?"

"I certainly hope so, if you are the one called Rodrick," she said expectantly, causing a sly smile to creep across the manager's face. "My name is Thedora Preston and I would like to inquire about the rental of your establishment and staff for a private event."

Upon hearing the code name and phrase, the manager's face betrayed caution.

"You realize that could get quite costly?" he asked.

Khabel feigned indifference. "I can assure you; money is no object. I want the best."

"Just how big an event are we talking about?"

"Fifty and I'm prepared to leave a sizeable deposit with you."

"I think we can handle that," the mysterious manager said, allowing greed to overcome prudence.

Khabel suddenly appeared haughtily satisfied, yet another service personnel bowed to her will. "Is there someplace we can discuss the details? I would also be reluctant to garishly display that much money in public."

"Of course, we can discuss it in my office."

"Splendid," she said, falling in behind him.

He led her back to a small windowless room with a desk, a few chairs, a filing cabinet and an employee's schedule mounted on the wall.

Before stepping through the threshold, Khabel discreetly tapped her Larimar talking stone, opening a channel so Taleeka and Alto could listen. Upon entering, she became startled when she saw another man with longer brown hair in the same manner of dress sitting in a chair beside the desk.

His clean-shaven face lacked the friendly deportment of the one who led her back.

"This is Draako, my assistant manager."

Khabel gave a condescending nod in his direction as the manager closed the door. Once in private, all pretenses of catering an event vanished.

"Your group has a reputation for getting the job done," Khabel said, watching him sit down behind his desk and motion toward a chair for her.

"Thank you, we draw from only the most elite the military has to offer."

"So I've been informed," she said, choosing to stand.

"You say you'll need fifty men, that's bordering on a sizeable force. What's the job?"

"I'm in textiles," Khabel said, following the rehearsed script. "One of my main competitors has opened a factory in the Narrow Lands and is threatening to undercut me with cheap Yupik labor and textiles. I want the factory destroyed and the management dealt with."

"When you say dealt with…"

"I mean removed!" Khabel said heartlessly.

"Opposition?"

"There will be a few guards, but the workers should be unarmed."

"Sounds simple enough, but the Narrow Lands is quite a distance from our base on Owling Island. We're used to doing jobs within the greater Goyan Islands."

"Are you telling me you can't do it?"

Hearing the subtle challenge, he gave a quick concerned look at Draako. "No, I'm not saying that. It's just that the distance and location will incur extra cost."

"As I have said before, money is no object. Name your fee."

"For that kind of an operation you're talking about five hundred gold pieces per soldier and a thousand for the commander."

Khabel paused and did a quick calculation. "That's thirty thousand gold. Agreed."

The two Zoldak traded satisfied looks and Roderick continued his negotiations.

"Good. Of course, we'll need more details. When did you want this done?"

"As soon as possible."

Rubbing the back of his neck, he considered the time constraints.

"It's going to take a cluster to put together an operation of that size. You said something about a deposit."

"I did," she said, moving toward the door. "My people are delivering your payment as we speak."

Both mercenaries' faces became perplexed watching her open the door. They gasped in shock when Taleeka and Alto stepped into the room. Khabel quickly exited and closed the door behind her.

"Hello boys," Taleeka said with a dangerous leer. "My father wanted to give you what you deserve, but you're unarmed, and he has a thing about that."

She then pulled her Mark Eight pistol from the belt in the small of her back.

"I on the other hand, have no problem with that."

○ ○ ○

Talib yawned and rubbed his eyes watching the buildings of the Shimol Plat go by from the passenger side of the unmarked police hackney.

"Shooting up a high-end lounge like Posh is one of those things you just don't expect," he said, sounding very tired.

"Expectations are going to be your downfall my friend," Tantei replied glibly from behind the steering wheel.

"Ugh, I'd just like to catch a case that doesn't have us traipsing around in the middle of the Kan."

"See, that's the problem with murderers, no respect for time."

"You're acting unusually chipper for the circumstances."

"What can I say, I just got laid and needed an excuse to get out of there. So, this worked out great!"

"Oh goodie," Talib groaned, rolling his eyes.

"Hey, I don't pick these guys for their sterling conversation."

"No doubt," Talib replied, watching them come up on the front of the lounge, blocked in by marked police hackneys and red cordoning rope.

"Got laid?" Cadi asked from the back seat.

"She was having sex," Talib said, turning to face her.

"Oh, and you say you didn't like this person you had sex with?" Cadi asked, clearly confused.

"Eh, I wouldn't go that far," Tantei said, parking the hackney. "Let's just say that their usefulness is kinda limited."

"I see," the Amarenian said, attempting to understand.

A few moments later, with badge placards around their necks, the two investigators and their consultant ducked under the ropes and entered the crime scene. Inside the open front doors, they could see the main room devoid of customers with the house lights shining brightly. The staff who witnessed the incident sat around several tables, nervously watched them enter.

"Alright, what have we got?" Tantei asked the patrol sergeant when he approached.

"Two bodies, manager and assistant manager, in the back office, shot at close range."

"Robbery?" Talib asked when the sergeant led them back.

"Nothing appears to be taken. The evidence team is just finishing up."

A lone patrolman stood guard outside the open office door and they saw the three-person evidence team packing up their suitcases.

"Tantei, Talib, how's it hanging?" one team member, a man in his mid-thirties with light brown skin and a continual stubble of hair and beard, greeted. "This is fairly cut and dry from my end."

"Hey, Doyle," Talib greeted. "What are you doing out in the middle of the Kan? I thought seniority had its privileges."

Doyle merely huffed and indicated the office itself. Two of the chairs lay blasted across the room as bloody kindling. Four arms, two of which contained blacked-out Zoldak tattoos, and four legs lay haphazardly where they landed on a red-soaked floor. The most disturbing part were the two heads, placed neatly on the desktop, leaking blood all across the desk's top.

Cadi followed the pair of investigators and gazed around in shock at the morose scene.

"So much anger and fear in this place," the sensitive said in a distant voice. "It still hangs on the air and permeates everything."

"They were shot at close range while seated," Doyle reported, indicating the destruction. "The shooter was standing right about where you are. We pulled two Mark Eight slugs out of the floorboard over there."

"Mark Eights, you say?" Talib clarified.

"Yep, whoever it was had the newest equipment."

"And that's it?" Tantei asked, surveying the office's new crimson paint job.

"Yep, like I said, cut and dried from my end."

"Alright, let's go talk to the witnesses."

The trio left Doyle to finish packing up and made their way back into the lounge.

"Listen up people!" Tantei addressed the seated group. "I'm Inspector Tantei and this is Inspector Talib and Cadi.

We're going to need to get a statement from each of you and then you can be on your way. Okay, who saw what?"

The original server raised his hand. "A rich-looking, well-dressed woman came in and asked to see the manager. I went and got him and I heard her asking about catering a private gathering. Then, they went back into his office. A few moments later, these two people came in. A young woman with a thin backpack and a man wearing black robes and carrying several blades. They went back into the office and the rich lady left. They were only back there for a few moments and then they left. That's all I saw."

A quick glance over at the Amarenian and she nodded, indicating he told the truth.

"Who found the bodies?" Talib queried the group.

"I did," a young waitress said, her voice still trembling. "That was about a half a deci later, when I had a question about my schedule. When I opened the door, I saw them… it was awful, just awful. Those heads sitting on the desk just looking at me. I screamed and someone called the guards."

The rest of the half dozen staff members gave fragments of the original server's story and all seemed consistent. Each time, Cadi confirmed that they all told the truth.

"Alright, thank you for your cooperation," Talib said and the group started to stand. "You can all go, just make sure you're available in case we have any more questions. If you think of anything, you can contact us at the Zorian Guards headquarters."

The group filed out with muffled assurances of their assistance and Talib peered over at his partner with a quizzical look.

"So, you tell me, because I'm still a bit confused, is this an investigation, or an *investigation*?"

Tantei huffed loudly. "You saw the tattoos on the victims' arms and heard the description of the assailants. There's very few who are sporting Mark Eight pistols, too. We both know who did this and I'll bet my next orgasm it's going to get worse."

"So, what now?"

"Looks like it's back to babysitting," Tantei replied. "We can fill out the reports while we wait."

○ ○ ○

Naza Kirkmon stared down at his daughter Panni lying unconscious in the infirmary bed at the Aris Clerria House and fought back a wave of tears.

"She lost a lot of blood to those, Hirudo," a Clerria said softly, coming up behind him. "They brought her in just before the Kan lifted."

"Will she be alright?" he asked, peering over at the purple-robed healer.

"Yes, thank the Goddess. The city guards got to her just in time."

"How many of those filthy leeches were on her?"

"Four," the Clerria replied, reaching down and feeling her forehead and neck. "The Hirudo Master said he didn't know how she got ahold of them. She only paid for one."

Naza's eyes narrowed in anger at the news, but he forced himself to calm when his daughter stirred.

"I'll give you some privacy," the Clerria said, then left the cubicle.

Naza forced a smile when she slowly opened her eyes and looked around.

"Hey there, Pooka," he greeted softly. "We're glad to have you back with us."

Panni scowled and turned her head away. "I don't want to be here!"

"I know it's been hard since your mother died. I miss her too, but we must be strong. We've still got each other."

"You have to be strong," she said curtly. "I don't have to be anything. I don't want to be anything."

"Please, Pooka, what can I do to help?"

Silence greeted the Riddle Master and he gave a forlorn sigh.

"I just lost your mother," he said in a hoarse whisper. "I couldn't bear to lose you too. I love you, little Pooka."

After a lengthy moment of tense silence, Naza felt the Larimar talking stone set into his wrist bracelet vibrate.

"I have to go, Pooka," he said gently, touching her arm. "I'll check back on you later."

When she gave no reply, Naza looked away sadly and left.

"Yes," he said, tapping the stone once outside.

"Sir, we just got the investigator's reports," came the voice of Gentry, his man in the Aris City Guards. "There was an incident at Posh Lounge in Zor during the Kan. Manager and assistant manager were killed and beheaded. The Konrads are suspected."

Naza scowled. He knew both of them to be Zoldak. Could it be the Konrads knew about their plot?

"Very well. Keep me informed if any more beheadings happen, or any Zoldak deaths for that matter."

"Yes, sir."

"And Gentry."

"Yes, sir?"

"Find out what Hirudo House my daughter was found in. Send a team there. Have them go through the records with a fine-tooth comb then beat the owner."

"Consider it done, sir."

◯ ◯ ◯

Tantei knocked on the door in the prescribed manner and waited. A brief moment later the door cracked open and a pair of suspicious eyes peeked out. Once he identified them, the male face with a dark beard relaxed and the door swung open.

Talib, Tantei and Cadi quickly stepped through the door of the modest apartment and watched the detective holster his Mark Six pistol and nod a greeting.

Miran lay on one of the room's two beds looking incredibly bored, while Kem sat reading in a chair by the window. Both looked over when the trio surveyed the room.

"Thanks, Erniee," Talib said. "We appreciate you sitting in for us."

"No problem," Erniee replied. "How did it go?"

"You know, two decapitated heads and an all-nighter investigation has left the two of us ready to party."

Erniee chuckled. "Well, it's been a million laughs here, too."

"So I see."

"Okay, I'm headed home to get some shut eye," Erniee stated, opening the door. "I'll see you all around the station."

All but Miran said their goodbyes and Talib plopped down in a chair next to Kem while Cadi sat on the bed next to Miran.

"Okay, so tell me, about this so-called investigation we're doing?" Talib asked, clearly perplexed.

"Like I said before, it's called going through the motions," Tantei replied. "Right now, our job is to get our witness here in front of an Imperial Judge tomorrow."

Talib's face scrunched in disbelief. "Going through the motions! Really?"

Tantei gave a wry chuckle. "Do you really want to be the one to try and bring the Konrads in? Tell ya what, I'll say nice things about you at your funeral. Look, House Aramos just grabbed a tiger by the tail and they're about to get clawed. I don't want to be anywhere around when that happens, and believe me, it's going to happen."

"You really think it's going to get that bad?"

Tantei threw him an 'are you kidding' look. "Alto Konrad has a reputation for being slow to anger and merciless in his vengeance. They killed his wife for pity's sake. It's just a matter of time before the bodies start piling up."

"I too sense great turmoil starting," Cadi said, peering around at the two investigators.

"What about Tally Konrad?" Talib continued.

Tantei sighed heavily. "Well, it *was* her mother. My guess is that she's been keeping her father sort of under control until the ones responsible were uncovered. Now that they know it was House Aramos, the Jomake and Mazie behind it, all bets are off. The two of them are already in the wind. See, the thing is, House Aramos thinks they're so big they're untouchable."

"Are they?"

"If the Konrads were pursuing this through legal channels I would say, yes, but that's not what's happening."

"And Mazie?"

"That's what the witness is for. Hopefully we can get Mazie before the Konrads can."

Kem put her book down and sat on the bed beside Miran, who placed her head in the intelligencer's lap.

"She'll be ready," Kem said, gently stroking her hair. "Won't you?"

Miran silently nodded and looked up at her with a lovestruck gaze.

"Then afterwards, we'll get you someplace safe," Kem assured calmly.

"But I love you," Miran protested. "I want to stay with you."

"That would be too dangerous," Kem reasoned. "They still have to take apart her organization. They will most assuredly try and retaliate."

"I guess," Miran said with a doleful sigh.

"Alrighty then," Talib said, standing. "At seventeen bells tomorrow, we've got a date with an Imperial Judge. Now, who's hungry?"

○ ○ ○

With the Kan lifting almost a deci ago, the morning business of the High Holy City of Zor hustled along at its usual frantic pace. In Judgement Square, the first hangings of the day rang out with trap doors opening and ropes jerking taut. All three of the gallows contained suspended bodies staring lifelessly out at a small gawking crowd.

Moving around the ghoulish gathering, a nondescript man dressed in a city worker's uniform listened to the group's morbid remarks about those hanged. Smiling at some of their comments, he shifted his large shoulder bag and headed through the field of stocks occupied by naked humans moaning in misery.

The five story Murdok Building stood on the far side of the plaza, housing the offices of the Imperial Court's support staff. He stepped through the double glass doors, an attractive human female receptionist smiled warmly at him and he returned the friendly deportment.

"You've got some fixtures out up on five," he said, briefly pausing.

The young woman furrowed her brow in uncertainty. "That's funny. I haven't heard anything about it. Usually, I'm one of the first and I make the call."

"We just got the call," the man explained in a friendly tone, when passing her towards the stairs. "I happened to be finishing up on a job close to here, so I drew the short straw."

"But..."

"Not to worry," he said patting his bag. "I have to haul around enough equipment to fix anything. Even if it's up five flights of stairs."

He ascended the stairs quickly and confidently, passing busy personnel who completely ignored him. On the fifth-floor landing, he looked around to make sure no one could see him before stepping over to the door leading to the roof. He tried the handle and found it locked. Reaching into his pants pocket, he retrieved a thin metal tool. Glancing around once more, he inserted it into the keyhole and jiggled it. The lock gave way with a soft click and the door opened.

Stepping out onto the flat roof, he closed the door behind him and locked it. The bright sunshine made him pause briefly, so his eyes could adjust, and he enjoyed the cool autumn breeze. Jobs on rooftops could often be unbearably hot and he really appreciated the cooler weather.

Once acclimated, he made his way over to the rear of the building. Reaching into the bag he removed a long coil of rope and secured one end to an exposed pipe. Then, leaving the length of cord coiled by the edge, he made his way to the front of the building.

He sat down near the edge and placed the bag next to him. Reaching into it again, he removed four parts to a Griesbach Two-Hundred sniper rifle and began assembling it.

He examined the weapon once assembled and then loaded four orange tipped bolts into the breech. Laying the rifle beside him, he discarded his city workers tunic and lay on it peering over the ledge. Assured of his vantage point, he grabbed his rifle and readied it.

○ ○ ○

The unmarked police hackney swerved slightly in the Zorian morning traffic when Tantei lurched in surprise behind the wheel.

"Wait!" she said, glancing over at Talib seated beside her. "You're telling me you're going out with her, whatever her name is, to dinner, *this* Kan?!"

"Her name's Husong and yes, in fact we've already been out a few times."

"You just met her a cluster ago!"

"Yeah, I know, but she's sweet and we really get along."

Tantei gave out a lecherous chortle. "Are you banging her yet?"

Talib stared at his partner with a curiously amused raised eyebrow. Tantei saw the look and her attention kept quickly shifting from the road to Talib's expression.

"What?" she asked innocently.

"I'm not sure I'm comfortable discussing that. It's kinda personal."

"What do you mean?! I'd tell *you!*"

"Yeah, well you're the more earthy type."

"What the fuck is that supposed to mean?!"

"It simply means you're more open about that kind of thing than I am."

The pair sat in tense silence, while Kem, with her arm around Miran's shoulder, attempted to comfort her in the back seat.

"It's going to be okay," the intelligencer soothed. "The judge's chambers will be cleared. Only the investigators, Judge, I.P. and an Imperial Scribe will be present."

Miran looked up in a panic. "Will you…"

"Yes, I'll be with you the whole time. The judge and prosecutor are going to ask you some questions. You have full immunity, so answer truthfully. At that point, they'll have you palm what the scribe recorded. Then we put you back in this hackney and drive you straight to the air station. We'll put you on an airship to an undisclosed location and you can begin your new life." Kem then glanced over at the investigators in the front seat. "She's packed, right?"

"In the trunk," Talib replied.

"We've got the entrances to Judgement Square covered," Tantei reported, turning to face them. "There are uniformed patrols in the square itself, so we've got you protected there. Remember, don't get out of the hackney until the four-man protection detail has a chance to surround the door."

Miran nervously nodded then looked over at Kem who gently stroked her hair.

"It's going to be okay," Kem assured.

"Alright you buggerers, it's show time," Tantei said, pulling the hackney to the curb.

True to the investigator's word, multiple uniformed Zorian Guards made a shielded route into the plaza. Tantei and Talib quickly exited and stood around the rear passenger door while four more uniformed guards got out of the hackney directly behind them.

"I still don't get why you won't tell me," Tantei said softly, watching the protection detail approach. "I'm your damn partner."

Talib sighed and rolled his eyes. "Will you let it go?!"

"I'm just saying, I'd tell you."

Tantei gave him a frustrated scowl then opened the door when the team surrounded the exit.

"Okay, let's go," she said waving Miran out.

Miran cautiously exited and looked around meekly at her guards. Kem slid out behind her then put her arm back around her shoulder and the group started off across the courtyard of anguish. The four guards positioned themselves five feet away in the front rear and sides. Talib walked beside Kem and Tantei flanked Miran's other side.

The only thing transpiring in the square happened to be the people agonizing in the stocks and the uniformed guards everywhere.

"Easy, I've got you," Talib overheard Kem softly comforting when halfway across the square.

Miran peered into Kem's face and managed a weak smile and a nod. Suddenly, her chest exploded in a small fireball. She lurched forward, following a torrent of burning gore spraying the cobblestones where they sizzled and seared. Likewise, her body became rapidly engulfed in magical Trinilic fire. She followed her internal organs to the ground, toppling into a blazing heap.

Kem screamed when the sleeve of her garment on the arm around Miran also went up in flames. Talib quickly removed his jacket and smothered the fire, then pulled her to the ground.

"Where the fuck is that shooter?!" Tantei screamed, as she pulled her pistol and crouched.

The area immediately descended into chaos, with Zorian guards drawing their weapons and running around in confusion. However, no other shots came.

"The roof of the Murdok Building," someone yelled and a crowd of guards rushed towards it.

Sensing no more danger, Talib helped Kem, wincing in pain, to her feet. He then pulled his pocketknife and cut away the remains of the burnt sleeve.

"Just in case there's any Trinilic residue," he explained. "We don't need this reigniting. Now let's get you to Clerria House for those burns."

Kem nodded and Talib summoned a uniformed guard to escort her.

Tantei stood appearing totally defeated, watching Miran's body burn with her pistol held limply at her side. All the while the smell of cooking flesh and noxious smoke rose quickly into the air.

"FUCK!" Tantei shrieked, watching the last of their witnesses' body being reduced to a sooty burn mark on the stones.

"Our case literally just went up in smoke," Talib said dejectedly, stepping over to his irate partner.

Tantei spun and glowered at him. "Jokes! We just got fucked and you're making jokes?!"

"I prefer to think of it as a witty assessment," Talib replied gloomily, ignoring her outburst.

Two uniformed guards rapidly approaching interrupted Tantei's next admonishment.

"The shooter was on the roof of the Murdok Building alright," one reported.

He got away by a rappelling rope off the back of the building."

Tantei scowled at the roofline five stories up and slowly holstered her pistol.

"The city worker's tunic explains how they gained entrance," Tantei noted, trying to concentrate on her job instead of her anger.

"Yeah, but who just ditches an expensive sniper rifle?" Talib asked, shaking his head.

"Somebody rich enough not to care," Tantei said, irritation still lingering in her voice. "Who the fuck are we kidding. We know who did this. Now, we gotta start all over again from scratch."

○ ○ ○

A shrouded *Vastus* slowly flew over Owling Island, a small, kidney shaped speck of land, one of five making up the Wouvian Islands in the eastern Shallow Sea. The fertile western half of the island is dotted with small to medium sized farms contributing to the overall agricultural output of the greater Goyan Islands. In contrast, the barren and rocky eastern half of Owling Island provided the perfect training grounds for the EEtah's Dakor Sunal.

Taleeka and Alto peered downward from the ship at the huge man-sharks charging from the waters of the Shallow Sea onto the rocky shore with their Yudon harpoons drawn and ready. This seemed a logical exercise to Taleeka, because each Sunal excelled in a specific martial ability. Dakor Sunal specialized in shock troops.

They flew three miles across the island past the shipping port of Turi, nestled away from the dangerous training grounds, and up to the far northwestern tip, where they found the Zoldak compound, an ominous looking fortification walled off from the sea.

"Okay Giddy, I've seen enough," Taleeka said, glancing back at Alto, who sat stone-faced staring straight ahead in his seat along the hull. "Take us back to the training area and put her down somewhere close but out of their way."

"You got it," the pilot said, scratching Brzo, riding in the seat next to her, on top of its head. "Yes baby, we're going to visit the big shark men, aren't we?"

The lizard responded by snaking out its tongue and licking her chin.

Giggling, Gidaria banked the airship and descended toward the rugged coastline. Once Taleeka felt certain they wouldn't be spotted from the Zoldak compound, she reached up to the overhead console between the pilot and navigator's chairs and turned off the shrouding device.

"I'd keep Brzo on a tight leash if you're going outside the ship," Taleeka advised. "He's the perfect size for a quick snack for an EEtah."

The visible craft slowly settled to the ground twenty yards away from the training exercises. Even though they landed well out of the trainees' path, they all stopped to watch. The instructor, at first irritated at the intrusion, smiled broadly when he saw Alto exit the ship with Taleeka right behind.

"Alto Konrad!" the instructor thundered enthusiastically. "It's been a while." He then faced his students. "Everybody, take five."

Alto managed a tight, sad smile walking up to him, and the contrast between the twelve-foot humanoid shark and Alto appeared stark, especially when they clasped forearms. Dakor Sunal, because of their specialty, accepted only the largest, most aggressive of their race.

"Taleeka, you've grown quite a bit since I saw you last."

He then placed a large comforting hand on Alto's shoulder.

"I'm so sorry to hear about Mal. She was a good friend and a fierce warrior."

Alto merely nodded his thanks, prompting a questioning look from the EEtah.

"Instructor Bakaar, it's good to see you too," Taleeka spoke up. "My father has taken a vow of silence until the ones responsible for her death are themselves dead."

"I understand," Bakaar said, nodding his approval. "So, what brings you to my surfside playground?"

"How many are in this class?"

"Fifty at this point. We've lost twenty so far. This group is about ready to graduate."

Taleeka nodded and peered over at the EEtahs resting with their harpoons, intently watching them, and knew when he said 'lost' he didn't mean dropouts. He meant killed in training.

"How would you and your trainees like to make a little pre-graduation side money?"

The incoming Kan fog made shrouding the *Vastus* unnecessary as it hovered a hundred feet over the Zoldak compound. Gidaria held the airship steady while Taleeka and Alto stared out the windshield, now thermal tinted a blueish orange. Along the walls and inside the fortification, they could clearly see the orange heat blooms and outlines of the mercenaries moving about.

The water just offshore glowed orange with building intensity just before fifty EEtahs and their leader broke the surface, charging ashore. A hulking wave of death from the sea swarmed up into the back of the complex. Bells and horns rang out when the guards posting watch duty spotted the surprise assault, sounding the alert from the walls.

"Split!" the EEtah commander screamed, standing with his back against the wall and holding his arms out pointing in opposite directions.

The EEtah shock troops divided into two companies, running around the inner walls and spreading out though the compound. The Black Talon trained Zoldak forces responded with rapid efficiency, but the suddenness of the stealth attack found many scrambling for their armor and weapons.

Zoldak mercenaries rushed from the gatehouse armed with Mark Five pistols and Firehammer Carbines. A squad of gunmen aimed down from the guard towers, opening fire on the EEtah shock troops. A couple EEtah suffered flesh wounds, as the rest flattened against the walls to avoid being shot.

Suddenly, with a loud roar, the EEtah fearlessly ran into the open fire of the few Zoldak able to get shots off. A handful of EEtah took serious wounds after the initial volley, but the rest of the Dakor Sunal battalion swept through, impaling the human mercenaries upon their Yudon harpoons and casting bodies aside like they were bailing hay.

This was when the blood frenzy set in. Gidaria turned away when she witnessed an EEtah rend a Zoldak in two, just before biting off his head. Taleeka, who watched the slaughter dispassionately with Alto next to her, placed a calming hand on her pilot's upper back.

The frenzied EEtah shock troops spread out through the fortress. The merciless man-sharks went from building-to-building ripping apart and eating the last resistance as well as those in hiding. The sound of humans screaming and EEtahs roaring echoed off the walls and over the water.

The entire attack took a half a deci and the Dakor Sunal battalion suffered no casualties. With the same methodical precision, they gathered their wounded before burning the fortress to the ground.

"I'd call this a win-win," Taleeka said watching the flames illuminate the thick Kan fog. "Dakor Sunal's latest class gets a practical final exam and we don't have to take on a small army. I'd say that was the best six-hundred gold we've ever spent."

○ ○ ○

The land office for the City of Zor sat in a governmentally nondescript two-story structure next to the forum. Tantei had never found a reason to set foot in the building before, so she didn't know what to expect. As she moved through the front doors, the sheer size of the operation caught her off guard. A large waiting area dominated the center of the room. Open-faced cubicles with desks and several chairs lined the walls. A wide variety of humans filled the uncomfortable-looking seats and the cubicles buzzed with the activity of city clerks diligently fulfilling citizens' needs.

A young male receptionist with short red hair smiled when she approached his desk just inside the entrance.

"Hello," she greeted. "Do you need permitting, inspections or deeds?"

"Neither," Tantei replied, returning the smile and retrieving her badge placard. "I'm Inspector Tantei from the Zorian Guards. I need to speak to one of your clerks, a 'Husong.'"

The clerk examined the identification, then stood.

"Husong is over in our permitting department. I'll take you to her."

"Thanks," Tantei said, following the energetic young man. "This place is so large and busy, I probably would've wandered around for decis."

"Yeah, they do keep us 'busy,'" he said over his shoulder. "Zor is growing so fast we're struggling to keep up."

He led her across the bustling floor to one of the cubicles along the far wall. Husong sat at a modest desk piled high with paperwork, studying a large architectural rendering at arm's length and tilting her head in confusion.

The receptionist knocked gently on the divider's pillar, snapping her out of her contemplative trance.

"Uh, Husong, there's an investigator from the Zorian Guards here to see you."

Husong looked up past the receptionist and smiled when she saw Tantei.

"Thanks, Clive," she said, placing the oversized sheet on top of her already voluminous workload. "Tantei! Good to see you," she added, standing as Clive slipped away. "There's not any trouble I hope?"

Tantei gave a reassuring grin and stepped into the small office. "No, no trouble. I just wanted to talk to you about Talib."

"Oh?"

"Yeah, I just wanted to clear up something before it gets away from us."

"Uh, okay, sure."

"You two are *still* seeing each other, right?"

"Yeah, he's sweet."

"Um, well, I'm not quite sure how to put this but... you know that date we all went on a cluster ago?"

"Of course. That's where I met him."

"You do know that was the only one I was paying for, right?"

Husong smiled and nodded. "Yes. I only infrequently escort, mostly when I need the extra money. That's why I go through the service you used. You know, I almost felt guilty taking your money, because we had such a good time and we didn't even have sex. In fact, we still haven't. He's such a gentleman."

"So, you two...?" Tantei said stunned, her eyes wide with disbelief.

"Yeah," Husong said, eyes sparkling, "if things continue like this, we could be a permanent thing. I've already decided that I'm not going to escort while we're seeing each other. It kinda feels like I'd be cheating on him. Weird huh? I haven't even slept with the guy."

"No, not weird," Tantei said softly as a warm fuzzy feeling swept over her. "It's *nice*. He's a good guy and he deserves to be happy. You both do. Okay, I gotta go harass some bad guys. I'm glad we got this straight. For the love of the Goddess, don't tell him how things got started between you two. It'll break his heart."

A look of shock descended on Husong's face. "Are you kidding? And *ruin* everything?"

Cedar Aramos heard the commotion in the outer offices of the Zorian Monetary Council but thought little of it. When a soft knock came, he looked up to see the face of his brother and sovereign, Dolan, poking his head through the opening—not his secretary.

"Brother! I mean, Your Majesty, please come in."

Dolan entered quickly and closed the door, but not before Cedar caught sight of his entourage in the outer office—the source of the commotion. The family patriarch carried a stern expression beneath his tan beret and sat down opposite Cedar's desk.

"Honestly, I don't know why you still wear that uniform. You're the king now for the sake of the gods!"

Dolan stared at his older brother, ignoring this often-repeated advice, knowing Cedar was one of the few people who could still admonish him.

"Cedar, we have a problem, and you may be in a position to help."

"Oh? How so?"

"I tasked Naza with derailing the Eldorian Amarenian Agriculture Compact, and I'm afraid he went a bit overboard."

"Why would you want to stop the compact?"

"It threatens to disrupt the prices of virtually anything grown—not to mention it potentially represents a dangerous coalition of power."

The senior economist scoffed loudly and waved his hand. "If you had thought to consult me on matters of, you know, *economics*, I would have told you that agreement would have little effect on the things you mentioned. And now you tell me you turned Naza loose? What in the name of the empire has the man done now?"

"He had Maluria Konrad killed and attempted to assassinate Shom Eldor. Both were architects of the plan."

Cedar sat in stunned silence, staring at his brother.

"By the gods, *why?*"

"I guess his thinking was… if he killed them, and the plan died with them."

"That's insane," Cedar gasped. "If history has taught us anything, it's that you can't kill ideas."

"Naza may be a top-notch sneak, but he's hardly a student of history."

Cedar shook his head, staring off into space. "And I should imagine the Konrads are out for blood."

"Oh yes. Naza used the Zoldak. Last Kan, the Zoldak compound on Owling Island was assaulted by the soon-to-be graduating class of Dakor Sunal. The EEtahs killed everyone and burned the place to the ground. Word has it the Konrads contracted them. I've requested a formal hearing before House Nur to question the instructor."

"And where, exactly, do I come in?"

Dolan leaned forward, his face grim. "The Konrads are in the wind and this revenge is only getting started. I'd like you, through your influence on the Monetary Council, to apply pressure on the other houses—to join us in attempting to bring the Konrads to heel and spare further bloodshed."

"That plan is unwise," Cedar scolded. "We need to keep finance out of this."

"But—"

"Brother, don't you see?! We may control the financial market, but the other houses hold the commodities our notes represent. If they pull their goods, we have nothing. At that point, the Calden Commodities Exchange folds like a house of cards. Then, my brother, a war between the houses becomes a distinct possibility. If this is Naza's doing, let the chips fall where they may. Keep this whole sordid mess out of the finance world. We have enough of our own issues."

Stepping out of the Kan fog through his front door, Naza felt both exhausted and depressed. The trips to Clerria House to visit his bitter, suicidal daughter after a cycle of dealing with House Aramos intelligence made it hard to even think.

To make matters worse, the dark interior of the residence drove home the point that his wife would not be there to greet him, nor would a meal be waiting. A little less than a grand had passed since she died suddenly from an unknown illness. Grieving his loss, however, needed to wait—Panni went into an immediate tailspin. Over the quintes, since that tragic day, she had tried to take her own life several times. This recent one came the closest to success.

He tossed his keys onto a small table by the door and contemplated making a meal, but realized he wasn't hungry. He considered lighting a fire but knew it would conjure too many memories of the Kans he and his wife would sit together by the fire after dinner and talk.

Sighing forlornly, he tapped the crystal by the door. A warm orange glow illuminated the room.

"Hello Naza," came a familiar voice from the common area.

The Aramos spymaster froze, then slowly turned to see Monteur sitting in his favorite chair, holding a pistol on him.

"Have a seat, sir," the Eldorian mechanic said, waving the pistol toward a nearby sofa. "We need to talk."

"You're in my seat," Naza said calmly.

Monteur chuckled and waved the pistol again. "I do apologize, but I won't be here long. Sit."

Naza took a seat, eyeing Monteur suspiciously.

"Alright. So, what do you want to talk about?"

Monteur chuckled again. "Oh, come now, Naza. Surely you can think of something, given recent events."

Naza's eyes narrowed and he smiled darkly. "Perhaps we should discuss you killing two of my Talons I sent to fetch you?"

"They were rude and brutish," Monteur said with a superior smile. "They shouldn't have pulled their weapons on me. After all, I do have a reputation to uphold. It was the greedy Zoldak handlers at Posh Lounge who led the Konrads to Owling Island... before they lost their heads over the deal, so to speak. And, while we're on the subject of things I didn't do—I didn't steal that intel from you either."

"Really?" Naza said, unconvinced.

"Yes, *really*. I have it on good authority that Taleeka Konrad was responsible for the theft."

"The Forsvara commander said you were there requesting information on Talons and Zoldak just a few cycles before the break-in. Are you trying to tell me that was just a *coincidence?*"

"Yes, because the trail from Maluria Konrad's murder to the attempt on my king's life leads squarely back to the mercenaries you use when you don't want to get too close and need plausible deniability."

"So, you're claiming Taleeka Konrad stole the data, are you?"

"Naza, look at me," he said sarcastically, indicating his paunch. "Do I look like a cat burglar?"

"You managed to get in here."

Monteur sighed in frustration. "Single-story residences are one thing. Climbing around on roofs and using sophisticated Magitech is for the much younger and nimbler. If memory serves, these actions fall well within Taleeka Konrad's skill set."

He watched Naza's face soften slightly as he weighed the argument. Sensing progress, Monteur continued.

"Riddle Master, we've known each other a long time. We've worked with and against each other on many occasions. I give you my solemn word as a gentleman and veteran member of the society—I had nothing to do with the theft of your data. Now, please call off your Talons so no more have to die."

"I thought killing was second nature to you."

"It is, but only out of necessity. Just be mindful of my code name."

"Reaper," Naza said with a sneer.

"Correct. Rest assured, any sent against me will not be returning, and their deaths will be needless. Besides, you're going to need every single one of those Talons."

A tense silence followed. Naza shifted nervously.

"So, what now?"

Monteur's face appeared unconcerned. "Myself? I'm going home. There's nothing more for me to investigate, and I'd just be in the way."

"Oh?"

Monteur stood, his expression turning grim. "The Konrads are coming, my friend. They don't need my help. And so, I bid you goodbye. It's been an honor and a privilege to serve both with and against you."

"You make it sound like we'll never see each other again."

"Yes," Monteur said coyly, putting the pistol away.

The Eldorian mechanic paused at the front door and looked back at the Aramos spy chief.

"Goodbye, Naza," he said flatly before exiting into the Kan fog.

Naza sat for a moment, contemplating everything he just heard. He looked down at his trembling hands. To calm them, he decided that only action would suffice. He needed an immediate audience with the king. Mazie and Serkel must be informed. He knew it would take all their efforts to thwart the Konrads' vengeance.

Naza led Panni out the front doors of Clerria House with his arm wrapped lovingly around her shoulders. She, however, stared downward, her face bathed in melancholy. The hackney waited by the curb, and he helped her into the back seat. Coming around the cab's rear, he slipped in beside her and the hackney pulled into Zorian morning traffic.

"Okay, let's get you home," he said, trying to sound positive.

Panni remained unresponsive, staring forlornly at the city passing outside her window.

"Don't you worry. We're going to take good care of you. You need to feel better and I've hired a full-time live-in nurse to make that happen."

"Don't you mean watchdog?" Panni said bleakly, not bothering to look away from the window.

"Pooka, no. She's there to make you feel better."

"I don't want to feel better. I wish I was dead."

"Pooka, don't say that. You've got your whole life in front of you."

"You can have it. I don't want it."

"You know, your mother would have wanted you to get on with your life."

"How do you know what Mom would have wanted? You were too busy sneaking around for House Aramos."

Naza felt a flash of anger, but he knew a heated debate wouldn't help. She needed love and encouragement, not contention.

"I'm sorry if I wasn't around as much as I should have been. We're together now. Pooka, we're all we've got."

"And it took Mom's death to make you see that."

"Perhaps, but we need to concentrate on moving forward."

"Maybe you do. I just don't see the point. If you had such a brilliant moment of clarity with Mom's death, maybe mine will be really enlightening."

151

"No, it wouldn't! It would be devastating! Please, give it some time. Things *will* get better. In the meantime, just know that I love you and want to keep you safe."

When the hackney pulled up in front of their upscale home in the Tuath Plat, Naza felt his talking stone vibrate on his wrist and tapped it.

"Naza here," he said, and the voice of Safir Bentley, the Aramos ambassador to Zor, rang out in his head.

Staring at the hackney's ceiling, he didn't notice Panni glaring scornfully at him.

"Riddle Master, I've secured you a place at the debriefing hearing for the EEtah instructor. Do I need to be present?"

"That might be helpful," Naza replied, hearing the car door slam and seeing his daughter running toward the house.

"The hearing is set for next cycle, at ten bells, in the Nurian Temple in Zor."

"I'll see you there, Ambassador, and thank you."

"Of course. See you there."

The line went dead and Naza stared at the front door. He considered going after her to explain but knew she probably wouldn't understand.

Sighing loudly, he faced the back of the driver's head. "Take me to the air station."

○ ○ ○

The room felt cramped, but then again, he mused, he normally wouldn't be here. Naza only remembered two times in his career visiting a Nurian Temple. Both times, on official business. This trip proved no different.

In the EEtah's typical austere manner, the room held no decoration with only two long wooden benches stretching its length. Instructor Bakaar sat in the middle of one bench, facing three female EEtah of House Nur, seated opposite him. Naza and Ambassador Bentley sat at the very end of the judges' bench. The two humans appeared dwarfed by the seven-foot-tall Nurians and the twelve-foot-tall Sunal instructor.

"Instructor Bakaar, would you please recount the events that took place on Owling Island," the middle judge requested.

Bakaar sat stiff and formal, surveying all three before he began. "Two cycles ago, just before the Kan, I was running the trainees through beach assault drills when an airship materialized and landed. Alto and Taleeka Konrad exited the craft and approached."

"Did you recognize them immediately?" the female on the end asked.

"Yes. I've worked with the Konrads before."

"Go on."

"I was asked if my trainees wanted to make some pre-graduation side money."

"Who actually did the asking?" the middle one asked.

"The daughter, Taleeka. Alto has taken a vow of silence until all involved in his wife's death are dead."

"And how did you respond?"

"I replied that all Sunal missions and payments were to go through House Nur, as per protocol. Taleeka then proposed that killing the ones responsible for her mother's death would make an excellent final exam and that she would arrange graduation gifts for the class. Seeing how we were already practicing seaborne assaults, I thought it an excellent idea."

"You didn't see this little technicality as unlawful?" the female at the far end asked.

"I broke no Nurian Edicts that I know of and assisted a great friend of Dakor Sunal in his vengeance."

"What happened then?"

"When the Kan set in, we attacked from the sea, taking the Zoldak garrison by surprise. We killed everyone and burned the fort to the ground."

"And you saw nothing wrong with that?"

"No. As I said, the Konrads are true friends of Dakor Sunal and the EEtah people in general. I was happy to be a part of their vengeance."

"Casualties?"

"None of my trainees were killed and only five were injured. Far below the average deaths and injuries in most of our final exams. The class graduated last cycle."

"And did your class receive their *graduation gift*?"

"Yes, one hundred gold pieces each."

The three leaned in close and spoke softly before addressing Bakaar, "Instructor Bakaar, even though your exam was unorthodox, you are correct. No Nurian Edicts were violated. This tribunal finds your actions within the law and you are free to return to your duties."

An incensed Naza could take no more.

"You must be joking!" he sputtered. "Well over a hundred men killed, an entire fortress destroyed, and there is *no punishment?* This is outrageous!"

"Riddle Master," the middle judge said calmly, "may I remind you this is a Nurian debriefing. You are here only as a courtesy. Not only did Instructor Bakaar break no laws, his testing, while unconventional, carried the spirit of the Sunal. This is what the Sunals do. We fight on others' behalf. It sounds very much like the quarrel you have is with the Konrads. I suggest you take this complaint up with them."

"I'll do more than that," Naza said angrily. "I'm going to lodge a formal complaint with the Zorian High Council."

"As is your right," she replied serenely. "This debriefing tribunal is adjourned."

The two humans stormed out of the temple with Naza grumbling to himself and the ambassador trying to calm him.

Even through his rage, it was clear the spymaster would get no help from the EEtahs in dealing with the Konrads.

○ ○ ○

Naza grabbed the first outgoing flight from Zor and returned to Aris by mid-cycle. A short hackney ride later, he arrived at the Aramos palace to seek an emergency audience with the king. Knowing the king reserved this cycle for his once-a-cluster target practice, the spymaster made his way to the west lawn of the estate.

Just as expected, he found Dolan Aramos lying prone on the ground, sighting in his favorite rifle. A young male attendant stood nearby holding a mobile armaments case.

"Now," Dolan said, once settled in position.

The attendant raised a red flag high above his head. Two hundred yards away, Naza barely made out a city guard muscling a shackled man to the center of the lawn. The guard removed the chains and quickly stepped away.

The condemned man looked around in a panic, before taking off running. Dolan calmly tracked him and pulled the trigger. Orange sparkles erupted from the barrel just before the man disappeared in a crimson explosion.

"Nice shot, Your Highness," Naza said, approaching the preoccupied monarch.

"Yes, Naza, what is it?" Dolan asked with a trace of irritation.

This time the attendant waved a green flag and another shackled prisoner appeared.

"Uh, sire, I just attended a Nurian debriefing. It's official—the Konrads hired Dakor Sunal to massacre the Zoldak garrison. Furthermore, the Sunal deemed the EEtahs blameless."

"I see," Dolan said, still focused through the rifle's sight. "Now."

The attendant raised the red flag again, and the guards released the next prisoner. This one bolted in the opposite direction, aiming for a wooded area along the lawn's edge. Dolan waited until he reached the tree line, then fired. The man exploded just like the last, this time painting the tree leaves a gruesome red.

"Ha! He actually thought he was going to make it," Dolan reveled, before sitting up and handing the rifle to his aide.

"Sire, I must convey the seriousness of the situation," Naza said, watching Dolan rise.

The Aramos patriarch studied his spymaster with concern. Naza rarely seemed this rattled.

"Walk with me," Dolan casually commanded.

They strolled across the lawn at a relaxed pace. A bodyguard appeared, seemingly from nowhere, and followed at a discreet distance.

"Naza, what is it that troubles you so?"

"Your Majesty, the situation with the Konrads is getting out of hand. They know we were involved in Maluria's death. Sooner or later, they're coming for us."

"You really think this is cause for concern?"

"I do, Sire. They're resourceful and deadly. Alto's reputation for revenge is legendary, and everyone seems to owe Taleeka a favor."

"Do we know their whereabouts?"

"No, Sire."

Dolan thought for a moment, watching the body parts being cleared from the lawn, then glanced back at Naza.

"Very well. I'll double the palace guard. You should consider a guard or two yourself. I'll contact Mazie and Serkel. They need to be made aware of the threat. Tell me— if Taleeka has disappeared, who's running her operation?"

"Her girlfriend, Sire. A woman named Zerga de Woon."

"I see. Naza, it's time we take a more aggressive approach. Have your people detain this Zerga. Even if she doesn't know where Taleeka is, it may flush her out."

"Yes, Your Majesty. I'll put a team together."

○ ○ ○

"Well at least this one wasn't in the middle of the damn Kan," Tantei said, staring at the two decapitated heads resting on a crate.

"I feel the same fear and anger I felt in the restaurant," Cadi said, turning her head in disgust. "There was a third. He was taken against his will."

"The bodies are in the rear of the alley," a female member of the evidence team said, walking past her.

She watched Talib examining the two headless bodies slumped against the back wall, sitting in a vast pool of blood, then looked back at the heads staring out with horrified expressions.

"Zoldak?" she asked, joining her partner beside the bodies.

"Yep. They've got the tattoo."

Tantei scoffed. "Like I *needed* to ask."

"They are consistent," Talib conceded.

"Unlike the managers at Posh, these heads were severed cleanly," Tantei noted.

"That's because they were armed," Talib said, pointing to the pistols still tucked into their waistbands. "It means Alto did this. Tally killed the Posh Zoldak."

"How do you know that?"

"Because Alto has a thing about killing unarmed people."

"Inspectors," a voice called from the alley's entrance. "We've located a witness."

157

The trio looked over to see a young patrolman with short blond hair beckoning.

"Hey, maybe we caught a break on this one," Talib said, starting off.

"Like we don't know what happened," Tantei said, falling in beside him.

"You never know. We might pick up some details. You were the one who talked about going through the motions."

"Shut up," Tantei muttered with frustration.

Trailing them, Cadi smirked behind her round blue sunglasses.

On the street, they found a female food vendor still wearing her apron, standing between two uniformed Zorian Guards. Her drawn, nervous expression and fidgeting hands told them everything.

"You saw what happened?" Tantei asked.

The woman nodded quickly. Her voice cracked with tension.

"Don't worry, ma'am," Talib said gently. "You're in no danger. Just tell us what you saw."

"I run the food stand over there," she said, pointing to an empty stall across the street. "I saw one guy enter the alley, then two more joined him a few centis later. All three had that military type of look. Then, I'm waiting on a customer and out of nowhere this guy in black robes and swords shows up with a young woman wearing this weird sort of backpack. They go into the alley."

"Then what?" Talib asked softly.

"A few more centis pass, and the guy in robes and the young woman leave—with the first guy who went in. He didn't look happy."

"What did you do?" Tantei asked.

"Well, I didn't think nothing of it. I mean, it ain't my business. That's how you get hurt or killed—poking your nose where it don't belong. I had customers to feed. A little while later, maybe a half a deci, someone screams from the alley. That's it."

A quick glance at Cadi confirmed she told the truth.

"Okay, thank you," Talib said.

The woman's face turned curious. "Hey, is it true they had their heads chopped off?"

Talib nodded, and the pair walked away.

"So now what do we do?" Talib asked as they climbed into the unmarked police hackney.

"We go back and file a report. Two dead, one missing, suspects unknown."

○ ○ ○

Zerga never really appreciated all the things Taleeka managed to do in a single cycle until she took on the lead role. Ever since the incident on Owling Island three cycles ago, Taleeka and Alto had disappeared from public view, leaving her to manage the day-to-day operations of the Konrad empire.

What an empire it turned out to be. Literally hundreds of informants required tracking. Several businesses, from manufacturing to shipping, needed monitoring. Then came the dozens of endeavors where she acted as silent partner or patron. And of course, the long list of those who owed Taleeka favors, from the lowliest to the most powerful in Lumina.

She felt nervous when first shown the scope of activities. Taleeka had assured her it wouldn't last long. All Zerga had to do was keep things running—no new ventures. Everyone she would need to deal with already knew her and the situation. There should be no challenges to her authority. That part proved crucial. She never anticipated the sheer amount of personal involvement and handholding required to keep things smooth. This late lunch meeting with the Antiquary's number two, Redati, brought the social part of the job front and center.

"I'll tell you what," Redati said over his plate of steamed oysters. "Your girlfriend and her dad sure have kicked the hornet's nest."

Zerga gave a coy smile and picked at her salmon. "They started it. I may just be a simple farm girl at heart, but where I come from, killing someone's kin would get exactly the same response."

"You have many blood feuds over in Otomoria? That's where you're from, right?"

"Yeah, a farm outside the town of Woon. Blood feuds don't really happen anymore. Folks finally realized how pointless they were. That, and the Lancers cracked down hard."

"So, as much as I enjoy your company and a free lunch— what's this little meet-up all about?"

"Tally expects things to start heating up."

"You mean more than it already is?" Redati replied sardonically. "Like a hundred dead on Owling isn't hot enough?"

"They're just getting started. Tally expects House Aramos to start pushing back any time now."

"I would imagine."

"Getting out ahead of that, Tally would like to call in a favor from your boss."

"He owes her enough of them."

Zerga leaned in and lowered her voice. "Just in case those good ol' boys at House Aramos try to harass or shut down our small but profitable shipping company, Tally would like access to the Antiquary's ships and warehouses. At a fair rate of pay, of course."

"Of course," Redati echoed. "Well, sounds doable short term, but I'll need to run it past Si. Bramoul."

"We shouldn't need it long. Tally says this whole dust-up will be over in a cluster or two."

That made Redati grin. "A little overly optimistic, don't you think?"

Zerga returned the smile. "We've already done the hard part. We know who the guilty ones are. Now it's just a matter of making them wish their mamas never bore them."

"At the rate the body count's stacking up, your Ms. Konrad might just be right," Redati conceded, finally picking up his fork.

The rest of the meal passed with small talk and laughter. Zerga appreciated how what started as a contentious relationship between Taleeka and Anak had evolved over the grands into a mutually beneficial friendship. They shook hands outside the eatery.

As Redati walked off, she reached for her talking stone to summon Gidaria. She made the call and had begun scanning the street for her ride, when a box truck hackney slammed to a stop in front of her. The rear door flew open and six large, intimidating men piled out.

"You're coming with us!" one of them growled as they charged.

Zerga barely had time to draw her pistol. She fired from the hip, obliterating the first man's torso and splattering gore across the others. The sudden bloodbath bought her enough time to bolt down the streets of Tuath Plat.

She darted around vendors and screaming pedestrians, scanning for Gidaria's hackney. The driver knew what working for the Konrads demanded. Their beloved pilot always took a flexible approach.

Zerga leapt over a small stack of crates outside a café and cut out into the street. Hackneys screeched to a halt, their drivers cursing her. Behind her, the thugs plowed through obstacles with far less care. She considered firing back but held off. There were far too many civilians.

Sticking to the main road, she took several more evasive turns until she spotted Gidaria's hackney pulling out of a side street. Zorian Guard whistles rang in the distance.

Relief washed over her when the sunroof opened and Brzo leapt out. The lizard scrambled down the hood, landed in its waiting collar, and the rear door swung open.

Without breaking stride, Zerga dove through the opening. Once she was safely inside, Gidaria shut the door remotely and loosened the tension on Brzo's collar.

The lizard took off at a blinding pace, dragging the hackney behind it. As they reached a wall, Brzo ran straight up it, and the Gyronite Etheria on the vehicle's base righted the craft instantly. The hackney sped off to the sound of bolts bouncing off its Ukko Wood hull.

"Thanks, Giddy," she said, sitting up in the back seat. "That was close."

"Yeah, I figured when you weren't where you said, there was trouble."

"I know I'm only supposed to call Tally in emergencies," Zerga said, pulling out her talking stone, "but she needs to hear about this."

○ ○ ○

Taleeka almost felt sorry for the man. Almost.

The nameless Zoldak sat naked, bound to a chair, his body glistening with sweat and crusted with dried blood. He stared out from behind long, matted hair plastered to his face and shoulders.

"Please, I've told you everything," he sobbed. "Please stop."

Taleeka stood by the door of the one-room building on the outskirts of Zor's Bogat Plat, saying goodbye to an obviously shaken Cadi. Alto levitated off the floor in a bare corner, eyes closed in meditation.

"He's telling the truth," Cadi said with a tremble in her voice.

Taleeka nodded and opened the door for her. "Thanks for taking time away from the guards."

"You know, this is my second torture session since I arrived a cluster ago. I don't think I'll ever get used to it. If you and your father weren't held in such high regard, I wouldn't have come."

"Well, thank you again. It's important we identify the right people. I don't want any innocents harmed."

"I'll convey that to the investigators."

"Thanks, but we've worked together long enough—they know me. I'm not a killer by nature, and I'm sure not enjoying this."

"I would say I understand, but I do not. Do you wish this incident to remain confidential?"

Taleeka shook her head. "Nah, I mean, keep your name out of it if you want, but I want this guy found. We're not going to be here much longer. I want them to know we're coming. Fear is the goal."

"Severed heads will probably do that."

"Believe me, if I could've thought of something more gruesome, I would've done it. But we're already committed to the severed head thing, so we'll stick with that."

"Once again, I do not understand your ways, but I recognize your need and justification for vengeance. Your mother was a national treasure to my people."

"You should've seen her before," Taleeka said wistfully. "She meant everything to me."

"I am truly sorry for your loss and wish you good fortune in punishing the guilty."

"You know that I'm now in your debt," Taleeka said, opening the door into the chilly Kan fog.

The Amarenian gave a weak smile. "From what I understand, that is as good as gold."

"Better," Taleeka assured her before Cadi stepped out and vanished into the mist.

Just as she closed the door, Taleeka's Larimar pendant vibrated. She touched it through her shirt, and Zerga's image filled her mind. That alone sent a chill through her—contact meant emergency.

"Hey baby, is everything okay?"

She listened as Zerga recounted the attack. Taleeka's face drained of color. Her mouth twisted in a sneer as she stared at the bound Zoldak.

"As long as you're safe," she said, her voice shaking with worry. "We need to talk face to face. Next cycle—I'll find you. I love you, babe."

She stood there for a moment, seething. Then she reached back, drew her pistol, and leveled it at the trembling man.

"This just got very bad for you."

$$\circ\ \circ\ \circ$$

For Zerga, Konrad House West could be a lonely place without Taleeka around. Even Peshk's constant activity running the home didn't ease the feeling. Standing by the master bedroom window with a teacup in hand, she stared out into the Kan fog and thought about the assault the previous cycle. To her surprise, she didn't feel frightened. The quinte she spent training at the Valdurian Combat School had prepared her well. The bad news she received earlier this cycle, however, wouldn't be so easy to deliver to Taleeka.

"Hey, babe," Taleeka's voice greeted softly from behind.

Zerga gasped in surprise and spun, nearly dropping her cup.

"Tally!" she said excitedly.

Setting the cup down, she rushed into her girlfriend's arms and kissed her passionately.

"Are you okay?" Taleeka asked, still holding her close.

Zerga nodded. "Yeah, and it's weird—I'm more pissed off than frightened."

"That's my girl," Taleeka said proudly, finally letting her go.

"Tally, how did you get in here?" she asked as they sat on the bed.

Taleeka's face scrunched. "You need to ask?"

"Sorry. Where's your dad?"

"He stayed on the ship. The *Vastus* is shrouded right over the house. Babe, I can't stay long. I had to see you in person to make sure you were alright. I also wanted to tell you things are about to heat up. So, handle as much business as you can from here. Only go out if you absolutely have to."

"Heat up how? It must already be bad if they're trying to snatch me."

"Most of the people at the bottom are dead. We're working our way up. Within the next few cycles, certain people at the top are going to get very nervous. That means desperate. So, keep your head down."

"For how long?"

"Like I said, I don't see this going on for more than two clusters. Maybe not even that long. We know who we're after."

Zerga lowered her head and sighed. "Tally, I've got some bad news."

Taleeka reached over, raised her chin with a finger, and gave her a questioning look.

"Tally, the Imperial Bank froze all your accounts. I can't pay bills or anything. They've shut us down."

"That figures, House Aramos runs finance."

"Tally, what are we going to do? We can't operate without gold."

"Give me two cycles. I'll take care of it."

Taleeka grinned mischievously when Zerga looked skeptical.

"Don't worry, you'll have enough money. My dad and I are really going into the wind until this is over. Important people are going to die and things are about to change, so you need to stay out of the line of fire. As for me—it's time to start calling in some of those favors I've been saving."

○ ○ ○

Dolan Aramos' eyes opened a full two decis before the Turine in the Aris harbor rang out that the Kan fog would lift—just like every morning. He sat up in his single bed and surveyed his sparsely furnished bed chamber.

He nodded in satisfaction when he saw his aide standing naked at attention by the bath chamber doorway. The baby-faced young man, in his early twenties with short black hair and light brown skin, held three towels in one hand. A freshly laundered uniform hung on a hook beside him.

Good, Dolan thought as he swung his legs over the side of the bed. *A disciplined start to the cycle means a disciplined cycle.*

"Good morning, Your Majesty," the aide said, staring at his king's lean, tightly muscled nude body as he stood.

"Good morning, Helmsley," Dolan replied, stretching and giving his aide a lustful side glance.

He's looking especially good this morning, Dolan thought, captivated by his hard dark nipples. *Perhaps a quick one before the duties of the realm.*

"Sire, your chamber pot and bath are ready," Helmsley said, noting the sovereign's rampant morning erection.

"Very good," Dolan said, walking into the bath chamber.

Helmsley followed and set the towels on a side table, moved up beside his king and removed the lid from a tall metal bowl. He gently took the hard organ in his hand and aimed it into the bowl. A long moment passed before Dolan finally relaxed enough to pee. Helmsley smiled in satisfaction when he heard his master sigh and gave his still stiff penis a few shakes when he finished.

The ten-foot-wide sunken tub was filled with clear cold water. Helmsley stepped in first, hiding any reaction to the chill. He picked up a bar of soap and dropped to his knees. Dolan entered and sat in the icy water, scoffing inwardly at the thought of civilians preferring warm baths.

Weaklings, he thought.

Helmsley started at the shoulders and moved down, cleaning his commander with methodical precision. He lingered on Dolan's sensitive spots, dragging a thumb across soapy nipples and feeling them stiffen.

When he reached between Dolan's legs, the cock began to rise above the water. Helmsley immediately knelt upright.

"Sir," he said with military precision. "Permission to suck your cock, Sir!"

Dolan nodded and leaned back so his erection rose fully into Helmsley's waiting mouth. A few moments later, Dolan grunted and Helmsley swallowed dutifully.

Afterwards, he toweled off the king and dressed him carefully, ensuring every piece of the uniform fit flawlessly. Boots and belt came last, with Dolan picking up his pistol from the nightstand and holstering it.

Helmsley quickly slipped into his own uniform in the adjacent room and met Dolan in the hall along with a lone bodyguard. Without a word, they headed to the first floor. Minimal early morning staff—mostly cleaners—swept and polished the corridors.

Spit and polish, Dolan thought, heading for his office. *Good.*

"Sire, your first meeting is in a few centis with your Master of Riddles," Helmsley said, keeping pace.

By royal protocol, he repeated this reminder each cycle— even though Naza's intelligence report always came first.

The king nodded. *Let's get this over with.*

When they reached the ornate double doors of the king's office, Helmsley pulled out a small key, but the door creaked open before he could use it.

Dolan clenched his fists. *What is this?*

"Funny," Helmsley said. "I know I locked this when we left."

The bodyguard's face tensed and he pushed past them, drawing his pistol. A second later, he cried out in shock, followed by the sound of retching.

Dolan and Helmsley stepped to the door. What they saw stopped them cold.

Naza's severed head, still wearing his fez, sat on the desk facing the door. Blood drenched the entire desktop, dripping in thick ropes onto the carpet.

Helmsley gasped. Dolan stood stunned.

The bodyguard staggered back, just in time to receive a sharp backhand from Dolan.

"Weakling!" Dolan snarled, sneering at the man's horrified expression.

Turning to Helmsley, his tone sharpened. "Find me a replacement. This coward gets ten lashes. I need a bodyguard with some balls!"

"Yes, Sire!"

This has gone too far, Dolan thought, his gaze locked on the dead spymaster's lifeless eyes.

"Get this office cleaned up immediately and then summon Colonel Kulina."

"Yes, Your Majesty," Helmsley said, already touching his talking stone.

He knew exactly what it meant. Colonel Kulina commanded the feared Black Talons. An escalation felt inevitable now.

ACT THREE

The Path Itself

For the past sixteen grands, the Imperial Bank of Zor recorded unprecedented growth. Branches opened in every major city in the greater Goyan Islands, as well as in the capital of Amarenia and Immor-Onn in the Twilight Lands. The original bank, located in the Forum and Baths Plat in the High Holy City, remained the largest and most lucrative.

An undisguised Alto and Taleeka stepped out of the back seat as the hackney pulled up in front of the bank's wide portico steps.

"Stick close and stay moving," Taleeka ordered Gidaria, behind the steering wheel.

"Got it, Tally."

The hackney pulled back into traffic and the Konrads ascended the stairs. Both took notice of the Outer Clan EEtah standing guard with a carbine that looked like a toy in the hands of the seven-foot-tall man-shark. He eyed them suspiciously but said nothing as they entered.

To Taleeka, the interior looked much the same as always. Six desks filled most of the space, where bankers tapped away on Larimar screens, the abacuses had vanished several grands ago. The vault still dominated the wall to the right, but they headed directly to one of the three offices at the rear.

They approached an attractive blonde in a business suit who sat at a smaller desk outside the far-left office.

"Hey Luci," Taleeka greeted warmly. "Is he in?"

The secretary looked up from her screen, genuinely surprised. "Yes, Mz. Konrad, but..."

She stopped mid-protest as Alto waved a forefinger in her face. Survival instincts suggested she shouldn't disturb the upcoming meeting. Without knocking, Taleeka opened the door and stepped into the manager's office while Alto positioned himself just outside.

"Hey Arrigo, what's going on?" Taleeka said jovially, closing the door behind her.

Arrigo, a thin, balding man with dark brown skin, looked up from paperwork with an uneasy expression.

"Why, Mz. Konrad, I wasn't informed that you had an appointment," he said nervously.

"That's because I don't," Taleeka said, plopping into the chair across from him.

A long, tense silence followed as the manager's eyes darted while Taleeka grinned in annoyance.

"So, Arrigo, I have a lot of money in this institution, don't I?"

"Yes, Mz. Konrad. You're one of our largest clients."

"You can imagine my surprise when an associate of mine the other cycle told me I couldn't access any of it."

Arrigo cleared his throat and gave a conciliatory nod. "Um, uh, yes, I'm afraid your accounts were frozen by order of the Assistant Director of the Zorian Monetary Council."

"Assistant Director, huh?" Taleeka replied, realizing they'd gone around Cedar Aramos, the director.

"Yes, I'm afraid my hands are tied."

Taleeka sighed. "Look Arrigo, I only want what's mine. This thing with the Aramos' isn't going to last more than a cluster or two. Meanwhile, I've still got businesses to run and that takes gold. I figure I'm going to need forty-two million to keep things moving. Nobody's going to notice such a small amount gone from my account. You can even date the withdrawal the cycle before the freeze order."

"But... but that would be falsifying bank records!"

"Whatever it takes."

"That could get me fired if anyone found out."

"And if it does, you'll immediately go on my payroll until this mess gets cleared up. Then I'll have you reinstated."

"You can do that?"

Taleeka gave an assured look, leaving little doubt in the banker's mind. "Yes—and with the added benefit of me being in your debt."

Outside the door, Alto watched the EEtah guards approaching with aggressive expressions. He cocked an eyebrow at them, extended his arm and wiggled his forefinger again. The two humanoid sharks stopped. Their expressions shifted to uncertainty. They stood for a long moment until one turned to the other.

"You know, something tells me this meeting shouldn't be disturbed."

"It's weird," the other replied. "I'm getting the same feeling."

One shrugged, the other nodded, and both returned to their posts on either side of the front door. Alto returned to his stone-faced vigil until several centis later, the office door opened and Taleeka stepped into the hall.

"I need that by close of business today, Arrigo," she called into the office, then closed the door and joined her father, who made several intricate gestures with his hands.

"I gave him a choice," Taleeka said. "Me being in his debt, or us making a forcible withdrawal."

As they reached the street, Gidaria pulled up right on cue.

○ ○ ○

"So, you saw Husong last Kan. How are things going between you two?" Tantei asked, taking a sip of tea.

"Good," Talib replied, sorting through the patrol reports on his desk. "She's really nice."

"So, have you two finally gotten around to doing it yet?"

Talib looked up with a sardonic grin. "What is with this fascination with my sex life?"

Tantei sat back and returned the smile. "I'm just checking to see how my matchmaking efforts are panning out."

Talib's face contorted in disbelief. "Matchmaking? As I recall, the only reason we were thrown together was so you could play 'ride the pony' with Si. Monster Schlong."

"Eh, you say potato."

"Well, if you must know, we haven't yet."

"What?!"

"We're taking our time."

"You're pathetic."

"Hey, just because I don't have a rampant libido like some people I know, doesn't mean…"

Tantei's talking stone went off in the breast pocket of her blouse. She held her hand up, cutting Talib's retort short.

"Hey boss," she said, tapping her pocket. "Yeah, he's right here with me… Yeah, okay, we're on our way."

She tapped her pocket again, ending the call, and stood.

"Boss wants to see us in his office," she said, grabbing the jacket off the back of her chair.

"Any idea what it's about?"

"None."

"Did he sound mad?"

"Nope."

"Hey, you're not mad at me for that 'libido' crack, are you?"

"Nope," she said, stepping into the hall.

"I don't know. I think you might be."

"I'm not mad! Give it a rest already."

"I'm just saying, if anyone should be irked, it should be me with that 'pathetic' jab back there."

"And all I'm saying is, with that tight little body of hers, I'd be hitting that every chance I got."

"You're not even into women!"

"That's if I was a man."

"We're just building up to it. We'll know when the time is right."

"Like I said, pathetic."

"That's the rampant libido talking."

The bickering pair stopped in front of Vanir's office. Tantei gave her partner a frustrated shake of the head. Giving two quick knocks, she opened the door and stepped in with Talib.

As usual, Vanir sat behind his cluttered desk with a half-full glass of whisky close at hand. A thin man with short black hair and light brown skin, wearing an expensive suit, sat in one of the chairs facing the desk. Both stood when the inspectors entered.

"Inspectors Tantei and Talib, this is Aramos ambassador Bentley."

The three shook hands. Tantei couldn't help but notice how weak and insincere the ambassador's handshake felt.

"What's up, boss?" Tantei asked after they all sat down.

"Ambassador Bentley is here checking on your progress in that string of beheadings."

Tantei gave a helpless shrug. "Uh, nothing much to report. We're working the case."

The Aramos ambassador pursed his lips. "Inspectors, I'm sure you're aware that the Aramos spymaster was found beheaded last cycle."

"Yeah, we heard about that," Tantei replied, not loving the ambassador's tone. "Any suspects?"

Bentley rolled his eyes and huffed. "Inspectors, you know as well as I do the Konrads are behind this!"

"Ambassador, in this business, jumping to conclusions is a bad thing," Tantei replied, her tone turning icy.

"He was killed in exactly the same manner as the others."

"That was all the way up in Aris," Tantei defended. "Last time I checked, I have no authority there."

"No, but you do have authority here. Heads keep turning up all around Zor. Already the Zoldak have been all but eliminated, as well as several other prominent citizens. Aramos citizens. And I can't help but wonder if your... Oh, what shall I call it? ...*lackluster* investigation is because of your cozy relations with the Konrads."

"Lackluster?" Tantei said incredulously. "Looky here, you prissy-assed bureaucrat. Don't tell us how to do our job! We put it on the line every time we hit the streets, while you sit shuffling papers in your comfortable office and attend cocktail parties."

Bentley's eyes widened. He sputtered in frustration. "I am a member of the Imperial Council and will not be talked to in such a manner by a common police officer."

Tantei shot an angry look at Vanir, who refreshed his drink with an amused grin.

"Boss, you better start writing me up on insubordination, because I'm about to tear this asshole a new one."

"Let's everyone take a deep breath," Vanir said, still smirking.

"I'm certainly glad you find this amusing, Captain," Bentley said sarcastically.

Vanir took a sip from his glass, then his demeanor shifted. "Ambassador, Inspector Tantei's temper has been known to ruffle a few feathers, but she gets results. And I'm not so crazy about that cozying accusation of yours."

"Well, she doesn't appear to be getting any *results* this time."

"Be that as it may," Vanir said calmly. "This is an ongoing investigation and we're not allowed to comment on it. So, Ambassador, your concerns have been noted. And now, if there's nothing else, we have work to get back to."

Bentley rose, glowering at Tantei. "I'm informing you as a courtesy that we've tasked the Black Talons to join in your

175

efforts to bring the Konrads to justice. As for you, Inspector Tantei, rest assured, your name will feature prominently in my next report to the Security Council."

"Well, moving paper around is what you candy-assed bureaucrats do best," Tantei replied snidely. "Just make sure you spell my name right."

Bentley's eyes flashed with anger, but Vanir intervened before the confrontation exploded further.

"Ambassador Bentley, you're well within your rights to bring in the Talons. But they also have a reputation. I will not have this city turned into a shooting gallery any more than it already is. If any innocent bystanders get hurt or killed by a trigger-happy Talon, they'll be arrested just like everyone else."

"I'll keep that in mind," Bentley hissed, storming out.

"Well, that was interesting," Talib said, unsure what to make of the exchange.

"Yeah, that last crack might've been a bit over the top," Vanir admitted.

"Asshole," Tantei muttered.

"So, what are we going to do?" Talib asked.

"Business as usual," Vanir said, taking another sip.

"So basically, what we have been doing?"

"Right. Look, if the Konrads are behind this—and who are we kidding, of course they are—every one of those severed Aramos heads had something to do with Mal's death, even if only indirectly. The Konrads are just doing our job for us. If the Talons want to rack up a body count by going after them, so be it. I'm not prepared to lose two of my best investigators unnecessarily."

"Uh, that was a kinda backhanded compliment, wasn't it, boss?" Talib said meekly. "You don't think we could bring the Konrads in?"

Vanir took another sip and shook his head. "No reflection on your abilities, but I don't think anything in the whole Annigan is capable of stopping them."

○ ○ ○

"It's been a while since I flew this thing," Taleeka noted to Alto seated beside her. Just leaving the Imperial Bank, she steered the *Mala* northward over the Zorian rooftops. She couldn't help but marvel at the increased air traffic over the High Holy City in the last few grands. In fact, the number of new crafts congesting the skies over the metropolis had grown so much, the High Council recently began considering additional air traffic and parking control measures—all under the supervision of the Air Workers Guild.

The vibration of her talking stone necklace broke her internal musing. Tapping it through her blouse brought Valindra Valdur's resting bitch face into her head.

"Ambassador, what can I do for you?"

The Valdurian ambassador gave a rare smile. "Mz. Konrad, I believe this time it's what I can do for you."

"You have my attention."

"A trip to Landagar might be in your best interests. Given recent events I won't be able to meet with you, but Da-Olman is eager for a get-together. Look for the green color code—you're expected."

"Understood. Thank you, Ambassador."

"You're very welcome. And this conversation never took place."

"What conversation would that be?"

"Exactly."

Taleeka tapped her stone again, breaking the connection, then watched Alto gesture with his hands.

"The Valdurian Ambassador has covertly requested our presence in Landagar."

Alto furrowed his brow and motioned again.

"Do I think I can trust her?" Taleeka shrugged. "I guess about as much as any politician. I don't think it's a trap or anything like that. It's in House Valdur's best interest, as well as everyone else's, to at least stay out of our way. The fact that the meeting is with Da-Olman probably means they're going to help. They want to see a change of management over at Aramos as much as all the other houses. House Aramos is a militaristic time-bomb just waiting for Dolan Aramos to set it off. Right now, we're the best bet to bring that change about.

"So, I guess we're off to Landagar. You know, in all my dealings with the Valdurians, I've never been there. This should be interesting."

○ ○ ○

"Would ya just look at that!" Taleeka said, while she and Alto stared in wonder out the windshield.

With the steep frigid peaks of the Atarian Mountains all around them, the six massive floating pods making up Landagar Station loomed ahead. Each resembled a giant disk hovering in a wide ravine. Bronze Ukkonite covered the entire underside of each disk, and an opening for airships rested just above the Etheria-lined base. A wide frame of different colors surrounded each opening. A driverless tram system connected all six pods.

Suddenly, Taleeka caught movement to her right as the Larimar talking stone in the dash began blinking. She whistled softly when two small teardrop-shaped, single-person airships zipped around a mountain peak and rushed toward them.

"Unidentified airship," a stern female voice echoed in their heads. "You are in restricted airspace. Identify yourself and state your business."

As the airships buzzed them like angry hornets, Taleeka noted the Trinilic mini-guns mounted in each of the noses. Keeping an eye on the fighters, she tapped the Larimar.

"Landagar control, this is the *Mala*. We are expected in Color Code Green."

The moment she identified herself, the interceptor ships stopped their chaotic paths and took formation beside Taleeka's converted scout craft.

"Roger that, *Mala*," the voice replied with a friendlier tone. "We'll guide you in."

"Okey dokey," Taleeka answered, making no effort to sound official.

They guided her to a windowless pod with green framing the entrance port, then peeled away. Inside, under a bright orange glow, an air boss directed them to an open slip. A clean-cut young man in a green jumpsuit stood beside it holding something in one hand. He approached when Taleeka popped the bubble top.

"Welcome to Landagar Station," he greeted flatly. "Here are your security badges."

He handed them each a thin Ukko Wood placard with a lanyard. Each card displayed a large green and yellow dot. They both noted the red dot on his own badge.

"Keep them on and visible at all times," he instructed firmly.

"I get the green dot because we're in a green area," Taleeka said, placing the lanyard around her neck, "but what's the yellow for?"

"Yellow's the lodging and hospitality unit," he explained, "in case you have to stay with us,". "You're only authorized for the Green and Yellow Zones. Now, if you'll follow me."

He led them through a door off the flight deck, guarded by a marine in a similar green jumpsuit holding a carbine.

Taleeka noticed him scan their badges before returning to attention. Above the door, a large green dot loomed, warning all who approached of the zone restrictions.

Beyond the door, humans and Piceans in white lab coats filled a wide hallway connecting several large labs where people worked on Etheria Magitech weaponry. In the pod's center, a wide circular staircase spiraled upward. He took them up three floors.

Da-Olman's lab stood out due to its size. The marine knocked, then opened the door.

"Sir, they're here," he announced, stepping aside for them to enter.

Inside, three long tables filled the room's center, each bearing two or more mobile Larimar screens, scattered Etheria parts, and partially assembled weaponry. Several lab techs tinkered at the stations. At the end of the far table, Da-Olman stood consulting with a very short human with round goggle-shaped glasses. Both examined a mostly assembled rifle mounted in a stand. The Gila's eyes rotated independently as he pointed to the rifle's breech.

"Ah, there you are!" the Gila exclaimed, noticing them with one roaming eye.

Taleeka hugged the humanoid lizard and tugged at his lab coat's sleeve. "Well, don't you look all official."

"I've still got my duster for off-duty hours, but they want me to wear this in here."

He clasped forearms with Alto and offered a sympathetic smile. "Good to see you, Alto."

When Alto nodded silently, Da-Olman glanced at Taleeka.

"He's taken a vow of silence until this whole mess is over."

"Really sorry to hear about Mal," Da-Olman said, nodding solemnly.

"I gotta say, the security around here is intense," Taleeka remarked.

"They've always been serious, but after Okawa made off with all those weapons at the end of the Etheria War, they've really tightened up."

"I can imagine. So, the ice queen said you wanted to chat?"

Da-Olman snickered at the nickname. "More like I have something for you. The ambassador asked me to make your current situation easier."

"Really?"

"Oh yeah. She's got no love for House Aramos. As soon as she found out what was going on, she called me. I was already developing these—she just bumped them to the front of the line."

He led them to a cabinet on the far wall and placed his palm on a Larimar pad. The lock clicked, and he pulled out two boxes—one larger and one smaller. Setting them on a nearby table, he opened the smaller box first. Two blue Etheria shards rested inside. He handed one to each of them.

"I know you're trying to stay low-profile. These should help. They're Lolite—psychic shields. If someone sends a sensitive or psychic after you, these will block it. Keep them on you at all times, even when sleeping. They're shaped to slide into a Ghost Suit's sleeve holster."

"That's all I've been wearing lately," Taleeka said, pocketing the gem.

"This box is for you, Alto," Da-Olman said, opening the larger container.

Inside, he found twelve, two-inch, double-edged, throwing daggers mounted in a circle with red tips touching.

Alto smiled.

"I know you don't want to use a pistol, but you need a ranged weapon these days."

Da-Olman pulled one free and handed it to Alto.

"The handle looks like a wooden coin—it's Ukko Wood. It'll boost velocity when thrown. The blade's made of Na-

Kab Carbon, and the red tip is Etheria Amber for attraction. They're nearly impossible to miss with."

Alto inspected the knife before nodding in appreciation. He extended his hand, and the two clasped forearms again.

"I've got one more request," Taleeka announced.

"The ambassador authorized full courtesy."

"I'm in the *Mala*. Zerga's got the *Vastus* and my hackney. I could really use a shrouding stone, and one of those cool Trinilic nose guns, like your interceptors."

Da-Olman grinned. "As I recall, the *Mala*'s a four-seater scout craft?"

"Yep."

"I can do the stone and gun easily. But here's the issue— you need a bigger PSI battery, and there's no room unless I pull the back seats."

"I almost never use them."

"Then let's get your ship over to Airship Research. You'll need a different pass, one with a blue dot included. Looks like you're spending the Kan with us."

◯ ◯ ◯

The sun felt good on her face and she could feel the autumn chill in the air on the other side of the window. Panni Kirkmon watched neighborhood children play in the street while she deftly manipulated the beadwork in her lap. Two cycles passed since they found her father's head on the king's desk.

She knew she had to come to grips with the fact she would be alone, but for some reason, she didn't feel any sadness. Watching the children play, she actually felt calm, relieved and happy for the first time in a long time. She realized staying busy would be the key to her relief.

Busy hands are happy hands, she said to herself, looping the final braid.

She continued watching the children until their mother called them home. Sighing, she considered their innocence and how long ago she gave hers up. It didn't matter. She felt content, like a giant weight had miraculously lifted from her shoulders.

Now things can be put right, she thought, with a sincere nod. *The way things ought to be.*

Closing her eyes and sighing, she allowed herself a moment free of any reflection, enjoying the calm.

When her eyes opened, she peered down and gave a surprised smile at the completed handiwork in her lap she had so diligently yet almost absentmindedly toiled over most of the cycle.

A thirteen-coil hangman's knot.

○ ○ ○

Paperwork, the bane of my existence, Talib thought, reaching across his desk for the next patrol report.

"Knock, knock," came a familiar female voice from the open door.

Looking up, a smile spread across his face. "Husong, what are you doing here?!"

"What, you're not glad to see me?" she teased with a pout, stepping into the office.

"Of course I'm glad to see you," Talib said, standing. "I just wasn't expecting you."

The couple hugged and gave a quick peck on the lips.

"So, to what do I owe the pleasure of this visit?"

Husong blushed slightly and put both hands on his chest.

"So, I was thinking," she said softly before pausing.

"Yes?"

She gave a shy grin before continuing. "Well, I've been having such a good time on our dates."

"Me too!"

"But they're always out somewhere, and we've really had no time to be alone with each other. You know, just us."

"Yes, that's what *alone together* means," Talib teased back, his pulse quickening. "What do you suggest?"

"Well, if you wanted to come by after work, I could fix us dinner and, you know, if you wanted to stay the night, that might be nice."

Talib's heart thundered in his chest and his palms began to sweat. "Well, uh…"

"Oh, if you're not ready—" Husong's quick caveat came with an embarrassed look.

"No, it's not that at all," Talib hastily replied. "It's just that I'm not really all that experienced and I wouldn't want to disappoint."

"Talib, are you a virgin?"

The investigator blushed. "Technically no, but past experiences have been few. Girls just don't seem interested in an overweight guy, and the ones I did manage to have were… let's call them lackluster."

A sympathetic grin crossed the former escort's face. "Well, there's a big difference between girls and grown women. With maturity, other things in men become more important than just looks. Honesty, kindness and reliability, to name a few. Talib, you've got all that and more. I'm not going to let a few extra pounds get in the way of my happiness. And you do make me happy."

"Well, okay, when you put it that way. What time?"

"Seven bells will be good. Make sure you bring a change of clothes."

"Uh, okay. Husong, are you sure about this?"

"Relax," she said, kissing him. "I'm going to take good care of you. Now, I gotta get back to work."

With another kiss, she quickly exited, leaving a trembling investigator smiling broadly as he leaned back against his desk.

"Hey partner, what's with the dumbass grin?" Tantei said, whisking into the office.

"Something wonderfully strange just happened and we need to talk. I need some advice!"

"Sure, but we'll have to talk while I'm driving. One of my informants just called and gave up the location of one Lopezz de Goya."

"That burglar we've been after, like, forever?"

"The same. They stumbled across his stash house. With luck, we'll nab him, along with his stolen loot. Let's go!"

The duo rapidly procured an unmarked hackney and made their way to Zor's Southern Docks.

"So, advice huh?" Tantei said, navigating through mid-cycle traffic. "Ask away."

"Well, um…"

Talib's hesitation made Tantei glance sideways with a raised eyebrow.

"All right, Tay, what's going on?"

"Well, uh."

"Yeah, you already said that. Now to the actual advice part."

"Well, Husong invited me to stay the night."

"My boy!" Tantei shouted, taking one hand off the wheel and playfully smacking his arm. "So, the noodle finally gets wet!"

"I really wish you wouldn't put it like that."

"Come on, man, this is great. When?"

"This cycle, seven bells. She's cooking dinner for me."

"Wow, dinner and a romp—she must really like you."

"Tee, come on, knock it off!"

"All right, all right. So, what's the advice you need?"

"Well, the fact is, I'm just not that experienced and I thought you might have some tips for me."

That made Tantei laugh. "Partner, it sounds like you care about her. Like you want a relationship."

"Yeah."

"I'm the last person you want advice from. Relationships are definitely not my thing."

"I mean the physical part. You're somewhat of an expert, right? I mean, you seem to get a lot of practice."

Tantei smiled at her partner's nerves but considered his date's former part-time job as an escort. She doubtlessly had to calm first timers and the inexperienced before.

"I think things will be fine. You don't have any problems with your equipment, do you?"

"No."

"And you know where all the important lady parts are, right?"

"Sure."

"Relax," Tantei said with a scoff. "You'll be fine. Remember to take your time and make sure she has a good time."

"Thanks, Tee."

"You bet. Now, we're here. Let's go bust some bad guys."

○ ○ ○

With a shrouded *Mala* parked safely overhead, Taleeka and Alto stood beside a food vendor's stall on Zor's southern docks. The pair watched sentients pass on either side of the busy street, keeping an eye on the entrance to the pub directly in front of them. Taleeka quickly gave in to the aroma of roasting meat and purchased a skewer. Returning to her father's side, she offered him a bite. He shook his head, never taking his eyes off the entrance.

"Come on!" Taleeka insisted. "You have to eat."

The swordmaster reluctantly accepted the meat stick, took a single bite, then handed it back.

In the Zorian harbor, the Grand Turine rang out the morning's passing and Taleeka wondered how long the Zoldak they stalked could drink the day away. Unease crept in—she never acquired visual confirmation of their target, only the word of an informant. They said he worked the Kan shift at one of the many warehouses on the docks and always ended up here at shift change. According to the contact, he would drink until mid-cycle, then stumble home with or without female companionship depending on whether it happened to be payday.

"And there's our boy," Taleeka said, watching the man exit the tavern.

The human male appeared just as described—well over six feet tall, dark brown skin, and an oddly shaped greying beard. He wore a soiled white t-shirt with pants drooping below his pot belly, and his heavy work boots clopped noisily on the cobblestones. For a brief moment, Taleeka thought he spotted them, but he pivoted right and turned down the alley beside the pub.

"Okay, let's go check this guy's arm," Taleeka said, starting across the street.

Alto followed close behind, readying six throwing daggers—three per hand—nestled between his fingers. Reaching the alley's entrance, they spotted him urinating against the wall. When he saw them, he took off running, still pissing as he went. The pair lost sight of him briefly when he turned behind the tavern. Rounding the corner, they halted abruptly. No longer fleeing, he stood smiling defiantly at them with arms crossed. Ten Black Talons surrounded him, staring menacingly.

"Trap!" Taleeka shouted. The pair ducked back around the corner just as several bolts chewed up the wall's edge.

Not wasting a moment, Taleeka yanked the Mark Eight pistol from her backpack. She flicked the lever to a three-shot burst, counted to three, then stuck her arm around the corner and blindly fired two bursts. Six bolts peppered the alley. Screams followed, telling her at least some hit their mark. Hopefully, it would make the survivors think twice about following.

Taleeka and Alto took off for the alley entrance, noticing a mysterious commotion in the street. Pausing at the intersection, they reeled in surprise. The sidewalk teemed with Bailian tourists of all ages wearing sunglasses, chattering and pointing at the sights. A Goyan woman using an amplified Larimar talking stone led the tourist group. A tall pole attached to the back of her belt displayed a flag so no one would get lost.

"And these are the famous Zorian Docks," the woman droned. "The largest commercial docks in the Annigan..."

Taleeka stopped listening to the monologue and glanced back. Their pursuers had found the courage to follow and now peeked around the corner.

Another three-round burst sent them ducking back, allowing father and daughter to vanish into the moving crowd of tourists, Taleeka reloaded and silently chastised herself for being so careless.

○ ○ ○

"Damn, I wish all cases were that easy," Talib said, watching the two patrol guards lead a bound Lopezz away down the alley.

"It's going to be pretty hard for him to burglarize places when they have his arm taken off," Tantei said. "That's if the judge doesn't order him hanged outright."

They had barely turned the corner out of sight when a commotion at the other end of the alley caught their attention. Both detectives spun to see a large group of Bailian tourists pass by. To their shock, Taleeka and Alto stepped out of the moving crowd and into the narrow side street. When they saw each other, all four of them froze.

"What are the freakin odds?!" Taleeka stammered.

Out of instinct, Talib drew his pistol and pointed it at the fugitive father and daughter.

"Don't move," he said nervously. "You both are under arrest!"

"Tay no!" Tantei said, reaching out to lower his weapon.

The young investigator sidestepped her arm, keeping the pistol trained.

"Tee, it's one thing to drag your heels in an investigation. When they're dropped straight into your lap, it's forcing us to do our job!"

"Tay, you're thinking like a patrol guy, not an investigator. We're interested in justice, not blindly following the law!"

"Talib, she's right," Taleeka said, slowly walking their way with palms exposed. "We've identified the guilty and no innocents have died."

Talib, now thoroughly puzzled, rapidly shifted his attention between his partner and the slowly advancing Taleeka.

"Stop right there!" he ordered with a shaky voice.

"Talib, come on," Taleeka coaxed, still approaching. "We're friends, remember? Think about how many times the name Konrad has helped out the Zorian Guards over the grands. That's gotta count for something."

"She's right," Tantei agreed. "They've always been friends to this city. Come on Tay, put the gun down."

"Not just the city," Taleeka added. "We're Heroes of the Realm. What does that tell you?"

"It doesn't matter," Talib said, on the verge of breaking down. "They're fugitives."

"Only if you count killing scumbags!" Tantei countered. "Tay, please..."

Four pursuing Black Talons rounded the alley corner with guns drawn, interrupting her plea.

"Hey, there they are!" one screamed, raising his weapon.

Talib, already facing them, got off a quick round, dropping the one who yelled. Alto leapt into the air and spun, launching blades from between his fingers into the remaining three. The struck Talons clutched at the lodged projectiles with stunned looks before toppling to the alley floor.

In the immediate aftermath, the distant sounds of the city mingled with Talib's ragged breath.

"Were those daggers initially meant for me?" Talib meekly asked Taleeka.

"He wouldn't have aimed to kill. Just enough for a distraction. We're friends, remember?"

The investigator finally lowered his pistol and stared around with a puzzled, defeated look.

"Come on Tay," Taleeka said, placing a gentle hand on his arm. "This is all going to be over soon. When it is, you have my word—we'll turn ourselves in."

With her final assurance, Talib weakly nodded and holstered his pistol.

"Now, we have to go," Taleeka announced. "And both of you can officially count me in your debt."

○ ○ ○

Bustani de Goya heard the Grand Turine in the distant Zorian harbor ring out five bells all the way across the city from his modest bungalow on the far west side of town. The Kan would be starting soon and he wanted to pick a few more vegetables before the fog set in.

Sitting back on his haunches, he stretched his lower back and inhaled the earthy fragrance of his garden. The fall coolness meant harvest time, and this grand's crop of squash shaped up to be his best ever. Once preserved, the yield would last all winter, with some extra to sell.

"Busty!" his sister Niabi called from the cottage door. "Dinner's almost ready. Come wash up."

The retired dry goods merchant smiled and waved. "Be right there."

He slowly rose to his feet and reached for the basket of fresh-picked squash. A shimmer in the air on the far side of the garden caught his attention. He left the basket behind and scrutinized the phenomenon, gasping when a shaft of light shot straight up from the shimmering field and the figures of Taleeka and Alto climbed from the visible cabin lights. Both hopped to the ground and made their way over to the startled gardener.

"Tally!" he said, opening his arms for a hug. "It's been forever."

"How ya doing, Bustani?" she asked as they embraced.

"Things are good—simple, quiet. It is just me and Niabi, and that is just the way we like it."

Taleeka smiled warmly. "That is good, Busty. I am glad. The reason I am here is, I need a favor."

Bustani felt a twinge of apprehension. He knew this day would eventually come. He owed Taleeka a great debt and always wondered when, and what, she would ask.

Twenty grands ago, he and his sister sold themselves into servitude to save the family's dry goods shop. House Whitmar managed to keep them together in service to a wealthy textile merchant in Nier. The unlucky part came in the form of a longer sentence for Niabi.

A free but brokenhearted Bustani returned to the family business to raise enough money to buy out her contract. He loved Niabi more than anyone. They shared their lives, secrets and a coital bed since their early teens. He promised to return for her and, for the next five grands, he toiled tirelessly, always keeping her in his heart.

One day, he heard about a special young woman who did favors for people she found worthy, asking for nothing but a future favor in return. He jumped at the chance and asked. Taleeka quickly came through, returning his beloved sister—and now the time had come to pay up.

"Of course, my friend. I owe you a great debt I will never be able to repay."

Taleeka chuckled and playfully swatted his upper arm. "Tell you what, Bustani—put us up for a few cycles and we'll call it even."

○ ○ ○

Three hundred crates of Wouvian rice filled the entire end of Pier Sixteen on Zor's Southern Docks. Captain Bors de Lomen stood on the bridge of the transport ship *Yanqul* and gave a satisfied smile. The crew had unloaded the ship in record time, meaning a faster turnaround and payment. His might be the newest ship at Konrad Shipping, but so far, it has turned out to be the top producer of the small fleet.

With the job done, he released the bulk of his crew for two cycles until their next run and popped open a fresh bottle of rum, drinking straight from it. He considered heading to the galley for a quick bite when a flatbed hackney truck slammed to a stop in front of the wharf. On its bed, about twenty Forsvara Guards and five Black Talons piled off and swept around the cargo, heading for the gangplank.

Bors, a veteran captain and survivor of several pirate attacks, instantly understood what appeared to be happening and felt his stomach knot. Reaching for the helm controls, he tapped the Larimar disk.

"Zerga," he said, calm but urgent. "The *Yanqul* just unloaded on dock sixteen. Forces from House Aramos just arrived. We're being boarded."

◯ ◯ ◯

Two cycles ago, Taleeka came through with the funds to keep operations running, which brought Zerga a wave of relief—short-lived, as expected. House Aramos moved against their shipping operations just as she'd feared. The call from the ship's captain didn't surprise her. If anything, it irritated her, as she had finally sat down to enjoy a late breakfast.

"Okay, Bors. I'm on my way. Hang tight, and for the love of the Goddess, don't give them rascals a reason to start shooting."

The last part of her warning made Peshk glance over from the stove, her Picean features etched with worry.

"Oh my, what's wrong?"

"Shipping issues. Nothing I didn't expect," she replied, tapping her talking stone again. "Redati, darlin', that thing I was concerned about—yeah, it's happening right now... Yeah, I'm on my way. I'll meet you there. Yeah, I've got the paperwork."

She stood and gave the family seneschal a frustrated look. "Sorry, Peshk. It smells great."

She tapped her Larimar one more time while walking to the table where she kept her pistol.

"Giddy, honey, fire up the hackney and get Brzo ready to run. We gotta be somewhere right quick."

○ ○ ○

Colonel Morto de Karo of the Aramos Black Talons took immense pride in the fact he never failed to complete a mission in all his grands of service. He followed every order without question, no matter how senseless it seemed. This time, however, babysitting an empty ship and a bunch of rice felt like a gross misuse of his and his men's talents. But the mission wasn't his to question.

"Is the ship secure, Captain?" he asked the Forsvara Guard after a salute.

"Yes, sir, but not before the captain called the Harbormaster and Zorian Guards."

"He can call whoever he wants. We're under orders."

"Yes, sir. What now, sir?"

"We wait for the hackneys to take this cargo away."

"Where?"

"Not my concern, Captain."

"Colonel, look!" called out another Forsvara Guard.

Morto turned in the direction the guard indicated. A luxury hackney, pulled by a lizard, zipped across the side of a building and headed their way. Just before reaching the dock, the vehicle slid onto the street, the creature threading it deftly through slower traffic. The hackney lurched to a stop beside the wharf, and a thin, attractive young woman with light brown skin and short dark hair stepped out of the back. She wore a messenger bag over one shoulder and marched over to them with a determined stride.

"My name is Zerga and I represent Konrad Shipping. What in the name of the Goddess is going on here?!"

"I am Colonel Morto of His Majesty's Black Talons. We are under orders to seize this ship and its cargo."

"Ordered by whom?!"

"Mundra, Lord of Currency, gave the order to my general and here we are. I don't know the reason for the order, nor do I care. I just follow orders."

Zerga instantly disliked the man and his flippant tone. She knew showing weakness or backing down would only embolden him, so she decided to throw him off by playing the sweet country bitch. Stepping forward, she locked eyes with him.

"Colonel, Sugar, I'm afraid that dog just won't hunt. You just landed in a briar patch of problems. First off, without a written directive from an Imperial Judge, your Lord of Currency can't seize anything. You got one of those?"

The Talon commander sneered but said nothing.

"I'm gonna take that as a no. Secondly, even if you did have one, it don't matter none. This rice don't belong to the Konrads. We were just transporting it, darlin'."

She reached into her messenger bag and pulled out several papers bound in the top corner.

"This here's a copy of the bill of sale," she drawled, handing it to the seething officer. "Now, I may be just a simple country girl, but it clearly shows that last cluster, one Anak Bramoul purchased this rice from my boss, Taleeka Konrad."

"Who is suspected of murder!"

"Aw darlin', what's that got to do with the price of milk in Otomoria? And speaking of the rightful owner, he's here now to take possession of his property."

A parade of large hackney trucks rolled to a stop in front of the wharf. One backed onto the docks and when it stopped beside the crates, Redati stepped out of the cabin's passenger side.

"Zerga," he greeted with a nod.

"Redati," she replied, nodding back.

"Nobody is taking anything anywhere until we get this sorted out!" the colonel barked.

Redati tapped his Larimar tablet and held it up for the Talon to see.

"This rice belongs to Si. Bramoul," Redati stated. "You have no right to seize it."

"Alright, what's going on here?" came an authoritative voice behind them.

All turned to see Harbormaster Ondrus—a giant of a man with a bright red beard and shaved head—approaching with two assistants. Both groups quickly explained their side of the story.

The harbormaster glared at Morto. "Colonel, just show me your seizure order from an Imperial Judge and you can have it. If not, I'm going to have to ask you and your men to stand down."

"We will do no such thing!" Morto bellowed.

"Sounds like we've got some tempers rising," came another voice from behind, as Patrol Captain Gasata and twelve Zorian Guards arrived. Gasata stepped up to the group while his men fanned out, prompting the Aramos troops to tense.

"Wow, I didn't expect the boss," Zerga said, surprised.

Gasata's smile tugged at his perfectly coiffed moustache. "When I heard who was involved in this little disagreement, I figured you might need a decisionmaker on scene. Okay, someone calmly tell me what's going on."

They laid out the situation again, and the Zorian Patrol Captain stared at the Talon colonel in disbelief.

"Colonel, they're absolutely right. Without a judge's seizure order, you've got no grounds to seize anything. I'm ordering you and your men to move on."

"I don't take orders from you," Morto growled.

"You damn well do if you're on *my* streets. Short of an Imperial Judge, I am the law out here. So, as the bartenders like to say, 'You don't have to go home, but you can't stay here.'"

"And if I refuse?"

Gasata sighed. "That's where things get tricky. If you refuse a direct order from a captain of the Zorian Guards to disperse, then this becomes an illegal gathering. That means I'll have to arrest the lot of you. And by the way you're postured, your men will probably resist. Then we've got real trouble. I know you guys are Black Talons and all, but we've got Red Division. It'll get ugly. People will die unnecessarily. If some of them are civilians, then you and I both end up in front of the Security Council. That's a career ender for you—and maybe worse.

"So, what do you say? One commander to another. Let's let cooler heads prevail."

Morto stood for a long moment, jaw tight.

"Colonel," Gasata implored gently. "The law is on their side. You didn't fail your mission. Your orders were bogus."

"Very well," Morto conceded with a scowl. "Aramos forces, fall back!"

○ ○ ○

One of the bigger perks of being manager of the main branch of the Imperial Bank of Zor happened to be a seat on the Zorian Monetary Council. Arrigo de Zor counted himself fortunate to hold such a prestigious position.

He felt frustrated at missing the council's afternoon meeting, all due to what he considered a wild goose chase. The appointment on Zor's Northern Docks with a wealthy ship owner allegedly in need of a sizable loan, turned out to be a no-show.

He sighed in frustration and stared out the side window of the hackney as it pulled up in front of his luxury apartment building. Paying the driver without tipping, he got out and made his way to the top floor and his penthouse apartment.

He immediately sensed something off when he opened the door and found the living room and bedroom lights on. The dwelling appeared empty and nothing seemed missing or out of place—until he stepped into the bedroom. A strange suitcase and briefcase lay on the bed. A folded piece of paper rested conspicuously atop the suitcase.

Furrowing his brow, he stepped over and picked it up. To his astonishment, he held an airship ticket to Immor-Onn, set to depart in two quintes. When he popped open the suitcase, he found it packed with his clothing. The biggest shock came when he opened the briefcase and found it filled with hundreds of secor notes. He estimated at least two million gold pieces worth.

His Larimar talking stone vibrated in his pocket, startling him and he looked around in a panic. Oddly, no one's identity filled his head. He let it buzz several times, debating what to do, before finally tapping it through his pants.

"So, me being in your debt just wasn't enough," Taleeka's voice resonated. "You had to *betray me?*"

"What did you expect?" Arrigo snapped. "You humiliated me!"

"It was genius, the way you and your buddy the monetary assistant director falsified those bank records. You almost got away with it too."

"I doctored those records to get that money *for* you!"

"It doesn't look that way on paper. Forty-two million is a lot of money. I figured I could spare two million of it to make sure you never betray me again."

The banker sputtered in anger and frustration against Taleeka's calm tone.

"Goodbye, Arrigo. I'm sure you'll find the Whitmar slave market interesting. Who knows, for forty-two million they might just hang you."

The line went dead just as a pounding on the front door echoed through the apartment. Arrigo turned anxiously, not sure what he sought.

"Arrigo de Zor," a thundering male voice boomed from beyond the door. "This is the Zorian Guards. Open this door immediately!"

"I'll be right there," he stammered. "Just give me a…"

A loud crash interrupted him. The door flew open and two brawny Zorian Guards rushed in. Talib and Tantei followed at a leisurely pace.

"Going somewhere, Si. Arrigo?" Tantei asked, picking up the flight ticket.

"No, I wasn't! I swear!"

She opened the ticket and read it while Talib popped open the suitcase.

"He's packed," Talib reported, then moved to the briefcase.

Tantei smiled at Arrigo. "Immor-Onn. One way," she said with an impressed nod. "I hear it's lovely this time of year."

"Looks like he was planning to travel in style too," Talib said, staring down at the commodity notes.

"I swear I've never seen any of this. I just got home. You have to believe me."

"Actually, no we don't," Talib said, closing the case. "You weren't at work or the council meeting today. And now here we are."

"Can't you see I'm being framed?!"

"I don't know," Tantei said, tapping her foot and surveying the luggage. "Looks pretty obvious to me. What about you, Tay?"

"I'd say we got here just in time before Si. Arrigo became a ghost."

"It's the Konrad woman! She's the one behind this!" Arrigo pleaded staunchly.

"Taleeka Konrad?" Talib asked in disbelief. "She's the one who falsified the bank records and withdrew forty-two million?"

"Tell it to an Imperial Judge," Tantei said with a skeptical smirk. "Let's go see what they have to say."

○ ○ ○

King Serkel of the Jomake empire stood at his throne room's floor-to-ceiling window and gazed down four stories to the first level of Quantara Keep. Far below the bridge fortress, at the bottom of the Quantara gorge, the river rushed from high in the Goyan Mountains out to the Shallow Sea.

He watched the Legate, who had just left his presence after setting up a Larimar tablet on a stand next to his throne, walk to the edge of the bridge. The old man's simple blue robes fluttered wildly in the late autumn winds and he held his head up to the sky basking in the sunshine. He reached into his robes' pocket and pulled out a small vile and lifted it to his lips. A brief moment after drinking it, he toppled over the edge, disappearing into the ravine and roaring water.

Satisfied no witness survived to tell their story, Serkel spun and returned to his throne. He reached over and touched the upper right corner of the Larimar tablet. The screen came to life with a hint of blue sparks and Serkel came face to face with Dolan Aramos in all his military bearing.

"Sovereign Aramos," the Jomake king said formally. "Serkel is pleased to see you. Serkel wonders what this communication is about?"

"You know," Dolan said sternly. "In every mission, the team is only as strong as its weakest member. Teammates rely on each other to pull their own weight."

"Serkel does not understand what this has to do with him."

"I'm saying the Jomake are not pulling their weight in this operation."

"Serkel still does not understand and is quite sure he doesn't appreciate your tone."

"Let me put it this way," Dolan said angrily, "they found the severed head of the last Zoldak two cycles ago in an abandoned warehouse. The Talons have been called in, but it's not enough. We need more men to aid in the search for the Konrads."

Serkel brushed back one of his long blonde ringlets and stared at Dolan incredulously.

"Are you telling Serkel that two people have eluded and continue to harass the forces of House Aramos?"

"Not just any two people. These are probably the two most dangerous humans in all of Lumina."

"And exactly what do you wish of Serkel?"

"We need men."

"Serkel would remind you that the bulk of his men are cavalry. They are not suited for urban missions."

"Can they walk?"

"Serkel demands to know what kind of question that was. Of course they can walk!"

"Can they shoot?"

"Yes."

"Then they'll do. There's a shoot-on-sight order for the Konrads. That should be simple enough for your men to grasp."

"Once again, Serkel does not like your tone."

"Let's get one thing straight. I don't give a crap what you like or don't like. The people at the bottom are dead. That leaves those of us at the top. They're going to be coming for us. That includes you. We need to stop them before they get that far. I've already doubled my palace guards. I suggest you do the same."

"Serkel is unconcerned. Quantara Keep is impenetrable."

"Oh, you mean like two grands ago when the Konrad woman broke out two of your prisoners?"

"Serkel learned from his mistake. Security has been increased and improved since then."

"I hope so for your sake. Now, what about those men?"

Serkel sighed deeply and glanced away from the screen.

"Very well. Serkel is prepared to spare a hundred men. Does that please you?"

"It's a start," Dolan said reluctantly, before the screen went blank.

Serkel sat back, considering he might very well be sending one hundred men to their deaths, but Dolan had reminded him of the vengeance he sought for Taleeka Konrad's raid. *Yes,* he thought, *this may be a golden opportunity to even the score with the brash young woman who made fools of him and his men.*

○ ○ ○

Captain Hollis de Goya of the Second Jomake Cavalry felt the irritation rising within him. He hated being away from the open plains and his beloved horse, Charger. But when the king tasked you with a mission, you obeyed. He had only visited Zor twice and hated it both times.

This time proved no different. The congestion, the noise, the smells—all made for a wretched assignment. Then came the danger. His detachment of nineteen men was one of five units ordered to assist their Aramos allies in hunting down Alto and Taleeka Konrad—two of the most dangerous people in the Annigan. Difficult enough, but now they must operate in unfamiliar territory.

Known for direct tactics and brutal methods, Hollis stood slightly over five feet tall and carried a bit of pudge. With light brown skin and a patchy short beard, he hardly cut a commanding figure, but what he lacked in appearance, he made up for in ferocity and ruthless efficiency. His strategy this cycle would be simple—assault and occupy Konrad House West. With her home and girlfriend captured, Taleeka would have no choice but to come out of hiding. And he'd be there waiting.

He split his force in half and would lead nine men to attack from the ground, while his lieutenant landed on the roof and rappelled through the second-story windows. They took several hackneys to 2400 Kasada Drive and approached the two-story house cautiously, weapons hidden beneath long coats.

"Alright, we're going in fast and hard," Hollis said, huddled with his squad. "Take the girlfriend. We need her alive. Kill anyone else in the house."

The men nodded and readied their carbines. None of them noticed the Aikin cloud floating lazily above them, glowing faintly blue.

O O O

"Zerga, bubby, we've got company," the humanoid lioness said into her talking stone.

"My mama taught me it was rude to drop by unannounced," Zerga drawled. "What's going on, Zau?"

"Well, I've been keeping an eye on Mazie's comings and goings. It's been pretty boring lately, so I took a peek around using my cloud friends. Looks like we've ten heading for the front door and ten landing on the roof in the back."

"Well, just because those fellas lack social graces doesn't mean we can't be neighborly."

○ ○ ○

Hollis hesitated at the six strands of large beads hanging in the doorway. The Jomake soldiers approached with caution and weapons drawn. They stopped just short of the Amarenian-style entrance.

"What is it, Captain?" a young corporal asked beside him.

Hollis nudged one of the outer Ukko Wood beads with his carbine. It swung easily.

"Some sort of beaded door," Hollis replied, pushing harder. "They look close enough together to keep the weather out. Behind these wooden ones are metal. Never seen anything like it."

He turned to the squad. "Alright, fast and hard. Spread out on the first floor. Everyone but the girlfriend dies. Ready?"

The men nodded and hefted their weapons.

"Go!" Hollis ordered, charging through the beads.

The fifth man in line, a young private named Mackeeo, halted when the rows of beads snapped tight with a loud clack. Screams echoed as bones crunched. The six remaining Jomake froze, staring in horror as blood seeped between the rigid strands.

"Sorry 'bout your friends, fellas," came a pleasant female voice from above, "but they didn't knock or anything, and that's just rude."

They looked up to see Zerga leaning from a second-story window, waving a pistol. The weapon's clear Calcite sights locked onto each man, syncing with the Calcite-tipped seeker rounds in the magazine.

"Sorry I can't stay and entertain y'all, but I can hear my mama callin'."

Jomake lieutenant Alabar led his nine men out of the airship and onto the rear roof of Konrad House West. Each carried a long coil of rappelling rope, which they promptly attached to the roof's lip and into a quick-release harness around their waists. Drawing their Mark Six pistols, they launched themselves, back-first, off the side of the building.

They swung out in a shallow arc, aiming the soles of their boots and the barrels of their pistols at the windows ahead.

None of them noticed the slight bronze hue of Ukkonite-treated glass.

Just as they had rehearsed hundreds of times, they fired a round just before their feet made contact, hoping to shatter the glass and disorient anyone inside. The lieutenant and six of the rappelling troops died instantly when their bolts ricocheted off the glass back at them, vaporizing their torsos and sending arms, legs and heads raining down. The final three screamed in agony as their legs broke on impact, flailing against the glass until their rapid-release harnesses dropped their broken bodies to the ground below.

Mackeeo's mouth dropped open in horror as the beads relaxed and the mangled bodies of his commander and comrades spilled out in a puddle of carnage. He stared, stunned, before snapping out of it.

"It's a trap!" he shouted to the five remaining men. "She's getting away out the back!"

They split into two groups and rushed around the house. When the teams converged on the rear, they froze. Ten ropes dangled uselessly from the second-story roofline. Body parts littered the ground. The only two still alive rolled in the gore, moaning, their legs bent at unnatural angles.

Thirty feet away stood Zerga, with arms crossed and pistol raised casually pointing into the air.

"Drop your weapon!" Mackeeo screamed, leveling his carbine.

The others followed suit and crept toward her.

"I said drop it!" Mackeeo yelled again, waving the barrel.

Still smiling, Zerga pulled the trigger. A burst of orange sparkles flared from the barrel and the rounds whistled into the sky. She dropped the weapon and raised her hands.

Seeing her currently unarmed, the Jomake rushed toward her with rifles still trained. They only managed to make it three steps before they heard the whistling and saw the seeker rounds turn in the sky and streak down towards them, each heading in its own trajectory.

They turned and ran.

The slowest of the Jomake soldiers took the first round in the back of his head, exploding his skull leaving only his lower jaw attached to a still running body. The second round caught the next Jomake as he dove for cover, leaving a hole the size of an EEtah's smile through his ribcage. The next three rounds hit their targets simultaneously, blowing massive chunks through the screaming soldiers.

The final Jomake ran for a hackney speeding past. Using his last ounce of adrenaline-fueled strength, he dove though the air, grabbed onto the rear end of the vehicle and pulled himself on board. Panting with relief, he couldn't believe his good luck as the hackney sped around the corner away from the scene.

Then he heard the whistling sound.

"No, no, no…" he plead, turning in time to see the last seeker round barreling around the corner, dodging vehicles and closing in on him.

He banged on the rear window of his hackney and screamed, "Faster!"

The horrified occupants of his hackney stared back at him as the driver punched the gas. The whistling grew louder and he turned just in time for the round to hit him right between the eyes. His head exploded and deadly shrapnel tore through the interior hackney, The vehicle fishtailed into a spin, throwing the Jomake soldier's decapitated body to the curbside, before crashing head on into another hackney.

Zerga just shook her head, retrieved her pistol and tapped her talking stone through her pants pocket.

Time to call Taleeka's cleaning crew.

$$O \ O \ O$$

"What a mess," Talib said, surveying the crushed corpses at the front of Konrad House West. Four bodies lay piled at the doorway, their remains tangled in loose hanging beads.

"They died instantly," Cadi said with a grimace.

"You think this is bad?" asked a patrol guard approaching from the corner. "You should see the back. Your partner's taking a statement from the victim."

Talib followed, pausing when he rounded the corner.

Blood and limbs blanketed the entire rear wall. Two men with shattered legs writhed on the ground. Five more lay dead, massive holes punched through them. A sixth body lay headless in the streets just around the corner. The two-vehicle head on collision and the subsequent traffic meltdown just exacerbated the crime scene.

Tantei spoke with Zerga off to the side while the evidence team documented the scene.

"The Vurr carts and Clerria are on their way," Talib said, joining them. "You did all this?"

"The house helped," Zerga answered with a sheepish grin. "Those boys didn't do their homework on whose land they were fixin' to take."

"The cleanup's on you, I'm afraid."

"I've got a crew en route."

Cadi knelt beside one of the bodies, eyes closed. After a moment, she stood and joined the others.

"These men were Jomake," she said. "The rashes on their thighs suggest they were horsemen."

"Makes sense," Tantei said, glancing at the carnage. "Mostly cavalry—bold frontal assault types. Which is probably why they got their asses handed to them."

"From what I gathered, their orders were to take the house and capture Zerga to lure out Tally. They were to kill everyone else."

"A frontal assault on the Konrads? That's a special kind of dumb," Tantei scoffed. "They got what they deserved."

"In this case, I'd agree," Cadi said.

"Well, nothing more for us to do here," Tantei said.

Cadi's brow furrowed. "You're not going to follow up with the Jomake?"

"Why reinvent the wheel? The Konrads have it handled. We'll reassess once the dust settles. For now, we've got reports to write."

Cadi looked between them. "Then I won't be returning with you. I feel compelled to explore other avenues."

"Oh?" Tantei tilted her head.

"Our missions aren't at odds, but they're not aligned either. The queen tasked me to bring Lideri Konrad's killers to justice. I'll be more useful elsewhere."

"I understand," Talib said. "Our hands are tied."

"It was good working with you," Cadi said, turning to leave.

They watched her vanish around the house before Tantei smirked.

"Ten says she's joining the Konrads."

"No way I'm taking that bet," Talib replied as the first Vurr cart pulled in.

○ ○ ○

The somber mood in the empty warehouse hung heavy in the air. Taleeka gazed around at the faces of Zau, Alto and a recently arrived Da-Olman, who peered quizzically back.

"You brought the cord?" Taleeka asked.

"Right here," the Gila said, displaying a thick coiled tubing with a plug at one end and what appeared to be a small basket lined with tiny Etheria shards attached to the other.

"Alright," Taleeka said seriously. "You all know what to do?"

Everyone nodded and Taleeka continued. "We need to be fast and precise. I don't want any time for them to give a warning. We move at ten bells to let everybody get nice and settled for the Kan."

She then glanced back at Da-Olman. "And the Valdurians are on board?"

The Etheriat nodded. "Unofficially."

Taleeka gave a sly grin. "And officially?"

"Officially, they know nothing about it," Da-Olman replied with a chuckle.

Taleeka nodded in satisfaction. "Okay, all we can do is wait. We've got about six deci before all the excitement."

Movement off to her left caused Alto to quickly tense and produce four throwing blades between the fingers of one hand, ready to throw.

"Hold up!" Taleeka said, when she saw Cadi step from the shadows.

"I am sorry to interrupt," she said meekly. "I'm here to help any way I can."

"How in the name of the Goddess did you find me?" Taleeka blurted out in surprise. "I didn't even know about this location until a few decis ago. And I thought you were working with the Zorian Guards."

"The Zorian Guards are only looking for you and your father. They've been purposefully dragging their feet. If I am to complete my mission of bringing your mother's killers to justice, you are the ones I need to align with. Finding you was actually easy. We've worked together before, remember? I've actually touched your mind. Once I do that, I have your psychic marker. I can find you just about anywhere."

"That might not be a bad idea for the rest of us. Just in case we get separated," Taleeka offered. "If everyone's agreeable to it."

Everyone nodded and, one by one, the Amarenian sensitive gently touched each forehead for a long moment with her eyes closed.

When she finished, Da-Olman looked around with a puzzled expression. "I didn't feel anything."

"What did you expect?" Cadi asked amusedly.

"I don't know, maybe visions or something."

"I am truly sorry to disappoint."

"Eh," the Gila said, shrugging.

"Okay, Cadi, welcome aboard," Taleeka said. "You're just in time. I've got an idea how you can help.

"Alright people, we move in six. These bastards harassing my girlfriend are about to come to a grinding halt."

The Grand Turine in the Zorian harbor rang out ten bells through the thick Kan fog while the residents of the High Holy City slumbered. The borrowed resistance-class cruiser dropped from its cruising altitude to just above the rooftops of the Shimol Plat. Taleeka, piloting the craft, turned on the craft's shrouding device as it approached the massive, well-lit opening of Air Station Three. Inside, a very confused ground crew reluctantly obeyed the order from no less than the Zorian Ambassador, herself, to vacate the charging station and take a twenty-five centi break on the flight deck.

To ensure no one's curiosity got the better of them, the Zorian mechanic Shurta stood guard in front of the large sliding door. One look at the burly Amarenian Hill Sister stuffed into her grey Ghost Suit and armed with a Firehammer Carbine would be more than adequate to quell anyone's attempt to pry.

"Wow, they really cleared this place out," Taleeka said, seeing the hangar oddly devoid of personnel.

"Yeah, we've only got half a deci to get this done," Da-Olman said from a passenger seat along the hull. "So, there's no time to waste."

Taleeka nodded, then tapped the Larimar disk in the console and thought of her mechanic friend. "Shurta, we just entered the main hangar. We're headed your way."

"Got it. Everybody's cleared out back here."

The Valdurian mechanic stepped to the side of the opening and, even though she couldn't see the airship as it passed, she definitely felt its presence. Once the craft traveled inside the large hanger, she slid the bulky door closed and resumed her vigil.

"I hate to put the Valdurians in this kind of spot," Taleeka said, turning off the shrouding, "but we sure can't use the charging station back at my place."

"I think you'll find there are plenty of sentients willing to help take House Aramos down a peg or two," Da-Olman reminded her.

The huge square hanger contained only a long, low island in the middle with three oblong monoliths jutting from it on either side. A long coiled cord hung plugged into each of the six charging stations.

"I sense a vast amount of psionic power very near us," Cadi said with a shake of her head.

"You should, being a psychic and all," the Gila replied. "Each one of those stations is tapped directly into a PSI well. They need it to charge the Obsidian batteries in the air fleet."

"Impressive, and we've got the place to ourselves," Cadi noted while staring out the windshield.

"Any one of these will do," Da-Olman said, pointing to the edifice.

Taleeka set the craft down near the first obelisk with the nose facing toward the door and dropped the side hatch. Everyone piled out with Da-Olman bringing up the rear.

"Okay, we don't have much time," Taleeka admonished. "Let's get this done."

Da-Olman pulled the coiled cord from its slot on the side of the charger and held up the end. "This is for ships."

He then held up the identical type of plug from the cord he had brought with him. "And this is for sentients."

"That much of a difference?" Taleeka asked, watching Zau sit cross-legged in front of the terminal while Da-Olman plugged his cord in.

"Oh yes. If you tried to use the ship refueling cord, it would fry your brain immediately. Come to think of it, with that much PSI flowing directly through you, it would probably fry all your insides. My cord tapers down the stream to a manageable level of flow."

Da-Olman handed the basket helmet to the seated Singa, and Taleeka knelt in front of her.

"You sure you can do this?"

The humanoid lioness flipped over a seashell on her belt, revealing the rune for Flavian Portals, and gave her friend a confident smile. "Tally, bubby, you keep me supplied with power and I can get you just about anywhere and back. I just hope your old man can hold on to his stomach. He never could take portals very well."

"Right," Taleeka said, standing. "Cadi, that's where you come in. If my dad looks like he's about to hurl or anything, use your powers to calm his stomach or whatever."

"That should be no problem."

"Have you ever gone through a Flavian Portal?"

"No."

"Well, it's not painful, but you may get a little lightheaded. My dad is an extreme case."

"I understand."

"Okay, Zau," Taleeka said, and the Singa placed the cage helmet on her head.

"Wow, I feel great!" Zau said, sitting up straighter with a broad grin. "I haven't felt this kind of power since the first time we encountered the Etherions over in the Land of Mists, remember?"

Alto solemnly nodded and Taleeka shook her head.

"Before my time," she said, waving her hand impatiently at her distracted friend. "Zau, time's a-wasting."

"Right, sorry," she said, closing her eyes and rubbing the rune with her thumb.

A short moment later, a field of blue sparks started emitting from a spot on the floor ten feet away. Slowly, the eruption of light churned and intensified upward into a seven-foot-tall swirling blue vortex.

"You say you have done this before?" Cadi asked, her face awash in trepidation.

"Oh yeah," Taleeka calmly replied. "This should be a fairly easy trip. We're not even leaving the Corporeal Reach."

King Serkel of the Jomake Empire hated two things most of all—women and thieves. He despised women because of the treatment he received when captured by the Amarenians as a boy. His hatred of thieves—deeply ironic—stemming from the fact that he originally formed the Jomake as a mounted bandit gang. Now, he had to deal with both. A serving wench caught stealing food from the kitchen commanded his direct attention. He insisted on doling out punishment to all female captives and took pleasure in administering the king's justice.

Lounging on his throne, Serkel twirled a long ringlet of blond hair and stared out the massive windows, pondering which disciplinary action to take. His spymaster and second-in-command, Chor—a bull of a man with stern chocolate brown features framed by a short black beard—sat beside him and advised lenience due to the nature of the theft.

However, a *woman* had committed the crime, and Serkel refused to be denied his twisted satisfaction. Two Jomake guards dragged her in. Serkel's eyes narrowed and his lips curled tight. She looked like she was in her late teens. Despite her shabby appearance, she struck him as attractive. He watched with callous detachment as her naked brown body trembled from both fear and the chill. Her tear-streaked face and long, sweat-plastered hair stirred the beginnings of an erection. When the guards shoved her to her knees, he leaned forward.

"So, you were caught stealing from Serkel's kitchens?" the king asked.

With her head bowed to the floor, she nodded and sobbed.

"Serkel now gives you the chance to explain yourself."

"Please, Your Majesty," she said without looking up. "My family is hungry. There was so much in the kitchen—I didn't see the harm in…"

"Didn't see the harm?" Serkel roared. "Any theft is a serious offense—especially against your king!"

"Please, Your Majesty, mercy."

A cruel smile replaced his fury.

"Chor here advised lenience, so very well. Since all women are cunts, and cunts serve but one purpose, Serkel orders this, cut off one of her fingers—your choice. Then clean her up and take her to my bedchamber. Once I've had my fill, restrain her in the main square for two cycles. Anyone who wants her may have her. Make sure she's visible from the windows. It will be amusing to watch. Serkel has spoken!"

The girl burst into hysterics as the guards yanked her to her feet. Serkel stood.

"I await the cunt in my bedchamber," he said, sweeping from the throne room.

○ ○ ○

She still trembled as the guards led her to the king's chambers. The pain in her left hand throbbed where they'd severed her pinky, but the terror of what Serkel might do to her overwhelmed even that. Given his reputation, it would likely be brutal. And then would come two cycles of public rape. She prayed her family wouldn't witness it. Would her husband even want her after this? Would she ever want any man again?

"The king's gonna have fun with you, missy," one of the guards sneered, slapping her ass hard.

"Yeah," the other chuckled. "Please him enough and maybe he'll keep you as his personal cunt. That'll spare you from the next two days."

They stopped at a pair of ornate double doors. One guard knocked. No answer. He knocked again.

"Your Majesty, we have your evening's entertainment."

Still nothing. They exchanged uncertain looks. One pushed the door open.

Inside, both men froze. The girl screamed.

King Serkel's severed head rested in the center of the massive bed. His face remained twisted in fury. Blood soaked the satin sheets, and a large stain on the far wall marked where the rest of him had exploded. Whoever had done it was long gone—but how?

"Lock down the keep!" one guard shouted. "The king has been assassinated!"

○ ○ ○

Mazie looked up from the hearth when the pulse of energy crackled through the room. She sipped her brandy and leaned back in her overstuffed chair, staring into the flames. A presence formed behind her.

"I expected you earlier," she said, taking another sip. "I suppose you're here to kill me?"

"No," Taleeka replied, taking the chair beside her, "But I am curious—why did you want my mom dead?"

"I suppose I do owe you an explanation."

A long silence passed. Mazie took another drink.

"Well?"

"I didn't especially want her killed. I only wanted to stop the agricultural compact she was drafting. Killing her was Naza's idea. Dolan was a fool to let that madman off the leash."

"But you set it in motion."

"I suppose so," Mazie replied wistfully.

"And now you're converting your soup kitchens into granaries?"

"With The Sisters rebuilt, the kitchens aren't needed. People gotta eat. I might as well profit. Between Jomake grain and Verlader shipping, I figured I'd clean up. That compact had to fail. I couldn't risk that kind of competition."

"Why involve House Aramos at all?"

"Money and manpower. House Aramos, through the Imperial Bank, owns most farm and ranch notes in the greater Goyan Islands. Convincing Dolan that the compact threatened his profits was easy. He's a military man, not an economist. Your mother's death was just an unfortunate result."

"I see," Taleeka said, turning toward the door. "Did you get all that, Vanir?"

"Every word," said the detective captain as he entered.

Talib and Tantei followed, flanking two Zorian guards.

"Mazie de Goya," Vanir announced as Tantei pulled her to her feet, "you're under arrest as an accessory to the murder of Maluria Konrad."

Tantei bound Mazie's wrists. Mazie stared at Taleeka, eyes burning with shock and fury.

"I wouldn't wait 'til next cycle to put her in front of an Imperial Judge," Taleeka told Vanir, holding Mazie's gaze. "She'll vanish. And you'll have dead guards."

"Don't worry," Vanir replied. "We've already pulled a judge and hangman from Kan rotation. She'll be swinging within the deci."

The patrolmen gripped Mazie's arms. The group moved outside into the thick Kan fog. Vanir reached for his talking stone, but Taleeka stopped him.

"Hold up, Vanir. This is ridiculous," she said, reaching into her jacket.

Before anyone could react, she pulled her pistol and stepped behind Mazie. She jammed the barrel into her back.

"You had my mother killed, you fucking bitch," she growled, and pulled the trigger.

Mazie's torso exploded. Blood painted the grass. Her head flew ten feet. Her legs buckled and fell. The stunned guards still held her severed arms.

"Konrad?!" Vanir shouted.

Taleeka looked around at the wide-eyed guards.

"What?" she said, holstering her weapon. "You were taking her to hang her. I just saved everyone the hassle. Also made sure she didn't escape..."

A stunned silence hung over the group as Taleeka raised her hands slightly.

"...You're welcome."

○ ○ ○

The Aramos ancestral palace stood sprawling at the far north end of Aris. The manor itself stretched across two stories with a wide portico in front. Half a dozen satellite buildings surrounded the rear of the estate, housing staff and offices. Since Naza's death eight cycles earlier, the king had ordered tighter security across the grounds, especially around the mansion.

On the side wall of one support building, blue sparks erupted and swirled into a vortex. The swirling cyclone grew until it covered half the wall. Alto and Cadi stepped out into the cold Kan fog. Almost immediately, Alto doubled over and began heaving. Cadi placed a hand on his back and concentrated. His stomach settled, and he slowly stood upright. He nodded his thanks. She smiled.

Alto's expression suddenly turned serious. He grabbed Cadi's arm and yanked her behind the building. Her expression turned fearful—until she heard horses' hooves clopping nearby. They flattened against the wall as a mounted patrol approached and stopped.

"I could have sworn I saw a flash over here," one said.

"Nah, nothing's going on," the other replied.

"I wonder how long the king's going to keep being paranoid," the first muttered as they rode off into the fog.

Alto and Cadi slinked through shadows between the buildings, making their way to the manor's porch. Cadi's face fell when she spotted two outer-clan EEtahs standing guard beside the ornate double doors. Both stood seven feet tall, wore Forsvara tunics, and carried Firehammer Carbines.

Alto shook his head to calm her and stepped into the open. The EEtahs immediately noticed and began unslinging their weapons.

He raised his hand and closed his eyes. *Do not be alarmed. Kindly open the doors and step aside.*

The man-sharks exchanged confused glances. Then, silently, they obeyed.

Close the doors and resume your watch, Alto instructed once they crossed the threshold. *We are not to be disturbed.*

Once inside, Alto scanned the richly decorated, militaristic interior. Cadi closed her eyes and extended her senses, then nodded toward a hallway.

They approached the office at the end and listened. No sound.

Alto drew four throwing blades between his fingers, then flung the door open.

Both froze.

Dolan Aramos stood at the picture window in full uniform, hands clasped behind his back.

"Do come in. I've been expecting you," he said calmly without turning. "I just got word from the Jomake about Serkel's death. Mazie's probably dead by now too."

He turned slowly. "Which leaves only me."

"Wait," Cadi said, eyes narrowing. "Something's not right."

Dolan whistled sharply.

Doors on all sides flew open. Two Forsvara Guards entered from each, pistols raised.

"I have no intentions of following them in death," Dolan said. "Take them out front and kill them. Heads on spikes at the gate. Leave the bodies for the Vurr Carts."

"Yes, my sovereign," one guard replied, gesturing toward the door.

They marched the prisoners through the manor's entry, passing the EEtahs, who stood at attention.

Save us, Alto silently commanded as they passed.

At the portico's edge, Alto heard carbines unsling. He shoved Cadi to the ground and dove with her.

The guards barely reacted before all six fell in a barrage of Na-Kab Carbon bolts from the EEtahs.

Alto and Cadi stood as the EEtahs held position, still bewildered. The pair ran past them.

Admit no one, Alto commanded as they reentered.

Back at the office, Alto opened the door. Dolan sat behind his desk, not looking up from a stack of papers. A Mark Six pistol lay beside him.

"I trust they've been dealt with?" Dolan asked, then noticed something was off.

Looking up, his eyes widened. He reached for the pistol.

Alto's dagger flew and pinned Dolan's hand to the desk. The king screamed and grabbed his trapped hand.

Alto extended his other arm, forming his fingers into a strangling claw. Dolan's screams became gurgles. He grabbed his throat, eyes bulging, foam pouring from his mouth. The psychic grip crushed the life from him. Finally, he slumped in the chair, hand still skewered.

"It is done," Alto said.

He approached the corpse, drew his short sword, and looked at Cadi. "You need not stay."

She stepped out.

Moments later, Alto joined her. Dolan's severed head now rested on the desk, face frozen in terror, beret still in place.

He tapped his talking stone. *Zau, are you there?*

"Hey, Alto, poppy, good to finally hear you."

"Thank you, Zau. My business is complete. Please bring me home. Have you heard from Taleeka?"

"She's back with Zerga. She got the job done."

"I am pleased to hear that."

"Hold tight, poppy. I'm opening a portal now."

○ ○ ○

Cedar Aramos packed the last few items from his nearly empty desk into a box, then closed the lid. He looked around the office he'd held for sixteen grands—minus the two stolen by Banavor.

"You gonna miss the place?" Taleeka asked, stepping inside.

"I've spent enough time in here. My new quarters should be an upgrade."

"As Aramos Sovereign, I'd say so. When do you find out?"

"The Bespoke Lords vote later this cycle. It should be unanimous. No one's going to miss Dolan."

"Any immediate plans?"

"First, demilitarize House Aramos. I'd say erase Banavor's name from the school of economics, but they already did."

Taleeka chuckled. "No more compulsory military service, huh?"

"First thing to go."

"The farmers and craftsmen will love that. They'll get their kids back."

"So, what brings you by?"

"It's about Dolan."

Cedar shook his head. "Brother or not, he had it coming."

"Yeah, and with Naza dead, I'm sure the Talons will stand down, but a royal decree would help."

"It's the least I can do. You cleared my name, took out Banavor and got me back on the council. I owe you big."

"Your Majesty, I hate calling in favors—especially big ones—but that's my trade these days."

Cedar smiled. "Okay. That'll be my first act. And hey, quit with the 'Your Majesty' until after the vote. Don't jinx it."

○ ○ ○

Karta Lushi, Imperial Prosecutor for Zor, looked across his desk at the two men before him and shrugged.

"Gentlemen, I'm at a loss. We've got a bunch of dead Aramos. We know who did it, but there's not much we can do."

Tad Bengoshi, the Konrads' barrister, leaned forward. His youthful, square-jawed face remained calm. "Si, Prosecutor, I agree. The only witnesses are dead. Whether guilt can be proven or not, justice was served."

"House Aramos may not love that outcome," Vanir said, pulling out his flask.

"Maybe," Karta said. "But as of late last cycle, the Bespoke Lords selected a new sovereign." He held up a document. "This came in this morning. A royal decree from Sovereign Cedar Aramos absolving the Konrads. It went to the Security Council, Forsvara, and the Black Talons. All Aramos forces are ordered to cease harassment of the Konrads, their charges and operations. We're still free to pursue prosecution, but…"

"That's not something I'm spending resources on," Vanir said, taking a sip. "Plus, she took out a violent mobster."

"We've been trying to pin something on Mazie since she opened shop in The Sisters," Karta admitted.

"So we're done?" Bengoshi asked.

"I believe so," Karta confirmed.

"I'm good," Vanir said, pocketing the flask.

"Splendid," Bengoshi said, standing. "I'll give my clients the good news."

○ ○ ○

Taleeka considered this moment as truly bittersweet. She stood with her father and a capacity crowd in the grand hall of the Zorian Forum for the ceremony her mother gave her life for.

In attendance, seated in their usual chairs, all human representatives of the High Council—except for the Jomake—watched Sovereign Shom Eldor and Amarenian Queen Omaris Atona officially sign the Eldorian/Amarenian Agriculture Compact.

"Do you think this was worth Mom dying for?" Taleeka asked softly.

"It was something your mother felt passionate about," Alto replied solemnly.

"I'm not so sure, Dad. I really miss her."

"As do I, little one. As do I."

○ ○ ○

"It sure is strange with Mazie gone from The Sisters," Talib said, looking over the latest patrol report from the area. "I mean, we don't have to deal with her schemes, but she did keep the peace with the street bosses. Now we've got escalating clashes between past rivals popping up."

"Yeah, well, for some, you can take the punk out of the ghetto but not the ghetto out of the punk," Tantei said, peering up from her own reading.

"Well, nature hates a vacuum, and that's what happened with Mazie's death."

"Maybe not for long," Tantei said, sitting back in her chair. "My contacts say Tally Konrad and her crew are setting up shop in The Sisters. She's rented out the top floor of a building on Wilson Street."

Talib chuckled. "That street was where I made my very first bust back in the day."

"And with her main rival gone, I'm betting the industrious Mz. Konrad is preparing to exploit her absence."

"It wouldn't be the first time she's worked an angle," Talib noted. "Hey, speaking of working an angle—is the boss back from the Security Council meeting?"

Talib discovered the answer to his question when the office door opened and Vanir's head poked through.

"Conference room, you two," he said seriously, then disappeared back into the hall.

224

"Well, I guess we're about to find out," Tantei said, standing and grabbing her jacket from the back of her chair.

By the time they reached the conference/interrogation room, they found Gasata and the twelve other investigators standing around expectantly, with Vanir at the head of the room.

"Okay kids," he said with a slightly hesitant look. "Given the growth of the city, the Security Council has decided to reorganize the Zorian Guards."

The statement caused a murmur to pass through the group.

"Basically, every plat in the city will have their own Patrol, Investigation and Fire Divisions with their own captains. That probably means promotions for some of you. All the individual captains will report to the main headquarters here in Judgment Square and a newly created office of Chief Guard. Records Division and the jail will remain here. The good news—we're getting our own crime lab. That will take over the second floor here. So, for us, it's probably going to be moving day. My team, along with Captain Gasata's Patrol Division, are relocating to The Sisters. The rest of you will receive your transfer notices soon."

"When's this supposed to happen, boss?" Talib asked.

"It should be completed by the end of the grand."

"That's like in three quintes."

"Yep."

Once again, muttering swept through the room.

"Hey boss, so who's this new Chief?" Tantei asked.

"A guy by the name of Sef Glaven."

Talib's brow immediately furrowed. "Hey, I know that guy! He's one of the commissioners for the Tuath Plat. He's a politician, not a cop."

"Yeah," Tantei said skeptically. "He's also one slice of bacon away from a heart attack. The guy must weigh four hundred pounds."

"What can I say," Vanir commiserated. "He's connected, and the Security Council didn't ask my opinion."

"Where's our new home, Boss?" Talib asked.

"We've got our own two-story structure at 1865 Union Drive." Vanir paused and scanned the faces in the room. "So that's all I got for you. If there are no more questions, you're dismissed."

The room slowly cleared out, investigators speculating in hushed tones.

"Hey Tay," Tantei said, stepping up beside him. "What say we take a ride and check out our new digs?"

"Yeah, sure," Talib replied with a nod.

"And while we're at it, let's check out the Konrads' newest offices."

○ ○ ○

"I'm really worried about Dad," Taleeka said, picking at her plate. "Now that we've exacted our vengeance, it's really hit him that Mom's gone."

"What about you?" Zerga asked. "She was your mom."

"I'll be alright in time. I can grieve. My dad's the master of controlling his emotions. He's never dealt with anything like this before. Keeping your feelings bottled up inside just isn't good."

"He has been distant."

"That's an understatement. He hasn't left his room in three cycles, ever since getting back from the signing."

A long, uncomfortable pause broke when Peshk rushed down the stairs with a folded piece of paper in her hands.

"Mz. Tally, I just went to check on your dad to tell him lunch was ready and he's gone."

Taleeka spun in surprise. "What?!"

"By the looks of things, he's been gone several cycles. He left his swords in their stands and this was laying on the bed."

Taleeka grabbed the note and opened it.

Little One,

Your mother has been avenged and I feel my usefulness in this place has come to an end.

The thought of going on without her haunts me and I now go to join her. Keep my swords as a remembrance of me. Know that I am proud to call you daughter and will always love you.

Taleeka lowered the letter and stared blankly.

"He's gone off to die," she heard herself say, causing Peshk to gasp.

Suddenly a determined look swept over her and she touched her Larimar necklace.

"Hey Cadi."

"Hey Tally. Something's wrong—what is it?"

"My dad's gone missing. You've got his psychic marker. Can you locate him?"

"Hold on, let me get someplace quiet."

"Time is of the essence."

Several tense moments passed before the Amarenian psychic's voice rang out in her head.

"Uh, Tally, I've got him way up in the Ice Lands on the Dra'Tar Glacier. What's he doing there?"

"Trying to die. I gotta go, thanks."

Tapping the stone broke the connection. Another tap opened it again.

"Hey Zau."

"Tally, bubby, what's happening?"

"I'm going to grab some cold weather gear," she said, bounding up the stairs. "I need a portal, fast!"

The Ice Lands sit at the top of the Annigan, and the Dra'Tar Mountains and glacier, running down its center, mark the dividing line between Lumina and Nocturn. The weak illumination of the sun far to the south keeps this frigid land in a permanent state of dusk.

The variable winds, blowing at a steady twenty miles per hour, sent small snow vortexes spiraling across the flat top of the glacier. When one vortex turned an iridescent shade of blue, it became stationary and grew. Taleeka stepped out of the tempest dressed in a parka with a fur-lined hood and surveyed her surroundings. Once completely out of the portal, the snow devil stopped glowing and resumed its random course dictated by the wind.

She saw her father, dressed only in his traditional robes, kneeling by the glacier's edge, facing the frozen tundra thousands of feet below. His eyes remained closed in silent meditation as drifts of snow piled up around his folded legs. In his hand, he held Mal's necklace. His cheeks appeared thickly crusted with frozen tears.

When she approached, his eyes opened, and she stopped and knelt in front of him.

"Hey Dad," she said sympathetically.

"Little one, why are you here?"

"To bring you back home."

"I have said my goodbyes."

"Dad, you don't need to do this."

"It is for the best."

"No, it is not! Your pain is great—I know, I feel it too—but my pain will be doubled if you die. I can't lose you both. Mom would not have wanted this. Please, we can get through this together. You said in your letter you weren't useful anymore. That's just not true. Dad, I need you! You can't leave me, please!"

Alto watched tears form in his daughter's eyes and gently wiped them away.

"Do not cry, little one. Your tears will freeze."

Taleeka sniffled, then smiled weakly and stood. "Come on Dad, let's get you home."

She extended her hand expectantly, and he slowly took it. Helping him to his feet, she tapped her talking stone through the thick fabric.

"Okay Zau, we can use that portal now. It's too damn cold here."

Taleeka could feel the Kan fog rising around her feet, accentuating the chill of early winter. All around her the new buildings of The Seven Sisters rose majestically, easily the tallest skyline in Zor. Hackneys flowed in either direction on the streets and sentients of every race walked past. She admired how much the former slums had changed. Not long ago, if she happened to walk these streets at this time, her pistol would be close at hand. Now, shops stayed open with patrons wandering in and out of well-lit interiors.

Listening to her boots on the cobblestones, she reflected on her life and all the changes and turns it had taken over the grands. Her next birthday would be her twenty-first, and she considered how much life she had managed to pack into such a relatively short time. Mostly, she thought of her parents— of which only one remained. Ultimately, they shaped her into who she became. Then she thought of all the sentients who came and went from her life, and a reflective smile crossed her lips.

Peering down at the twin rings on the ring and forefinger of her right hand, she sighed. The thin gold bands, funereal gifts from the Cevot queen, would be the latest symbols of friendship toward her. Spreading her fingers in a V shape activated the rings, and an intricate asymmetrical spiderweb of light connected them. She smiled, watching the shimmering pattern—an exact but modern version of the Cevot pass given to her as a child.

She'd been busy since returning with her father from the Ice Lands a cluster ago. With Mazie's death, peace between street bosses began to fray. The Security Council covertly suggested her presence in The Sisters would help stabilize things. She and her associates would work separately yet in concert with the Zorian Guards. As always, she'd be given a wide berth to solve problems, and her service would be free of charge to the city.

Turning down Wilson Street, she caught the comforting aroma of roasting meat from a nearby food cart. Even with The Sisters' modernization, some things didn't change—and such familiarities always made her happy.

The building at 3219 Wilson Street reached five stories, making it one of the tallest in the city. A blue Air Workers tower on the roof made it seem even taller. The ground floor held a haberdashery and cobbler, separated by a foyer. The deep alcove dead-ended with stairs leading up to an Air Workers transport tube running directly to the top floor and her new offices.

Standing directly under the tube's mouth twelve feet above her, she placed her palm on the Larimar plate set into the wall beneath the small sign reading: *Mal and Company*. A gentle whooshing sound preceded her hair flying about as she lifted into the clear tube. This, she thought, would definitely take some getting used to.

She arrived on the fifth floor to a mostly empty room filled with the people she knew and trusted. Smiling at the reception, she stepped out of the tube and over to Alto, who hugged her. Making her way past Zau, Larzz, Cadi, Sister Ravitseja and Zerga, she situated herself by the windows.

"Thanks for coming," she addressed the small group. "I've been asked by the Security Council to make sure The Sisters don't revert back to their more lawless days. It's finally making money for the city, and they're eager to see their investment protected.

"This is going to be my base of operations, and as you can see, I'm just now getting around to furnishing it.

"I've called on you in the past to assist me in my endeavors, and I hope you will continue. Just like before, you'll be well compensated."

"Aren't you and your dad in hot water with the Security Council for cutting through House Aramos?" Larzz asked.

Taleeka chuckled. "No. An Imperial judge, friendly with Mazie and with a big old stick up his butt, filed a motion in the Security Council. He wanted to strip us of our Hero of the Realm title. It was soundly rejected by every house—except House Whitmar, who abstained. So, we're good to go.

"If everybody's on board, I'm calling this entity *Mal and Company*—in honor of my mom."

GLOSSARY

Spoiler warning: *The following is a master glossary for all the books in this series. Reading beyond a specific word or phrase searches could result in spoilers.*

Adad Sunal – EEtah war collage belonging to House Bran, specializing in conducting internal security for House Bran.

Agress – A green Etheria Crystal with red striations which opens and closes doors, windows and hatches, negating any locks but not traps or wards.

Aiken – Semi-sentient clouds sent out across the Annigan from Mount Ghas-Tor, recording everything they witness on the ground and in the air. They are indistinguishable from other clouds against the backdrop of a blue sky. Aiken constantly send visuals back to the mountain, but recent images remain in their limited memory. Those possessing psychic abilities can access their recent memories by flying through and communing with them.

Akina – Humanoid fox creatures native to the Barrens in the Twilight Lands. Often sly and excellent thieves.

Amarenian – Female human race formerly noted for their hatred and slavery of men and piracy.

Angona – Roasted eel on a stick. Sold from vendors' carts all over the City of Immor-Onn.

Annigan – The name of the world which is the setting for the various stories in the Tales of the Annigan Cycle. It includes the two hemispheres of Lumina and Nocturn separated by the Twilight Lands.

Anointed Sister – The title for the Amarenian Queen.

Aquamarine – Pale blue Etheria Crystal which reveals something's true nature.

Ara-Fel Party – Political party of Amarenian farmers.

Arapa Fish – A large fish native to the back waters and tributaries of the Otoman River. Their tough scaly skin is coveted among the Dreeat as armor. The scales by themselves are so abrasive they are also sold as nails.

Ash-Ta – Avion term (winged monster) for the widespread colonies of humanoid bats inhabiting the rocky crags stretching across of the Spine of the World. Avion scholars record six tribes: the Molossi, Acero, Chiro, Ptero, Diaemus and Desmodus. The Ash-Ta allied with the Tiikeri due to their shared enemy, the Do-Tarr.

Astute Sister – Amarenian title for high level politician.

Aur-Quaz – Iridescent Etheria Crystal stimulating energy.

Available Regions – Uninhabited areas of Immor-Onn waiting for the residents displaced by the recent Black Pearl Revolution to return and inhabit.

Avion –Proud sentient rulers of Lumina's sky. Incredibly beautiful and graceful to behold and unabashedly elitist, especially towards their distant cousins, the Humans. Avions refuse to wear any armor and yet have led the way in almost every major war fought. Their scholars contributed a great deal to the knowledge of Lumina. Their four Great Houses occupy the airspace and mountain tops of the Goyan Islands.

Avion Great Houses:

House Azar - Avion House inhabiting the City of Mitar, on the Island of Dal, in the Tellasian chain, ruled by Queen Averin. Their territories include the skies over the Tellasian Chain, Otomoria, Zer-Tal Twins, and the Zerk Atoll. They are known for their healing Clerics of Neami and their beautiful music.

House Eacher - Avion House inhabiting the Island of Wou, City of Picon & surrounding airspace. Ruled by King Sindil.

House Solas – Smallest of all the Avion houses. They inhabit the city of Adean on the Island of Temil in the Outer Zerians and control the surrounding airspace.

House Pyre - Eldest, largest, and most powerful of all the Avion Houses. They inhabit the skies above the Island of Goya. Their city stronghold, Darmont Keep, sits on the north face of volcanic Mount Goya. Unlike the other Avion Houses who utilize Air Magic, they mastered Fire Magic drawing their power from the volcano.

Awal – First of the ten Quinte Grand Cycle, Spring.

Azurite – Purple Etheria Crystal which connects to the Middle realms.

Bailian – Predominate race of the western Twilight Lands. Descended from the Piceans, they are a beautiful humanoid race with pale blue skin and large eyes.

Banja – The seventy-seven Amarenian noble families, eleven for each of the various seven provinces called Dors.

Banok Atoll – Island ring in the Southeastern Occan of Lumina housing one of the largest permanent Flavian portals. Its psionic ripples extend out hundreds of miles and affect the entire southeastern Deep Ocean of Lumina.

Banok Run – The final test for admittance to the elite Brightstar Sailors where they must navigate a tight circle around the turbulent seas surrounding the Banok Atoll without being pulled into its giant Flavian portal.

Bespoke Lords – Members of prominent families who have Bespoke Names and serve as advisors to the sovereign in a respective noble human house in the Goyan Islands.

Bespoke Names – Honorary family names only bestowed by a Goyan Island governor or higher as reward for exemplary service to the crown.

Black Mural – A magical record of the Annigan located deep in the Rod-Ema Trench in the Ocean Deep of Nocturn. It slowly grows in size as it records every act of imbalance on the planet. If it grows too large, it will penetrate into the planet's core, killing all life and allowing it to start anew.

Black Talon – Special forces of the Aramos Army, the Fosvara Guard.

Boustian Mage – Bards who perform magic by singing, playing music and storytelling, found predominantly in the larger cities of the Goyodian Chain of islands.

Brightstar – Elite sailors of House Calden qualified to sail the Deep Oceans and the storm-tossed seas of the Twilight Lands. Captains in the Calden Navy must be Brightstar qualified. Brightstar only allows acceptance to their ranks upon completion of the treacherous Innaca or Banok Runs.

Brom – Horse size dragonflies inhabiting the steep southern foothills of the Amaren Mountains.

Calcite – Clear Etheria Crystal which aids in navigation.

Caldani – Privateers hired by Human House Calden to patrol their waters.

Calden Intelligencer Service – House Calden's elite spy agency and secret police. They draw recruits mostly from the Calden Maritime Legion.

Calden Maritime Legion – Marines for House Calden

Calisma – Main library in the University of Marassa.

Cali – Branch libraries and scriptoriums in the five Human capital cities in the Goyodian Island Chain.

Carbana – Chewing tobacco rolled into a tight tube.

Cavernite – A pale green Etheria Crystal with pink striations that can increase the physical dimensions of the interior of any structure it is placed within. The size increase depends on the amount of Cavernite used and the level of PSI used to power it. Without a constant supply of PSI power, the dimensions revert back to their original size. Often used with an Obsidian PSI battery backup.

Centi Elipse – Called a Centi for short. Unit of time in the Goyan Islands equaling a minute.

Celot – Amarenian term for a priestess.

Cevot – Large sentient spider creatures known for their silk, inhabiting the Os-Oni Mountains of the Twilight Lands.

Ched – Seventh of the ten Quinte Grand Cycle, Autumn.

Chanakans – An ancient race of sentient octopoids dwelling in vast underwater cities in the Ocean Deep of Nocturn. They worship the ancient ones of the abyss and practice a powerful water magic.

Cluster – The name for ten cycles, the Annigan's version of a week. There are five clusters to a Quinte (month).

Cobalcite – Deep pink Etheria Crystal used for healing.

Code of Tisina – Mobster code of silence in the City of Zor. Because of Zor's zero tolerance for organized crime, the various independent criminals adopted a "no cooperation" rule with city officials. The slightest violation of this code is punishable by death.

Common – The Common Tongue, a spoken only language used mostly by humans and those in business with them.

Cocoonessa – Cocoon city of the Tinian Moth people on Mount Natal in the Land of Mists. Also called the Silk City.

Corporal Reach, The –The prime material plain of the middle realms where the Annigan resides.

Coxeter – Both the language and magic system of the Tinian race based on a complex form of three-dimensional geometry. The written language is made up of cryptic mathematical notations using lines and dots. Tinian minds perceive all math as the three-dimensional mapping, best displayed in their silk weavings of intricate geometric patterns. When combined with Etheria Crystals, these patterns can be used to perform spells.

Croquis – Magitech mapping devise projecting a scalable three-dimensional holographic image of a desired location, including the other planes of the multiverse.

Cub Prince – A rare black tiger heir to the throne of the Tiikeri Empire. Once every generation, the Tiikeri king must breed an heir. All prominent Tiikeri families offer their most eligible daughters for breeding, but only one will conceive of a black tiger. All other cubs produced from this royal union are killed at birth. They move the complete family of the female who gives birth to the Cub Prince into the palace and considered them nobility. They immediately begin grooming the Cub Prince for the throne, and, when he comes of age, he must kill his father to take it.

Cul-Ta – Humanoid rat creatures found in almost every City in Lumina.

Cycle – Time period equivalent to a day.

Dag – Amarenian term for a common slave. A derogatory slang word for a male.

Darek Witch – Amarenian earth shamans acting as midwives and performing other shamanistic duties.

Darian Silk – High quality silk spun by the Cevot Spiders traded to the On'Dara.

Darwan – A cross between the Balians and the Fudomi, this race is the most prolific humanoid native to the Barrens. They situate their villages around Ghorn temples and must pay tribute to the Onay hordes of the region. Villages close to the borders of the hordes remain under constant threat. Darwans raise a herd animal called the Ng'Ombe which provides the major staple food in the Barrens.

Dasam – Tenth of the ten Quinte Grand Cycle, Winter.

Deci – Time unit equivalent to one hour.

Derde – Third of the ten Quinte Grand Cycle, Spring.

Diamond – Clear Etheria Crystal which transfers power.

Doggin – Derogatory term used for slave dock workers in the city of Aris.

Dolin – Etheria gem hunters, mostly of the Gila race, traveling the Barrens in small caravans and harvesting raw Etheria Crystals to sell to the Zadim lapidaries of the Oasis in the Dark Waste Desert.

Dor – Title of the seven various provinces in Amarenia. Taia-Dor, Denat-Dor, Mivira-Dor, Amoso-Dor, Kinning-Dor, Rackam-Dor, Durik-Dor.

Do-Tarr – Sentient, hive-minded mantid creatures from the Land of Mists in Nocturn. They comprise two large hives in the north and south with precise subterranean tunnels connecting them. They are expert builders and remain neutral in all forms of politics.

Dreamer in the Lake – Demi-God of the Os'Tor Forest and a Harbinger of Balance. She rests at the bottom of a large lake encased in mud and manifests herself on the lake's surface as a multicolored lotus. Her accolades, sentients from every race, sleep around the lake's shore, sending their ethereal bodies out into people's dreams and guiding them.

Dreeat – Humanoid crocodilians inhabiting the end of the western fork of the Otoman River in Otomoria. They grow sugar cane and make magical healing candies from it. They harvest river fish as a major part of their diet. For thousands of grands, ever since the arrival Human race, the Human families have tried to eradicate them.

Dronning Mare – Female horse chosen to breed with the On'Dara chief.

EEtah – Large, powerful and aggressive sentient humanoid shark creatures trained in martial schools known as Sunals to become the professional warriors of Lumina. After their egg birth in the hatcheries and their first year in the nursery, they are sorted into one of the various Sunals of their House. Females enter House Nur and the males go through a highly competitive Sunal scouting and recruiting process with the nursery's called the Garess. Sunals hire out bodyguards, sentries, mercenaries and virtually anything martial. This, along with weapon manufacturing and sales, provides the main revenue stream for the great houses.

EEtah Great Houses:

> **House Nur** – This Noble house is female only. Co-ruled by a secular Queen Mother and spiritual High Priestess.
>> Temple of Drulain headquartered in the High Holy City of Zor.
>> Specialty: Scribes, Clerics, Healers, Politics, Domestics.
>
> **House Crom** – Three Sunals in the Tellasian Chain.
>> Sedar Sunal on Roe Island. Specialty: Bodyguard.
>> Boril Sunal on Uma Island. Specialty: Crom Internal Security.
>> Zorod Sunal on Tel Island. Specialty: Castle and Town Defense.
>
> **House Bran** – Four Sunals in the Goyodian Chain.

Garf Sunal on Quell Island. Specialty: Long term inland duty.

Tukk Sunal on Mobis Island. Specialty: Shipboard Security.

Adad Sunal on Creos Island. Specialty: Bran Internal Security.

Farak Sunal on Roust Island. Specialty: Bounty Hunter, Vengeance.

House Zed – Three Sunals in the Wouvian Islands.

Dakor Sunal on Owling Island. Specialty: Shock Troops.

Jut Sunal on Tor Island. Specialty: Zed Internal Security.

Morrak Sunal on Billow Island. Specialty: Police, Executioners.

Elipse – A unit of time equaling a second.

Ellie – Slang and abbreviation for an Ellipse.

Esteemed Sister – Amarenian title for Ambassador.

Etheria Crystal – Crystals containing magical properties mostly found in crystal trees in the Barrens of the Twilight Lands. Residents of the Dark Waste Desert harvest and process the oases' crystals. These crystals provide the primary form of magic in Nocturn.

Flavian Portals – Portals through space making different points in the Annigan instantaneously accessible by passing through the inter-dimensional Middle Realms. Each portal is different. There are several large, fixed portals on both Lumina and Nocturn and hundreds of smaller dedicated Flavians. Certain animals, intoxicants and magical items can open smaller portals.

Frozen Sea – The vast expanse of ice flows covering the majority of Nocturn and the largest centrally occupied area in all of Annigan. The ice ranges from a slushy mixture with icebergs near the land masses to several hundred feet thick in the eastern areas.

Forsvara Guards – A rank-and-file foot soldier army of House Aramos.

Fudomi – Sentient humanoid ram creatures inhabiting the western Os-Oni Mountains of the Twilight Lands. They steal and sell the Cevot Spider broods' silk and eggs, which they consider a delicacy.

Galeb – Sea Gulls with a psychic connection to a handler. They are used to transport messages across Lumina.

Garf Sunal – EEtah War college belonging to House Bran. Their specialty is long term inland duty.

Gar-Kal – Fish head humanoids living on the ocean floor of Nocturn. They are of low intelligence and aggressive.

Geta – Amarenian title for a master at a skill or craft, especially if they teach it.

Ghas-Tor – This is the tallest peak on the Annigan. It reaches upward 32,000 feet in the Os'Ani Mountain range of the Twilight Lands. More than a mountain, it is a sentient being and the epicenter of Air Magic in the world.

Ghorn – Necromancers of the Barrens in Twilight Lands.

Ghost Suit – A gray, skintight jump suit used mostly by Valdurian forces to blend into the Kan fog.

Ghosts of the Kan – Mariner's term for Rayth raiders. Due to their ghost white chalk covering their bodies and acting as camouflage when they attack during the Kan fog.

Gila – The main sentient race populating the Dark Waste. Hybrids comprising Bailian pilgrims and a now long-gone sentient lizard native to the region. They are an advanced race occupying the three large oases of the desert.

Golden One, The – Otick term for the Golden Avatar.

Goy-Ardia – Goyan fire mages trained at the University of Marassa.

Goyan Calendar – Method of time keeping found only in the Goyan Islands. It consists of a Grand Cycle (year) which is comprised of ten Quinte (months) named; Awal, Teine, Derde, Kvara, Peto, Sesto, Ched, Merve, Tisa and Dasam. Each Quinte is divided into fifty Cycles (days) with each cycle being divided into fifty Deci (hours) twenty-five in sunlight and twenty-five in Kan. Ten cycles equal a Cluster (week) with five Clusters per Quinte.

Goyan Rise – A 300-mile-wide sea mount in central Lumina acting as the floor of the Shallow Sea. Its volcanic vents fuel the volcano of Mount Goya.

Grand – Short for Grand Cycle. Unit of time equivalent to a year.

Grass Eater – Singa insult

Gustare' – Amarenian bath house and tavern.

Hackney – Etheria driven floating carriages found throughout the major cities of Lumina.

Hand of the Wind – The Assassin's Guild of Annigan. All members worship Orad, Goddess of death. The upper levels are clerics of Orad.

Hakim – A judge in the High Holy City of Zor.

Harbingers of Balance – Sentient creatures of all types called to a secret society monitoring the balance of the Annigan and warning when something upsets it.

Hasteen – City of the Dreeat crocodile people.

Hill Sister – Hermaphroditic warriors inhabiting the northern foothills of the Amaren Mountains in Amarenia. Though they possess both male and female sex organs, they cannot procreate. Popular with Amarenian nobility as seneschal/bodyguards partly because they can have sex with them and not violate their "no man" pledge.

Hoon – Word used in Zor to denote a pimp or the manager of a brothel.

Howlite – Gray Etheria Crystal used for glamour, disguise and polymorphing.

Humans – The Human race descended from the Avion race. In 5070 PA, the rebellious Avions which joined Xandar the Mad's doomed Great Kraken Incursion had their wings severed as punishment before being banished and scattered to the Goyodian Chain. 171 years later the Seventh Avatar sang the "Song of Rebirth" evolving them into a separate race. They formed their Great Houses, spreading out across the Goyan Island Chain and beyond the Shallow Sea.

Human Great Houses:

House Aramos –The largest and wealthiest of the great human families directly descended from the First Men. The capital city of Aris is located on the Island of Vakai in the Goyodian Chain of Islands in the Northern Shallow Sea. They control banking and finance in Lumina and constantly hatch Machiavellian plots to expand their power over the other houses.

House Calden – This great house controls the seas with the largest military and commercial fleets. Their Capital City of Nader is on the Island of Tarla in the Goyodian Chain, but they command the island chain of the Zerk Atoll where their sailors are trained.

243

House Eldor – This great house controls virtually all the agricultural islands of the eastern Goyan Islands. Their Capital City of Rophan is on the Island of Tolle in the Goyodian Chain of Islands in the Northern Shallow Sea.

House Valdur – This house is known for their incestuous practices to keep the family bloodline pure. Their capital city of Dryden is on the Island of Atar in The Goyodian Chain of Islands in the Northern Shallow Sea. All but destroyed in a surprise invasion by House Eldor called the Unification War, only the discovery of lighter than air travel and a fleet of war balloons saved their home island. They lost the rest of their agricultural lands to Eldor. Their entire culture revolves around their powerful air guild, the Valdurian Air Service.

House Whitmar – This family runs the organized and sanctioned slave trade on Lumina from the City of Nier on the northern Goya coast. Their Capital City of Brinstan is located on the Island of Umin in the Goyodian Chain in the Northern Shallow Sea.

Immor-Onn – Large city known as "the Shining Jewel of the East" located on the western coast of the Twilight Lands. Home of the Bailian Empire.

Idonian Philosophy – The Avion prejudice that Humans are a scourge which should be wiped out. The driving belief of the Idonian Cabal of Avion House Pyre and Solas.

Innaca Deep – Giant whirlpool in the Northwestern Ocean of Lumina housing one of the largest Flavian portals. Its psionic ripples extend out hundreds of miles.

Innaca Run – The final test for admittance to the elite Brightstar Sailors where they must navigate a tight circle around the turbulent seas surrounding the Innaca Atoll without being pulled into its giant Flavian portal.

Ironmark – Brutal enforcers of the Quartermasters in the Goyan Islands of Lumina. Each island chain has their own Ironmark specializing in their own unique form of torture.

Itori – Insect Shamans found throughout the agricultural western Goyan Islands. Although they control mostly locusts, they can command any insect and are immune to all insect venoms and stings.

Jangwa – Elite desert commandos defending the outer parameter of the two civilized oases in the Dark Waste Desert. Capable of traveling under the sand and rapidly over the surface of the desert, they make frequent scouting missions to the untamed Qua-Raman Oasis and the Buried City of Nof-Saloom.

Kaefom – Traditional Amarenian breeding ritual overseen by the Darek Witches.

Kan – Period of the day in the Goyan Islands when the thick sea fog rises blotting out the sun, used mostly for sleep. It is an effect caused by geothermal activities only found in the Goyan Islands and Shallow Sea.

Kel – Flying lizards bred and tended by Avions for food and as beasts of burden.

Kharry Institute – Tiikeri medical facility located outside the Tiikeri capital city of Hai-Darr and run by the brilliant and ruthless Dr. Met-Ge, specializing in crossbreeding Mawl races to produce Mongrels for specific duties. The Institute created Cheepas and the Ves-Lari.

Kinjuto Dominator – Sex mage using BDSM techniques.

Konaleeta – Called the Island of the Lost. The entire island is caught in a permanent Flavian Loop. It bounces around from location to location across any of the planes of the Middle Realms, never staying in anyone place for very long.

Kusars – Mawl bandits from the Dasos region in the Land of Mists.

Kvara – Fourth of the ten Quinte Grand Cycle, Summer.

Ky-Awat – Sentient rat creatures of the Dark Waste Desert. They have bred them up from the Cul-Ta and are larger and more aggressive, but no smarter. Various factions use them as cannon fodder. They breed quickly and are plentiful, especially around the three main oases.

Land of Mists – The largest land mass in Nocturn. So named because the mixture of cold temperatures in the air combined with the warmth of the ground results in a uniform constant low hanging fog over the entire continent. Three distinct landscapes cover the surface of the land, separated by the Kel-Raku Mountain range and dimly illuminated by bioluminescence, outcroppings of Etheria Crystals and the moon and stars. The thick rainforest of Arboro lies to the north, and the vast savannah of Rovina runs to the south. They're connected by the Bor-Kaa Pass. The dense jungles and swamps of Dasos lie to the east.

Landagar Group – Research and Development Division of the Valdurian Air Service located in the balloon city of Landagar high in the mountain peaks of the Valdurian home island of Atar.

Larimar – The "Talking Stone," a milky white Etheria Crystal with blue striations, used for psychic communication between parties within proximity of the gem.

Learned Sister – The title given to Amarenian teachers, scribes & academics.

Legates – Suicide messengers hired through House Whitmar. Candidates are usually elderly or terminally ill. Upon their death, House Whitmar agrees to care for their surviving family for their remaining lifetimes.

Lor-Danta Oasis – The eastern most major oasis in the Dark Waste Desert. The large Obsidian field stretching from its shore contains six Tanum Charts of the skies used by the Arron-Nin Astrologers dwelling there.

Lumina – The hemisphere of the world in constant sunlight.

Luna – Term for the lunar cycle used by every culture in the Annigan except the humans in the Goyan Islands, who cannot see the moon.

Luroh – Bolo/sash weapon used by the Mahilia. The sash contains the person's rank and record. The two metal balls at either end become an effective weapon when twirled.

Magitech – The fusion of magic and technology. Mostly referring to the use of Etheria Crystals and specific mechanical items. i.e., Airship engines.

Mahilia – City guards in Mostar, the capital of Amarenia.

Makari – Inter-dimensional race of sentient spiders from the Pasture Plain of the Middle Realms. They seeded the Cevot race in the Os'Tor Mountains in the Land of Mists. The males resemble hairy wolf spiders, the females resemble black widows. The females have been known to allure any male of any race. They compulsively kill after sex.

*Mala*chite – Light green Etheria Crystal, absorbs energy.

Marassa – A professor at the University of Marassa.

Masha – Amarenian for master.

Maudo Grass – Tall grass with a bright blue flowering tuft growing in the Land of Mists. The flowers are a favorite intoxicant for Mawls and especially coveted by the Tiikeri.

Mawl – Overall name for the humanoid cat races of the Land of Mists. It is also the term used for the common language they share.

Medikua – Medical officer aboard Calden naval vessels.

Merve – Eighth of the ten Quinte Grand Cycle, Autumn.

Middle Realms – Constantly shifting inter-dimensional plane between worlds. Sometimes referred to as the Fairy or Dream Realms.

Mongrel – The product of cross breeding between the Mawl races found all over the Land of Mists. Pure breeds mostly shun them and the Tiikeri use them for slave labor.

Moonfall – Period of the cycle when Nocturn's main illuminating body, the moon, dips below the horizon issuing in the Moonless

Moonless – The "night" period of the cycle when Nocturn's main illuminating body, the moon, orbits around to the Lumina side of the Annigan.

Mora – Term used for teacher or master in the Whovian Sword Schools of Rohina Takki.

Morasian Puff Boy – Male prostitute from the Port City of Moras on Goya's west coast. Known for their distinctly feminine demeanor.

Mostas – Capital City of the Amarenian Empire on the western shore of Amarenia.

Najuka – Amarenian emasculation ritual performed on all males except those used for breeding purposes in the Kaefom Ritual.

Na-Kab – One of the three insectoid groups originating from below the Land of Mists. They occupied the easternmost hive closest to Mount Natal. Their exoskeleton is made up of fire magic. Their tail has a penis shaped stinger capable of impregnating any living thing they sting.

Namesake – Term used for spouse when they share a bespoke last name.

Narrows, The – Remnants of an old iron mine forming the slums of the Hidden City of Toriss in Otomoria.

Nocturn – The hemisphere of the world in constant night

Nolton Boat – Ships made of Ukko Wood in a secret shipyard on the Island of Zer, mostly used by Brightstar sailors. Hovering less than an inch above the water, their Ukko rudder guides and propels. The specific construction of the hull makes the boat unsinkable.

Noma – Poison from the Noma Viper.

Nurian Edicts – EEtah rules of conduct set down by House Nur forming the basis for all Sunal laws. The various Sunals add their own individual laws to this baseline.

Nyanja – Large seahorses ridden as sea cavalry by the Calden Navy.

Obsidian – Black Etheria Crystal storing psychic energy.

Ocean Deep – Name referring to any of the deep oceans of Lumina or Nocturn.

Ol'daEE – Person able to cast spells while having sex under the influence of Oldust.

Oldust – Hallucinogenic powder derived from the spores of the rare Impia Mushroom, increasing magical abilities and is essential for individual travel to the Middle Realms.

Onay – Humanoid wolf men of the Barrens, banding their various packs together in three distinct hordes.

On'Dara – Sentient horse creatures living on the Plains of Taka-Vir in the southeastern Twilight Lands. They raise and train horses, trading them for silk with the Cevot Spiders and selling them to the rest of the Annigan.

ooD – Shell worn on the back of the male Otick warriors as armor. They mark the warrior's rank and house on the outside of the shell and inscribe a record of their deeds on the inside. They place the ooD over the entrance to their homes in the sand.

Oracle of the River – Demi-God who dwells in the cypress swamp at the end of the western fork of the Otoman River for thousands of grands. It appears as a partially submerged giant catfish with its many whiskers sunken into the water. These whiskers perceive anything happening in, on, or around the waterway.

Orad – Air Goddess of death and predominate deity of the assassin's guild, the Hand of the Wind. Her creed: *She comes as the wind. And takes whom she wishes. Her name is Orad. And she is death.*

Orad Dex – Initiates to the Orad priesthood. Street/entry level assassins.

Orad Con – (Taker of the Divine Wind) These are full priests of Orad. Their special skills are the Kiss of Death, the Poison Breath and the Phantom Dagger.

Orad Sto – (Giver of the Divine Wind) High priests of Orad who can also restore life.

Otick – Humanoid crab people inhabiting the Shallow Sea. Among the first sentient creatures to rise from the ocean floor they evolved into a proud, deeply spiritual and noble race. Goya's volcanic warmed waters provide home to the Otick's prolific oyster beds littering the floor of the Shallow Sea. From these beds arose the five great Pearl Avatars, creation gods whose songs brought life and sentience to Lumina. Otick society is divided into a highly structured caste system: Worker Class, Warrior Class and Mother Class, and organized into two main categories: domestic and military. The Shelled Triad, the three Otick Great Houses, tend their own oyster beds and compete for the birthplace of the next Avatar.

Otick Great Houses:

House Awa – Home of the last two avatars. Located in the Tellasian Chain, in the capital city of Hidet on the Island of Zod. Mother Class specialization.

House Pewa – Located in the Goyodian Chain, in the capital city of Oniack, on the Island of Zak. Worker Class specialization.

House Sensu – Located in the Otoman Group, in the capital city of Sunico, on the Island of Lakia. Warrior Class specialization.

Otomoria – Large Island continent in the western Goyan Islands. The main grain producing agricultural island.

Outer Clan EEtah – Humanoid shark creatures smaller in stature than regular EEtahs and cast out from the three great EEtah Houses hatcheries. The survivors band together into loose clans, contracting themselves out as deck hands or recently volunteering in the Valdurian Marines.

Padi – Regional demi-god of water worshiped in and around the High Holy City of Zor, associated with the peace and calming effect of water and represented by a calm pond.

Palu EEtah – Rare hammerhead EEtahs. They are as big as the Outer Clan EEtah but extremely intelligent. They tend to be reclusive loners.

Pappia – Members of the child street gangs of the Hidden City of Toriss in the slum section of The Narrows.

Pa-Waga – Lawful evil god of greed worshiped mostly by the Tiikeri. Its clerics practice binary blood rune magic comprised of the letters "X" and "I."

Peace Babies – Children born of a union between any of the five major Human noble houses.

Peto – Fifth of the ten Quinte Grand Cycle, Summer.

Piceans – Humanoid fish people of Lumina. Capable of breathing above and below the water and impervious to the ocean's depths. They have gill flaps large enough to fold over their ears and when the vocal sound waves pass through the membrane, it translates it. This makes them valuable translators in the seaports of the Goyan Islands.

Piety Watch – Militant, religious police faction of the Pa-Waga church. They arrest anyone caught begging, idle, or not being productive. Minor offences are punished by a beating with thin cane rods. They wear red shirts under black capes with high pointed collars resembling cat ears.

Pisar – Bailian title for a scholar.

Pomaku – Humanoid leopard people (Mawl) native to the Arboro region in the Land of Mists, Nocturn.

Protocol 13 – EEtah House Nur code phrase requesting a meeting between an intelligence asset and their handler.

Qua-Raman Oasis – An oasis in the central Dark Waste Desert. Due to its location just south of the Tur-Qua Pass, it serves as a major trading post for gems harvested in The Barrens to the north.

Quartermaster – Collector of taxes and tariffs in the Goyan Islands who use the Ironmark to enforce their rule.

Queen's Envoy Service, The – The Amarenian Empire's spy service and member of the Society of Whispers.

Quinte – Time period equivalent to a month.

Ramu – A gambling dismemberment game banned everywhere in Lumina, except the Free City of Tannimore.

Rayth – Pirate faction of the Amarenian people in open revolt and attempting to form their own nation.

Rod-Ema Trench – Massive abysmal fissure running along the equator in the western ocean floor in Nocturn. At its head is the Agar Goyot and the Black Mural is found on its north wall dipping into the ocean depths.

Rohina Takii – Sword school originating on the Island of Wou. Known for its strike while drawing technique.

Sardor – Amarenian title for a female warlord.

Salar Winds – Turbulent winds surrounding the peak of Mount Goya which must be navigated to enter the Avion City of Darmont on the mountain's northwestern face. Avion term of exasperation, "By the mighty Winds of Salar!"

Secor – Street name for the Imperial Gold Ingot equivalent to ten struck gold coins.

Sesto – Sixth of the ten Quinte Grand Cycle, Autumn.

Shallow Sea – The body of water surrounding the greater Goyan Islands covering the Goyan Rise. The depth is no more than thirty feet deep at its lowest point.

Si – The term for "mister" in the Common Tongue spoken in the Goyan Islands.

Sikari – Female Singa hunter/killer squads, traveling in groups of two or more. They arm themselves with crossed bandoleros covering their chests and filled with sickle shaped throwing blades.

Silent Partner – Seven cabals of organized crime families in the Goyan Islands.

Simikort – Round engraved coin acting as an Amarenian noble's calling card.

Singa – Humanoid lion people (Mawl) inhabiting the southern Rovina area of the land of Mists.

Skirting the Upwinds – Dangerous maneuver practiced by few airship pilots. It involves taking the airship up to the edge of the atmosphere and then plummeting down to your destination. Allowing long-distance travel in a short period.

Society of Whispers – The general intelligence cooperative of the five Human noble houses, the Zorian Spymaster, the Calden Intelligencer Service, Suusho, and the Queen's Envoy Service.

Spice Rat – Smugglers operating in the Spice Islands chains (Zerian Reef Chain and Outer Zerians) and occasionally in the entire western side of the Goyan Islands.

Spooks – Street term for spies and operatives in the Society of Whispers.

Strasta – Ancient prophet in the folklore of the Cevot spider people of the Os-Ani Mountains.

Sunal – EEtah war college specializing in martial skills.

Suusho – The Bailian Empire's spy service and member of the Society of Whispers.

Szoldos Mercenaries – One of several small private armies for hire on the Goyan continent.

Taking it Upstairs – Airship slang for skirting upwinds

Tanum Charts – Six maps of Nocturn's night sky. The Arron-Nin Astrologers use them for divination and sometimes the opening of Flavian portals.

Teine – Second of the ten Quinte Grand Cycle, Spring.

Ten/Fifty— Cliché phrase in the Goyan Islands referring to the ten cycles (days) in the cluster (week) and fifty decis (hours) of the cycle (day). The equivalent of 24/7.

Tenable Sister—Title given to Amarenian lawyers.

Tiikeri – Sentient humanoid Tiger creatures of the Dasos region in the eastern Land of Mists.

Tisa – Ninth of the ten Quinte Grand Cycle, Winter.

Trinilic – Orange Etheria Crystal, fire magic connection.

Turine – Tidal clocks used in the Goyan Islands.

Twilight Lands – Area between Lumina and Nocturn in constant state of Twilight. Due to converging hot and cold air masses its weather remains perpetually stormy.

Ukkonite – Bronze Etheria Crystal with natural repellant properties. It is the crystal equivalent to Ukko Wood found only in Nocturn.

Ukko Wood – Magical wood from the World Tree, harvested only on the Island of Zer in the eastern Goyan Islands. Its natural repellant properties are used in shields, weapons, Brightstar Nolton Boats and used as currency.

Ulana – Chaotic evil sea Goddess worshiped by a small sect of Amarenian Rayth in the province of Durik-Dor

Unification War – Conflict started by House Eldor in 2 P.A. against the eastern agricultural islands of House Valdur. It ended as quickly as it began when House Aramos forced them to the negotiating table by threatening to freeze both houses' accounts in the Imperial Bank.

Valorous Sister – Amarenian title for heroic acts which affected the realm.

Vedette – Small fast Nolton Boats crewed by a single ex-Brightstar sailor and used for fast, anonymous travel around the oceans of Lumina.

Velocomite – Pale blue Etheria Crystal with red bands, increases or decreases an object's speed travelling.

Veros Pearls – Highest quality pearl cultivated in the Otick oyster beds. They are capable of holding a magical charge.

Ves-Lari – Mawl mongrels bred by the Tiikeri for rowing and poling. They are a combination of Pomaku (leopard) and Duma (Cheetah). Crews can pole or row for hundreds of miles at a time without stopping.

Vurr Carts – Carts used by the Vurr Clerics to collect the City of Zor's dead and garbage. There are two types: stationary carts situated on every major street where citizens can deposit their waste and roving carts mostly dealing with collecting the bodies of the dead.

Vurr Clerics – Accolades of the Free God Vurr serving as waste disposal in the City of Zor. Once maintaining constantly pyres burning everything from corpses to ordinary refuse. The city upgraded the pyres to full crematoriums. Vurr clerics smell of smoke and generally work nude, wearing only a simple cloak.

Wraith – Deep cover agents for House Aramos drawn from the elite Black Talons unit.

Yagur – Humanoid jaguars (Mawl) from the Arboro region of the Land of Mists. They are seers, healers and shamans, serving all the various Mawl races.

Yudon – Harpoon with a rifled the shaft for throwing accuracy. The standard weapon of every Sunal EEtah.

Yupik – a.k.a. the Ice Clans, one hundred and sixty-five clans divided into three major groups. The nomadic wanderers of the Western Flows compete for resources while the Ash-Ta constantly hunt them as prey. The largest group inhabits the vast Eastern Flows with semi-permanent settlements surrounding the Ice City of Mos-Agar'.

Zadim – Lapidaries operating in the Dark Waste Desert.

Zerian Rangers – Woodsmen fighters belonging to any of nine different clans occupying the forests of the Island continent of Zer in the Goyan Islands.

Zoldak Group – A private mercenary army comprised of former Black Talons of House Aramos.

Zorian Monetary Council – A ruling body founded in 3850 P.A. controlling all banking in the High Holy City of Zor. The council coordinates with the Calden Commodities exchange to regulate the exchange of money, goods and services, and uses the Quartermasters Guild for the collection of taxes and tariffs.

R.W. Marcus

MAPS

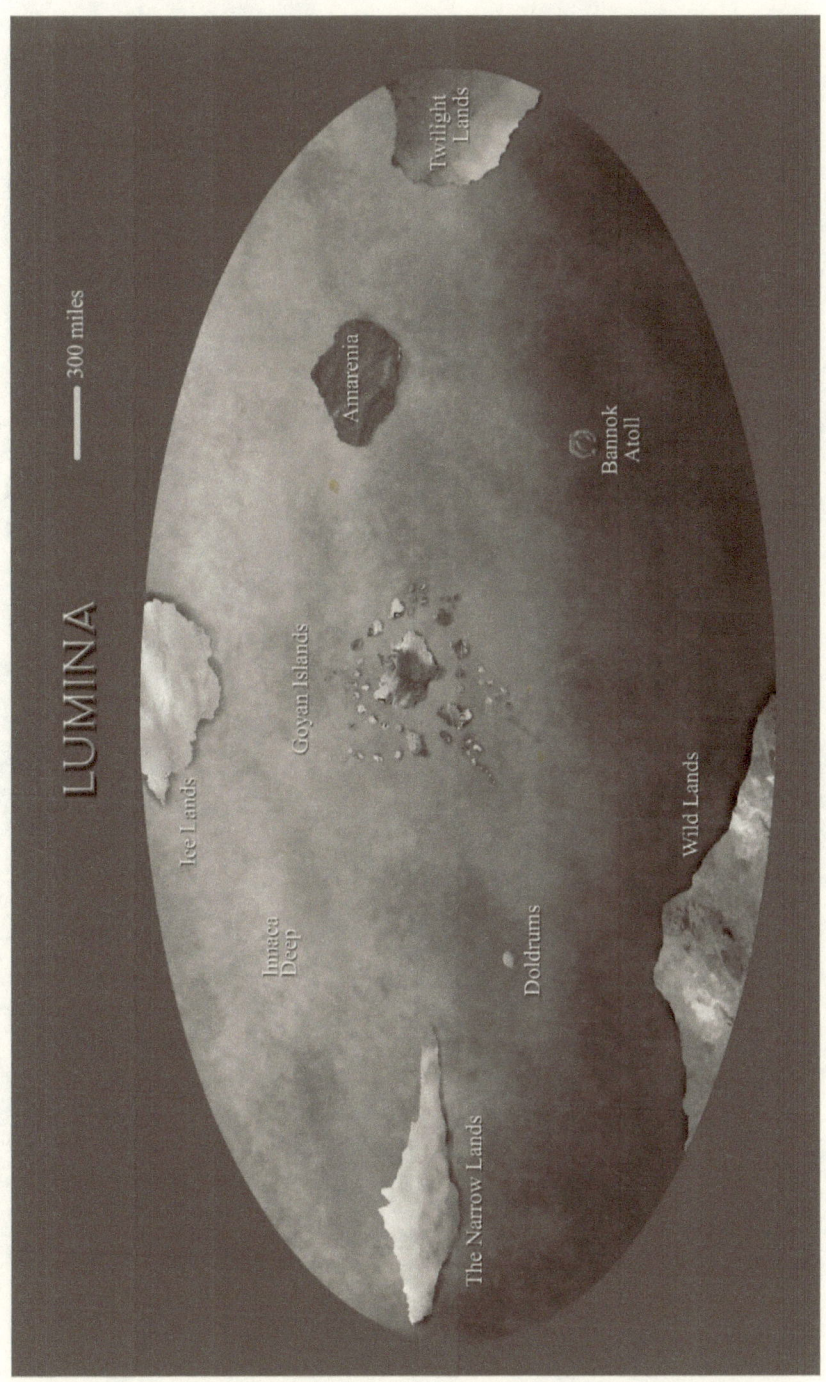

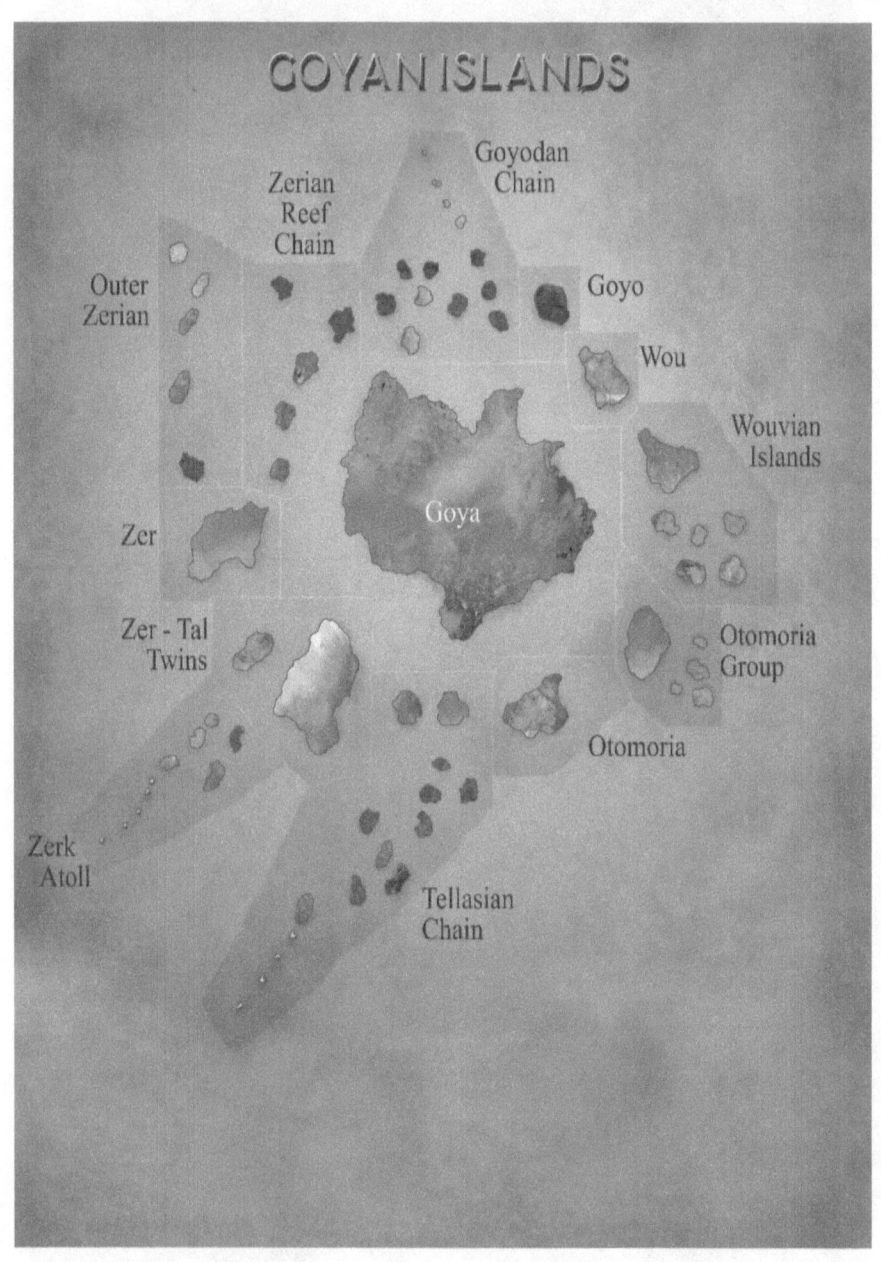

GOYAN ISLANDS

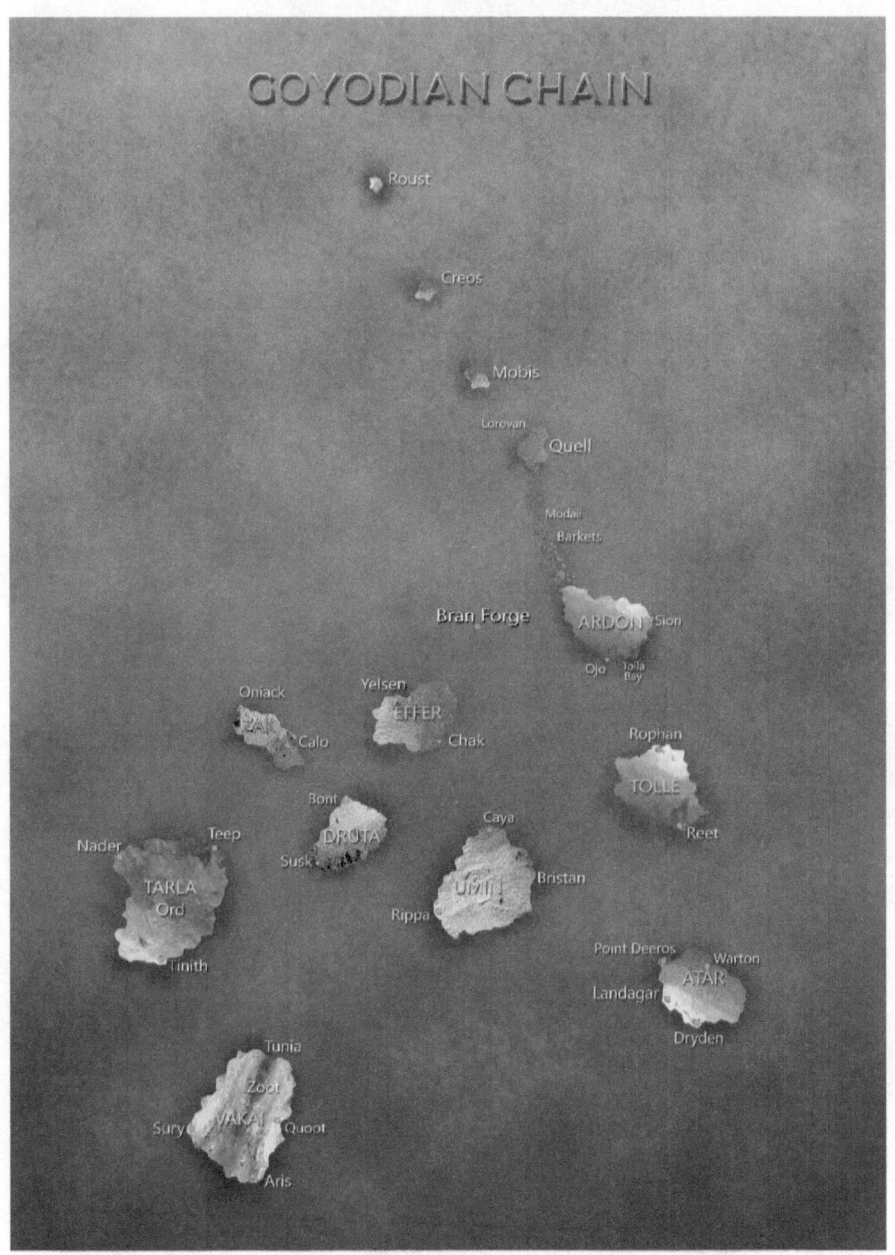

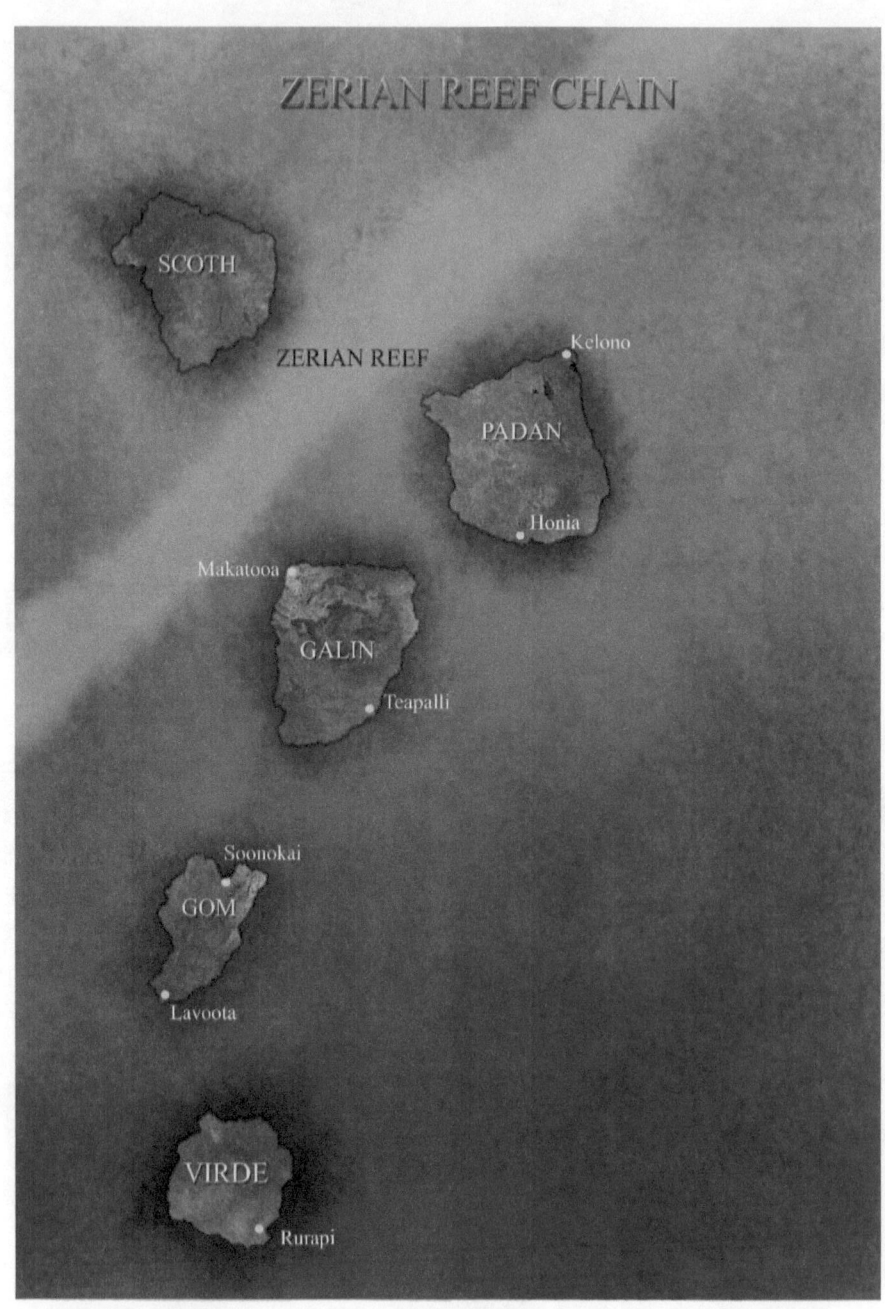

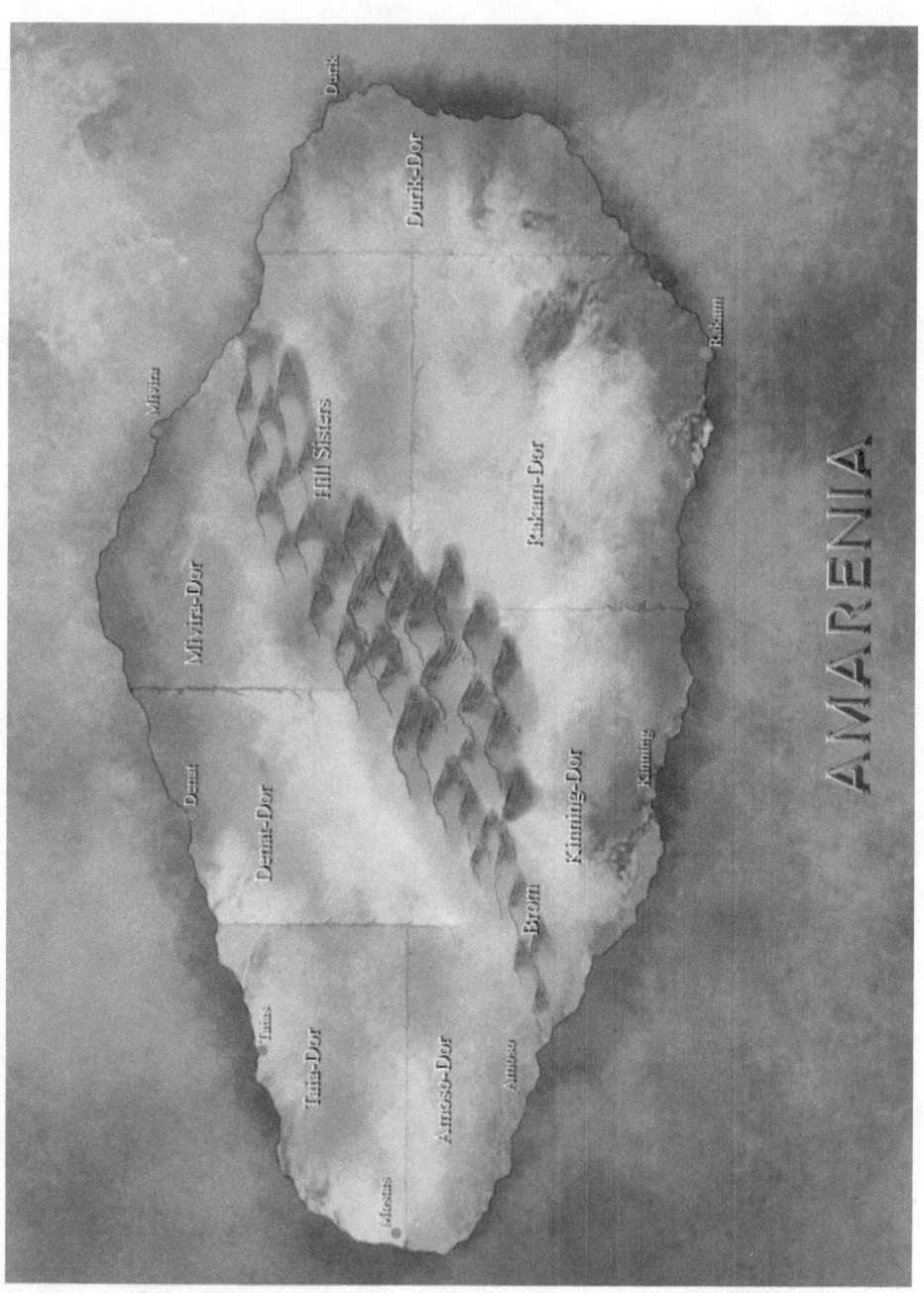

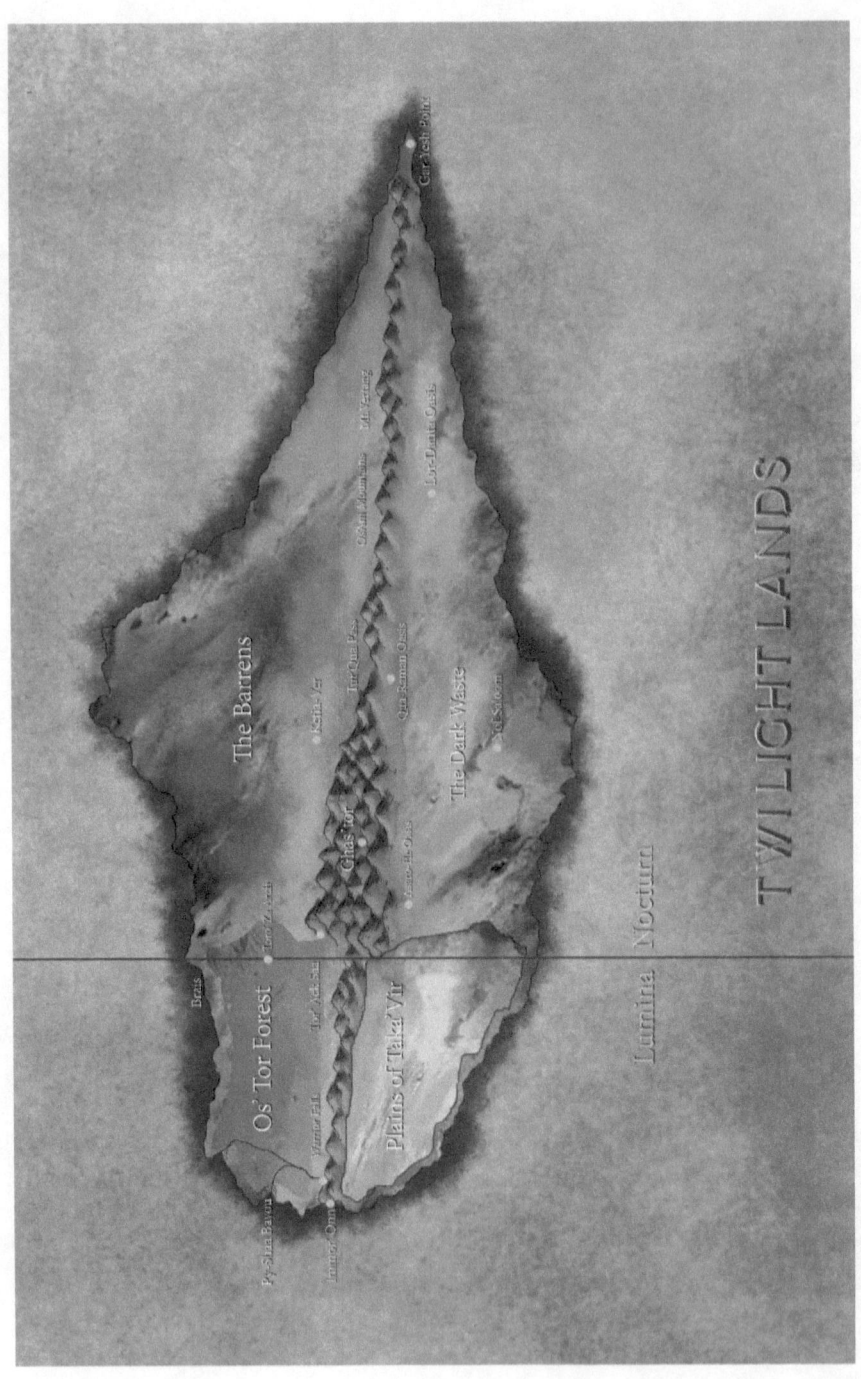

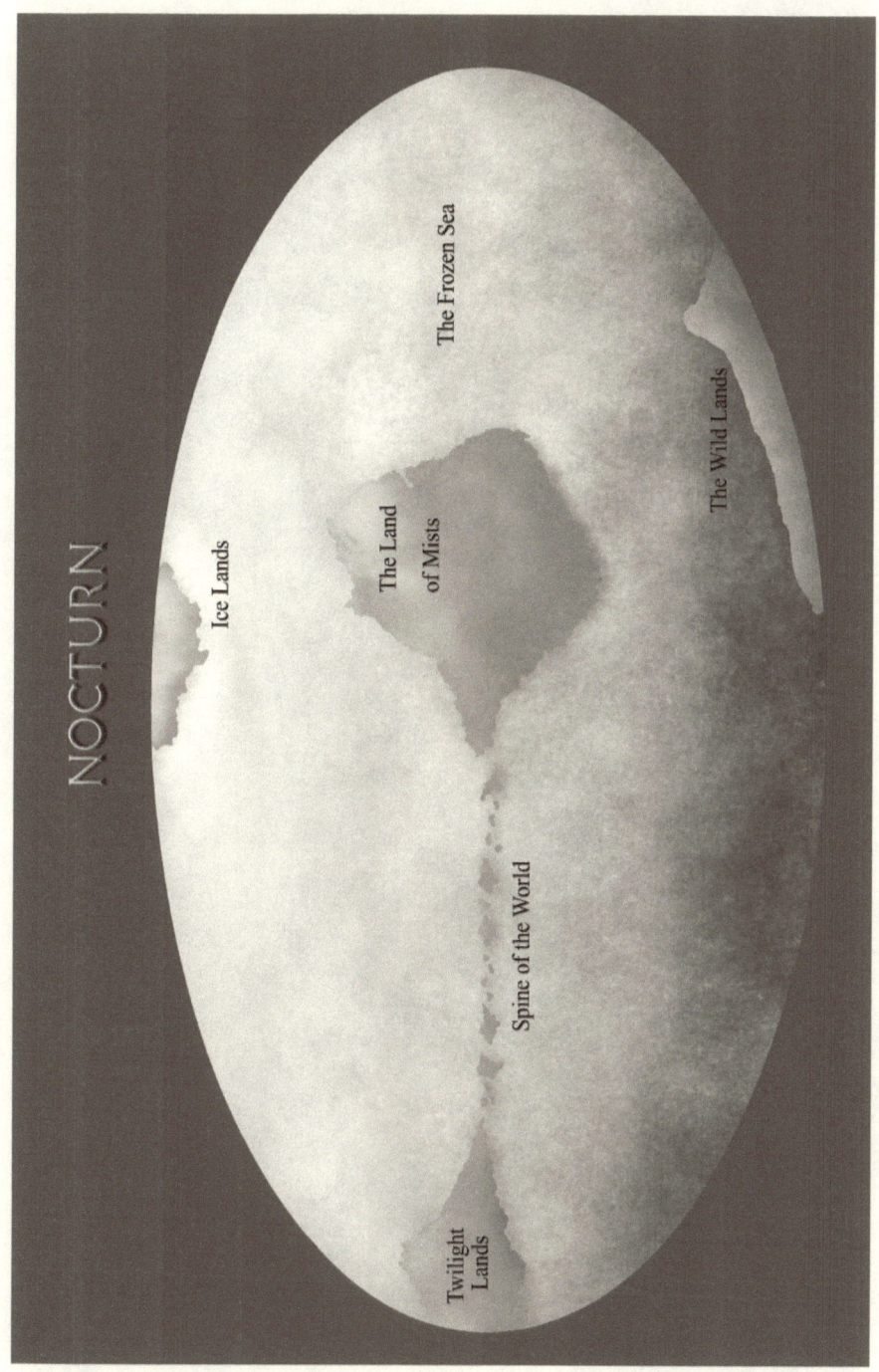

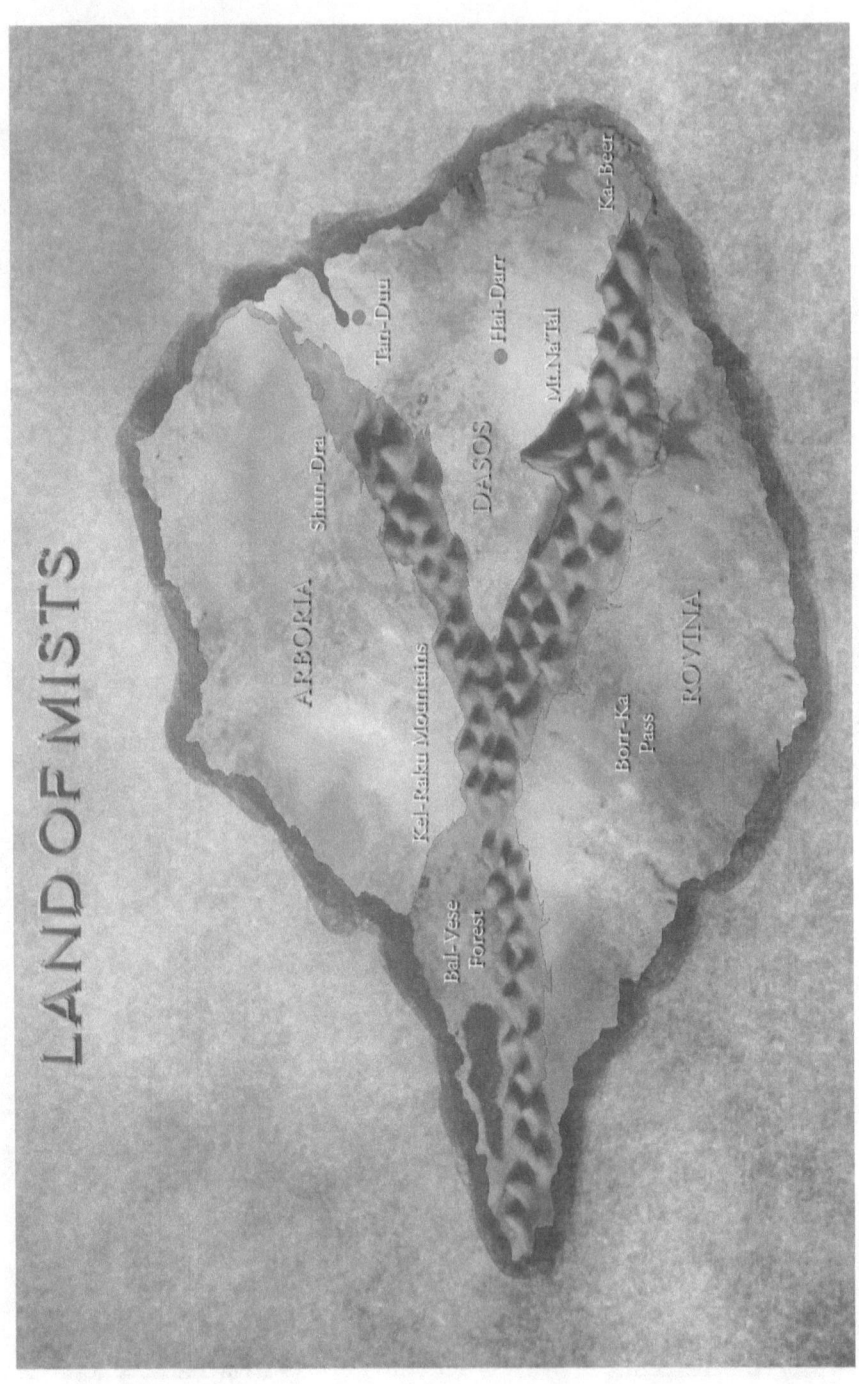

LAND OF MISTS

ARBORIA

Shun-Diru

Tiu-Duu

DaSOS

Hai-Darr

Mt. Na-Tal

Ka-Beer

Kel-Raku Mountains

Bal-Vese
Forest

Borr-Ka
Pass

ROVINA

ABOUT THE AUTHOR

R.W. Marcus spent most of his life selling books. Along the way he managed to become a Falconer, 3rd Dan Black Belt in Yoshukai Karate, Freemason, Freelance Photographer, Ad Copywriter and WMNF Radio Disc Jockey. Marcus' radio commercials and freelance photography won numerous awards, including Best of Shows and Best of the Bay Addy Awards for work with Creative Keys and Laughing Bird Productions. R.W. Marcus was also Founder and Creative Director of United Game Masters, where he cowrote the UGM Universal Gaming System which he used to create and playtest a role-playing game based in the world of the Annigan Cycle. He formally held the title of Director

of Incunabula at Griffon's Medieval Manuscripts, where he penned his first nonfiction title, *The Ship of Fools to 1500*, which Amazon called "an authoritative guide to one of the most popular works of secular writing." Now retired, he created a new genre of fiction— Pulp Fantasy Noir—to exorcise the darker side of his good nature.

CONNECT
WEBSITE: https://AnniganCycle.com
FACEBOOK: https://www.facebook.com/noirrwmarcus/
TWITTER: @NoirRWMarcus
EMAIL: RWMarcus@yahoo.com

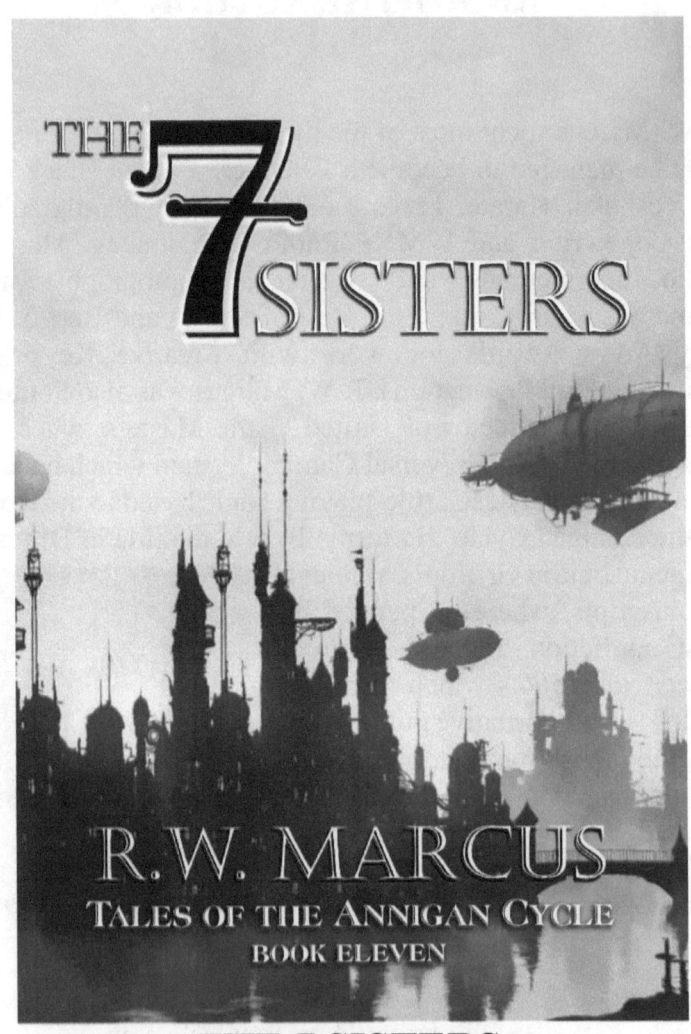

THE 7 SISTERS
TALES OF THE ANNIGAN CYCLE
BOOK ELEVEN
FROM LAUGHING BIRD PUBLISHING